Will

Notes on Comparative Anatomy

Anatiposi

William Ord

Notes on Comparative Anatomy

Reprint of the original.

1st Edition 2023 | ISBN: 978-3-38210-210-4

Anatiposi Verlag is an imprint of Outlook Verlagsgesellschaft mbH.

Verlag (Publisher): Outlook Verlag GmbH, Zeilweg 44, 60439 Frankfurt, Deutschland
Vertretungsberechtigt (Authorized to represent): E. Roepke, Zeilweg 44, 60439 Frankfurt, Deutschland
Druck (Print): Books on Demand GmbH, In de Tarpen 42, 22848 Norderstedt, Deutschland

COMPARATIVE ANATOMY.

NOTES ON

COMPARATIVE ANATOMY:

A SYLLABUS

OF A

COURSE OF LECTURES DELIVERED AT ST. THOMAS'S HOSPITAL.

BY

WILLIAM MILLER ORD, M.B. LOND., M.R.C.P.,

ASSISTANT-PHYSICIAN TO THE HOSPITAL, AND LECTURER ON PHYSIOLOGY AND ON COMPARATIVE ANATOMY IN ITS MEDICAL SCHOOL.

LONDON:

J. AND A. CHURCHILL, NEW BURLINGTON STREET.

1871.

PREFACE.

THE following Syllabus has been prepared for the use of my class in Comparative Anatomy. It embodies the substance of about three annual courses of lectures, in each of which the several regions of the whole Animal Kingdom are examined; in each of which, successively, one-third of the Kingdom is more minutely surveyed than the rest. In the whole survey, the position of a student fairly acquainted with human anatomy is assumed. For things near and familiar, but few words of general description are enough; for the rare and distant, some kind of picturing must give comprehensive ideas. Of his own neighbourhood, much is assumed to be known, and surface-differences—of teeth, of skin, of symmetry of limbs,—are here talked of; what is further off is mapped, and photographed, and catalogued for him with increasing minuteness as we near the horizon.

There is set before us in teaching the necessity of imparting, in the beginning, clear ideas of the objects of our demonstrations. To this necessity all things are subordinated in this Syllabus; and thereby must be explained, if not justified, certain inequalities in the attention paid to the several groups of animals, and a certain free use of theories as scaffolding for facts. In the discussion of rival theories, especially, first a compact summary, and then an orderly use of facts, will tend to fix in the memory clear ideas of things hardly remembered without some such assistance; as, for example, the nature and value of "squamosal" and "mastoid" bones, the composition of the "shoulder-girdle," or the constitution and homologies of a Tunicate and a Polyzoon.

The course is too short to include much systematic detail, and is therefore arranged so as to present to the student a chart in which a few principal centres of life are clearly indicated, as opposed to that sort of chart in which the paper is filled to confusion with closely-packed names of places of all grades of importance;—a traveller's hand-book as opposed to a bare, lifeless list of countries only illustrated by instantly-to-be-forgotten tables of such things as latitude and longitude, of value of produce, or of articles of commerce.

Finally, it will be obvious that the Syllabus is intended to guide the student in his reading and preparation, not to take the place of a complete and systematic treatise.

CONTENTS.

COMPARATIVE ANATOMY.

(SYLLABUS.)

Object of this Course, "The Animal Kingdom."

The Animal Kingdom and the Vegetable Kingdom together constitute the world of life.

Of Distinctions between Not-living Matter and Living Beings.

I. External form: in not-living, regularly angular and facetted where a definite form possessed; in living, rounded and geometrically irregular.

II. Internal constitution: homogeneity of crystal opposed to heterogeneity of living body.

III. Mode of growth: in not-living, additions of like matter to surface; in the living, absorption and remoulding of matter into conformity with the substance of the body (assimilation). And, further, cyclical growth or development.

IV. Relations to surrounding circumstances: not-living matter comparatively indifferent, its changes without self-regarding purpose; in living bodies, perpetual change a constant characteristic, such change having a definite relation to the conservation of the whole organism. Life "the continuous adjustment of internal to external relations." (Mr. Herbert Spencer.)

Of these, the last the most important; the others subordinate, not always available, and, standing alone, severally inadequate.

Of Distinctions between Animals and Plants.

I. Chemical composition. Ternary compounds (CHO) specially characteristic and largely component of plants. Quaternary, (CHNO) of animals. But this a distinction of degree only.

II. Reactions. Plants assimilate inorganic matter directly; animals indirectly, using material put together by plants, excepting in the case of oxygen. Incidental to this, the readily observed distinction that plants decompose CO_2, and set free O, while animals absorb O, and set free CO_2.

III. Animals eat; plants do not eat.

IV. Locomotion, general or partial, is universal in animals; rare in plants.

V. Sensation general in animals; rare, if anywhere existent, in plants.

All these grouped together form two distinct pictures; but, as we travel low down in the scale on both sides, we lose one after another of the list, till we come to minute forms where eating and the gas-reactions are our only guides.

These guides, indeed, are not always trustworthy.

But the animal type altogether higher than the plant type—"higher" meaning more perfect relations and wider correspondence with surrounding circumstances.

Method of the Course.—More prominently morphological than physiological, the object proposed being the knowledge of animals in their totality.

Given the animal kingdom, upon what principles shall it be subdivided as a prelude to the consideration of its constituents?

In classification, different principles will prevail, according to the extent of knowledge. The method may be—

1. Alphabetical, as in early stages of science.

2. Superficial, or quasi-alphabetical, where easily-recognised surface-marks are chosen for the basis of arrangement, as in the Linnæan system.

Both kinds being tentative and provisional.

3. Natural, or judicially comprehensive, as in the so-called "Natural System" of classification of plants—wherein things are placed together according to their total affinities, and not separated by counting of toes or hairs. They are joined together by likeness to a type; not cut asunder by the unyielding lines of definition (Whewell). In table of characters preliminary to ranking, a law of order and precedence recognised, some characters being noted as deep-seated and essential, others progressively less constant and less important. Classification will be perfect in proportion as subordination is understood and applied; and all classifications of large groups of animals founded upon the form or development of single parts or organs are to be regarded as doubtful or imperfect.

In the organization of animals at least two factors,—(1) the original type, (2) the habits, their history, and the changes or additions of structure therewith correlated. Origin of the various forms constituting the animal kingdom.

1. Doctrine of Special Creations.
2. Theory of Progressive Development (Lamarck).
3. Theory of Natural Selection (Darwin).

Of these—

1. Needs no explanation.

2. Proposes the idea of an innate tendency to the development of higher and more complex forms in successive generations of one line, from monad to elephant or man ; but allows the modifying influence of surrounding conditions.

3. Regards surrounding conditions as the grand moulding agencies, inasmuch as forms most in harmony with them will most certainly survive and perpetuate themselves. The particular adaptations will be rendered possible by the law of variation, and the perpetuation by the law of race-likeness, or atavism.

PLAN OF CLASSIFICATION.—Five great groups recognised as togetherconstituting the whole kingdom :—

VERTEBRATA.
MOLLUSCA.
CŒLENTERATA.
PROTOZOA.
ANNULOSA.

Observations.—The Vertebrata very probably equal in value to the whole of the Invertebrata. The Mollusca subdivided by Huxley and others into the Mollusca proper and Molluscoidea, the Annulosa into the Articulata, Arthropoda, or Annulosa proper, and Annuloida, the Protozoa into the Infusoria and Protozoa proper. The sub-divisions of the Mollusca and Annulosa, however, can in no sense be equal to such a group as the Vertebrata. The Infusoria and Protozoa still imperfectly understood. (Note that the Protozoa, Cœlenterata, certain low forms of Mollusca (Polyzoa), and certain low or aberrant forms of Annulosa (Scolecida, Echinodermata) constituted the Radiata of Cuvier.) In the case of the first four groups, it is possible to construct type-forms applicable to all the animals comprehended in each severally. In the case of the Protozoa, this is not so practicable, a circumstance which demonstrates our knowledge of the group to be imperfect. Divided or not, the group is provisional, comprehending doubtless one or more true groups, and, mixed with these, stray forms, mostly embryonic or larval, belonging to the higher and better established groups—in this sense a "refuge for the destitute." (E. Forbes).

Scheme of distinctive characters of these five groups in succession.

I. Vertebrata.

Segmented vertebral column, with dorsal and ventral arches in segments corresponding to those of the column.

The arches embrace two longitudinal and parallel canals—one dorsal, enclosing cerebro-spinal axis; one ventral, enclosing viscera of organic life, which are arranged within it as follows: Alimentary canal in centre, heart ventral to canal, sympathetic ganglion-chain dorsal to canal. Blood red, containing two kinds of corpuscles; circulates everywhere in closed channels, not communicating with the perivisceral cavity. No hermaphrodism.

In form, symmetry of two kinds:

a. Horizontal or bilateral; on each side of flat vertical longitudinal plane.

b. Vertical; consisting in division of body by transverse planes into a series of segments, each of which has, homologically, the same constitution with the rest: this symmetry, however, less perfect than the first.

c. Skeleton internal.

d. Limbs jointed; in pairs; never exceeding four.

In development:

a. Primitive trace. Declaration of Vertebrate type.

b. Umbilical vesicle communicates with ventral aspect of embryo.

II. Mollusca.

1. No vertebral column or dorsal tube.
2. Body contains only one tube, corresponding in the main

to the lower tube of the Vertebrata, but inverted; the alimentary canal being central, the nerve-chain ventral, and the heart dorsal.

3. Blood has only white corpuscles, and circulates partly or entirely in lacunar spaces belonging to the perivisceral cavity.

4. Hermaphrodism common.

5. In form, symmetry only of horizontal kind, on each side of curved vertical plane. Body not jointed, nor provided with jointed external skeleton. Limbs, if present, soft, and non-articulated; mostly single and median.

6. Development. Umbilical vesicle connected with head or dorsum.

III. Annulosa.

1, 2, 3, 4, as in Mollusca.

5. In form, both symmetries.

  a. Horizontal; on each side of flat vertical plane.

  b. Vertical; very perfect; the body being divided into a number of rings or somites accurately repeating one another, and with their parts much individualised.

  c. The body invested by an external horny skeleton, highly developed as to its morphological aspect.

  d. Limbs in pairs; as numerous as the rings; jointed.

6. As in Mollusca.

Note.—The physiological development of the Annulosa less perfect than that of Mollusca; greater distribution.

IV. Cœlenterata.

No vertebral column, &c.

No distinct nervous system.

No heart.

Alimentary canal opens into perivisceral cavity.

Form.—Symmetry, at first sight, in radial vertical planes around centre of body-tube; in reality bilateral.

Skeleton internal or external.

Wall of body-tube consists of two membranes (ectoderm and endoderm), comparable to the serous and mucous layers of the vertebrate germ. Thread-cells. Histologically, tissues areolated or multicellular.

V. Protozoa.

All negative characters of Cœlenterata.

No symmetry.

Positive characters:

1. Nucleus, with nucleolus.
2. Contractile vesicle.
3. Encystment, preliminary to multiplication by fission.

Histological constitution, for the most part unicellular.

Classes Comprehended in the Animal Kingdom.

Sub-kingdom, Vertebrata. Classes—Mammalia.
Aves.
Reptilia.
Batrachia.
Pisces.

2. Sub-kingdom, Mollusca. Classes—

Mollusca propria {
Cephalopoda.
Pteropoda.
Gasteropoda pulmonata.
Gasteropoda branchiata.
Lamellibranchiata.

Molluscoidea {
Brachiopoda.
Tunicata.
Polyzoa.

3. Sub-kingdom, Annulosa. Classes—

Articulata	Crustacea. Arachnida. Insecta. Myriopoda.
Annuloidea	Annelida. Scolecida. Echinodermata.

4. Sub-kingdom, Cœlenterata. Classes—Actinozoa.
Hydrozoa.

5. Sub-kingdom, Protozoa. Classes—Infusoria.
Spongidea.
Rhizopoda.
Gregarinidea.

Description of Constituents of Groups.

Take lowest form, and work upwards, beginning with—
Sub-kingdom—Protozoa.

Four classes—Gregarinidea.
Rhizopoda.
Spongidea.
Infusoria.

The first three closely associated together, having amœba as their central form.

Amœba;—microscopic; a little mass of sarcode (rudimentary flesh or protoplasm) usually differentiated into an outer and an inner portion—ectosarc and endosarc. Pseudopodia, simple contractile projections, agents in locomotion; locomotion by extension and retraction; no distinct mouth or anus, though existence of oral and anal regions asserted; feeding by engulfing; nucleus and often nucleolus; contractile vesicle. No separate organs of digestion, respiration, circulation, innervation. Reproduction by (1) fission; (2) conjugation, said to occur, but results imperfectly known; (3) encystment, also with imperfectly known result; (4) true reproduction by spermatozooids developed in nucleus, and ova developed in the mass of the body (Carter).

Cl. GREGARINIDEA.—Minute parasitic animals, with amœbiform zooids.

Type-form: Gregarina. Microscopic: A spherical or oval body, sometimes provided with hooklets for attachment, parasitic in alimentary canal and other parts of Invertebrata, and less commonly in Vertebrata. Body invested by a well-defined imperforate membrane, contractile in somewhat regular undulations or peristalses; within this a semi-fluid, granular mass (ectosarc and endosarc); embedded vesicular nucleus, with nucleolus. No mouth; nourishment by absorption. No other organs. Reproduction;—encystment, possibly after conjugation, followed by transformation of contents of body into pseudo-navicellæ; from ripe pseudo-navicellæ issue tiny amœboids, growing, according to some authors, to gregarinæ.

Psorospermiæ, found in cysts, parasitic in Vertebrates; the pseudo-navicellæ of amœboid gregarine (Huxley).

Cl. RHIZOPODA.

Starting-point, amœba, growing to great diversity of form; by restriction of pseudopodia to certain parts of surface; by several variations in form and arrangement of pseudopodia; by development on non-pseudopodial surface of a single or many-chambered shell.

TABLE OF ORDERS OF RHIZOPODA.
(CARPENTER).

Orders.—

1. Lobosa.	2. Radiolaria.	3. Reticularia.
Fam. Amœbina.	Fam. Actinophryna.	Fam. Gromida.
	Acanthometrina.	Foraminifera.
	Polycystina.	
	Thalassicollina.	

Order 1.—Lobosa. Type-form : Amœba.

This simple form, altered by several processes :—

1. By limitation of pseudopodia to ventral surface ; Amœba limax.

2. By development of test on non-pseudopodial or dorsal surface. Pseudochlamys-test soft, yielding. Arcella-test membranous or horny. Difflugia-test arenaceous.

Order 2.—Radiolaria. Type-form : Actinophrys.

Actinophrys ; microscopic ; body spherical ; consisting of sarcode, often much vacuolated ; endosarc and ectosarc ; pseudopodia extended from all parts of surface, slender, simple, rarely fusing, flexible, not usually retractile, displaying slow circulation of granules ; nucleus, and one or more contractile vesicles ; no mouth or anus ; mode of feeding ; doubtful ova and spermatozoa.

Acanthometrina.—Actinophryna, with siliceous spicular internal skeleton.

Polycystina.—Actinophryna, with siliceous much perforated external shell.

Thalassicollina.—More differentiated Actinophryna, interior fluid, exterior gelatinous investment, with spicules, vacuoles, and cells, through which the pseudopodia radiate. Compound forms, with spicular siliceous skeleton (sponge affinity).

Order 3.—Reticularia. Simple form, Lieberkuhnia. Body subspherical, or flask-shaped, invested by thin pellucid membrane, except at mouth of flask, from which issues a sort of stem, branching out into pseudopodia. Pseudopodia emitted as threads of different sizes, branching and fusing where they come in contact, so as to form a constantly changing network of great comparative extent ; circulation of particles along the threads. No nucleus or contractile vesicle.

The great variety of forms comprehended in this order

produced by differences in investment of body and mode of growth.

Thus, body may be invested by membranous or horny test, or by shell. Shell may be, as to texture, porcellanous, vitreous, or arenaceous ; as to structure, imperforate or perforate ; as to mode of growth, single-chambered or many-chambered. Many-chambered shells indicate growth by successive additions of more or less similar, but usually larger, masses of shell-forming sarcode to the original animal, and the form of such shells is determined by the way in which the new parts are attached to the old. The forms may be straight, spiral, or cyclical, and radiating, and among these severally there will be distinctions founded upon the degrees of insulation of the several segments. Application of term "foraminifera." Geological value of these forms ; chalk ; Atlantic bed ; recent deep-sea dredgings ; bathybius ; coccoliths and coccospheres.

Cl. Spongidea.—Type-form : Grantia or Spongilla.

As Rhizopoda are amœboids which form an external investment of test or shell, the Spongidea are amœboids which form an internal spicular skeleton, the two classes being connected by such forms as Thalassicolla and Carpenteria.

Spongilla or Grantia.—Each a fixed body. A mass of associated amœbæ, invested by a structureless cuticle, perforated by two kinds of orifices—pores inhalant, oscula exhalant. The oscula permanent, the pores subject to variations, according to the activity of the circulation. Pores lead to subcuticular spaces, from which channels pass into the mass beneath, ramify, dilate, anastomose, and finally reunite to form large tributaries to great out-flowing channels ending in the oscula. The flow always from pores to oscula through the sponge, the direction being given by vibratile cilia in the deeper parts. The mass kept together, and its several parts maintained in proper position by spicules, calcareous in Grantea, siliceous in Spongilla, and varying infinitely in the long series of siliceous sponges, in size and form according to their special uses, or by horny anastomosing tubes, as in the soft sponges of commerce; feeding; food-circulation; breathing-circulation; variations of pores; contractility of oscula and mass of sponge in certain forms. Reproduction, (1) ciliated gemmules; (2) fixed winter-gemmules, composed of a box, usually in part siliceous, enclosing young sponge matter, and allowing it to escape, when circumstances favour, through micropyle; (3) ova and spermatozoa found in deeper parts in certain cases—*e.g.*, Tethea (Huxley).

Classification.—Dr. Bowerbank's used, as convenient, though, of course, not final:—

Order:	1. Calcarea.	Grantia.
	2. Silicea.	Spongilla, Euplectella.
	3. Keratosa.	Sponge of commerce.

In relation to this, the various forms of spicule and horny reticulation noted.

Cl. INFUSORIA.—Microscopic animals, possessing, in addition to the characters of amœba, various differentiations connected with locomotion, feeding, and reproduction. Type-form: Epistylis or Vorticella.

Epistylis. Microscopic: egg-shaped body, supported upon a stalk, and fixed thereby to submerged surfaces. Body of sarcode invested by thin, non-contractile cuticle. Sarcode in two layers—outer, firm, contractile; inner, soft. Around distal end of ovoid runs a line of cilia, attached to a rim (peristome), and forming rather more than one turn of a spiral; where the two ends overlap, a depression between them leads to the mouth; from the mouth a pear-shaped pharynx, lined with cuticle, depends into the inner mass of sarcode, ending blindly, and having no obvious continuation. A line of cilia (one large cilium, Auct.) runs from the mouth down one side of the pharynx; contractile vesicle, a simple spherical vacuole, appearing and disappearing from time to time. Nucleus, granular, refractile, with attached nucleolus. Vesicle and nucleus imbedded in ectosarc.

Mode of feeding, by pinching off end of dilated œsophagus at a point where the cuticle ceases so that vacuoles are successively formed, and perform a cyclosis in the endosarc. A mistaken view of this arrangement gave origin to the name Polygastria, applied by Ehrenberg. Anal region, close to mouth.

Reproduction, by fission and gemmation. More doubtful meaning of encystment. Asserted alternations of Acineta and Podophrya forms with vorticellids (Stein). True reproduction said to have been observed in some larger forms of Infusoria (Bursariæ), the nucleus appearing to have an ovarian, the nucleolus a testicular function.

In working out the homologies of the class, it may be noted that the stalk appears to be continuous with the cuticle. Placed in position unfavourable to existence, the body detaches itself from the stalk, and swims freely, often becoming after a short time encysted. At certain stages of existence, these forms are free swimmers, with extra circlet. Stalk, simple or branched, may have spiral retractive muscle (Vorticella, Carchesium); may expand to form urn (Vaginicola); or, still further, a lidded box (Opercularia).

Among free-swimming forms, the cuticle may be soft (Bursaria), or rigid (Euplotes), in which case the cilia become developed into stout crawling bristles.

Cilia and flagella; suctorial processes of Acineta.

Note also fascine-like addition to œsophagus of Nassula; tooth of Chilodon; variations of contractile vesicle in Stentor and others; of nucleus in Spirostomum; thread-cells; chlorophyll.

Classification: Provisional and imperfect. Claparéde and Lachmann followed.

Order:	1. Ciliata.	Vorticella.
	2. Suctoria.	Acineta.
	3. Cilioflagellata.	Peridinium.
	4. Flagellata.	Euglena (of disputed animality).

Sub-kingdom—Cœlenterata. Established by Frey and Leuckart; accepted pretty generally among English zoologists; opposed by Agassiz.

Positive characters:

1. Free communication of alimentary canal with body cavity.

2. The division of wall of body into two layers—endoderm and ectoderm.

3. Thread-cells.

Division into two great classes, Hydrozoa and Actinozoa.

Cl. HYDROZOA.—Body has but one cavity, partly digestive, partly somatic, the digestive cavity being never suspended within the somatic; reproductive organs external.

Cl. ACTINOZOA.—Alimentary canal suspended within the somatic cavity by mesenteries; reproductive organs internal, on the mesenteries.

Hydrozoa. Type-form: Hydra.

A cylindrical body, rarely more than half an inch long, and on an average one-thirtieth, or less, in diameter. At one end, closed by a disc of attachment; at the other, perforated by a transverse slit—the mouth—round which, from the margin of the end of the cylinder, project tentacles, very moveable, extensible, and armed with thread-cells. The body contains but one cavity, divided into a digestive region near the mouth, and a somatic region near the base. In body walls, the two membranes easily seen, growing from a central structureless plane, the ectoderm outwards, the endoderm inwards. So also in tentacles. Thread-cells, their sac, filament, armature, and mode of discharge. Hydra has at least two kinds: one permanently projected (palpocil), one explosive (nematocyst).

Terms: Digestive portion, Polypite, or Polype.
Somatic portion, Hydrosoma.
Disc of attachment, Hydrorrhiza.

REPRODUCTIVE ORGANS.

Male.—Little volcano-like projections of ectoderm just beneath arms; spermatozoa formed within, and emitted from apices.

Female.—Eminences of ~~ectoderm~~ mesoderm lower down; form ova, which, after fecundation, become ciliated, and are said to swim away, find a surface of attachment, lose their cilia, and, beginning with Hydrorrhiza, gradually grow to polyp form.

Reproduction by gemmation goes on during active life of polyp. Buds given off from the sides of the body. Regeneration of parts after mutilation.

Habits.—Mode of feeding; probable use of thread-cells in numbing small organisms. Progression, creeping, floating. Hydrozoa divided by Huxley into seven orders, founded upon various additions to the simple structure of Hydra. The more recent arrangement of Hincks and others is placed by the side of Huxley's.

Hydroida	1. Hydridæ	Gymnochroa.
	2. Corynidæ	Athecata.
	3. Sertularidæ	Thecaphora.
Siphonophora	4. Calycophoridæ.	
	5. Physophoridæ.	
(To Hydroida)	6. Medusidæ.	
Discophora	7. Lucernaridæ.	

DETAIL.

1. *Hydridæ;* includes only genus Hydra.
2. *Corynidæ.*—Fixed; permanently compound.

Parts: Hydrorrhiza, *cænosarc*, *polypites*. Stem soft, with or without horny investment (*polypary*); polypites never with horny investment; third, middle, layer in walls. Circulation in cænosarc; spiral tentacles of Hydractinia (modified polypites).

Reproductive organs more developed than in Hydra. *Gonophores* of about three kinds:—

1. Simple processes of both membranes of body, containing offshoot of somatic cavity.

2. In various stages medusiform, permanently attached.

3. Medusiform and free; swimming as independent zooids, far more highly organized than the parent form (*gonozooid*).

Gonophores vary in position; they may be developed on the polypites, on special modified polypites (*gonoblastidia*), or on the cænosarc. Ova and spermatozoa formed in ectosarc.

The Medusæ are, in fact, only locomotive polypites, the canals of the bell corresponding to tentacles, and the bell itself to a web joining them at their bases. The circular canal of the Medusæ, however, a new structure. Compare Campanulina Acuminata, zoid of Clavatella, and any Medusoid (Hincks—Allman).

3. *Sertularidæ.*—Fixed; always compound; have always a chitinous polypary, mostly ringed at root of polypites; polypites supported by chitinous cups (*Hydrothecæ*). *Nematophores* in some forms; snake-like appendages of Ophiodes; both probably modified polypites.

Gonophores tolerably uniform; developed on gonoblastidia; gonoblastidia protected by *gonothecæ.*

4. *Calycophoridæ.*—Type: Diphyes.

Free swimming. To proximal end of cænosarc, replacing the hydrorrhiza, are attached *nectocalyces*, or swimming-cups, having a lateral, not a median, relation to the stem (altered polypites ?). Other parts;—*stem* naked, retractile within, *hydrœcium; somatocyst; stem-polypites* without tentacles; *free tentacles;* and *bracts* (*Hydrophyllia*). Gonophores always medusiform, growing on peduncles of polypites, and eventually independent.

5. *Physophoridæ.* Type: Physophora.

Free-swimming. Proximal end of cænosarc modified to form *pneumatocyst* and *pneumatophore*, or float, which is, in the natural position, the uppermost part of the whole structure; below this a cone, having for centre a delicate stalk, or cænosarc, supporting a number of three-lobed swimming bells in many transverse rows, developed from above downwards. Below the cone the cænosarc expands, and forms a hollow disc, to which are attached three circlets of organs—1st, a ring of long hollow closed sacs (*hydrocysts*) brilliantly coloured; 2nd, below and within, reproductive organs; 3rd, alimentary polypites, with long tentacles sprouting from their peduncles, the mouth having no tentacles, but very flexible lips.

Note Physalia, Velella, and Porpita.

Gonophores medusiform, with marked distinction between male and female.

6. *Medusidæ.*—Naked-eyed Medusæ of Forbes. Type: Thaumantia. Consists of one polypite, fixed in the middle of the concavity of a nectocalyx. Polypite has four flexible lips; cavity communicates with a second median cavity at the base, partly hollowed out of the bell (somatic cavity); from this radiate four or six canals, like the ribs of an umbrella, to the margin of the bell, where they are united together by a circular canal; these canals rarely branch, and never anastomose; from the edge of the bell hang down tentacles, with often dilated bases and *pigment spots* (eyes ?); on the margin of the bell are eight *lithocysts* (ears ?); within these a circular valve (like an iris), called the veil or *velum*, extends inwards, and narrows the mouth of the bell. Reproductive organs, male or female, developed in the peduncle, from which also, or along the line of the radiating

canal, budding may take place. The true Medusidæ reproduce themselves directly without intervening fixed or compound stage, and must be distinguished by this fact from the medusiform gonophores of the preceding orders.

7. *Lucernaridæ.*—In this order a sexless Hydra gives rise to medusiform reproductive zooids. The Hydra (H. Tuba, with further working out of complexity in Lucernaria) is fixed by a Hydrorrhiza, has the Hydrosoma expanded into a sort of inverted umbrella or disc, and the polypite fixed in the middle of the concavity of the disc. Polypite four-lipped; its cavity leads to a somatic cavity, from which canals radiate to the margin of the disc : tentacles supported on the margin of the disc. This reproduces itself by lateral or basial gemmation for a given time, but at length exhibits a number of annular constrictions, gradually deepened, so as to divide the column into a number of segments, joined together by only short, narrow, tubular processes. The segments finally break away, and grow to medusiform reproductive zooids—*hooded-eyed* Medusæ. These, when perfectly grown, consist of an *umbrella*, or swimming disc (which, it will be observed, is a section of the whole body of the Hydra), and one, or many massed, polypites suspended from its concavity (Monostoma or Rhizostoma). The umbrella differs from the nectocalyx of the naked-eyed Medusæ in having eight radiating canals, which give off many lateral anastomosing branches; in having a festooned *hood* or fold of the edge of the margin overhanging the lithocysts, and in having no velum Its developmental relations in some sense also different.

Short notice of Rhizostomidæ.

Reproductive organs, in sacs at base of polypites.

From the egg emerges "planula," presently growing to form of Hydra Tuba.

Cl. II. Actinozoa.—Type, Actinia.

A short, stout cylinder with disc of attachment and free disc. Free disc traversed by slit-like mouth with extensible lips, and a tubercle at each end; round the mouth tentacles in many rows. Mouth leads to sub-globular stomach marked with longitudinal folds and grooves, and communicating with somatic cavity by a circular orifice, opposite the mouth, said to be provided with a sphincter. The stomach hangs in the somatic cavity, suspended by a number of vertical lamellæ or *mesenteries*, which are attached to the outer side of the stomach, and inner side of the vertical walls of the body, not to the base. While, therefore, all around the stomach they divide the somatic cavity into *loculi*, below the stomach the cavity is undivided, and has merely the concave edges of the mesenteries presented to it. Some of the mesenteries complete, others not (*primary* and *secondary*).

Tentacles sprout from loculi, are hollow, and perforated at their extremities.

Muscles.—Body-wall has two layers; external circular; internal longitudinal; mesenteries have four muscles each; opposing surfaces of mesenteries correspond.

Reproductive Organs.—Ova or spermatozoa developed in transverse folds on surfaces of mesenteries. Animals mostly diœcious.

Craspedum; "cinclides" of Gosse; *eye-specks; grasping tubercles; spicula* in a few; *basial horny secretion* of Adamsia; ciliation of surfaces.

Habits.—Feeding by engulfing; indigestibles rejected by mouth; locomotion by creeping movements of disc; floating with disc upwards.

Reproduction direct from ova, without metamorphosis. Out of the elements here presented the complex forms of corals are obtained, the form becoming compound by various processes of fission, budding, and extension of the base; and supported by skeletal structures corresponding homologically either to the spicula or to the basial secretion above alluded to.

In composite structures we recognise—1. Polypes. 2. Cænosarc. 3. Sclerenchyma (spicular skeleton). 4. Sclerobase (secreted, really external, skeleton).

In skeleton, besides *cœnenchyma* (skeleton of cænosarc), we have hardenings of several parts of polypes, viz.:—

Theca, wall skeleton.

Columella, base skeleton.

Septa, and *pali*, = mesenteries.

Dissepiments, regular transverse plates joining septa.

Synapticulæ, irregular and oblique processes joining septa.

Costæ, external vertical ridges corresponding to septa.

Circumstances Determining the Form of Corals.

1. Fission; its extent, direction of growth, horizontal or vertical.

2. Gemmation; *a*, basial (in sclerobasic corals, and the like of Zoanthus).

b, parietal; giving rise to branched forms—*e.g.*, Dendrophyllia.

c, calicular; pyramidal forms—*e.g.*, Cyathophyllum.

Three Conditions of Hard Parts.

1. Cups; perfect (Tubulosa), or wanting (Fungidæ).
2. Cups imbedded in Sclerenchyma or free (Astræa).
3. Tendency to excessive development of septa on the one hand (Fungidæ), or of dissepiments on the other (Tabulata).

Classification.

Orders.—1. Zoantharia.	Types.—Actinia,	Zoanthus, Madrepores.
2. Alcyonaria.	Alcyonium,	Gorgonia, Pennatula.
3. Rugosa.	Extinct.	
4. Ctenophora.	Beroe.	

1. Zoantharia.—Type, Actinia. Tentacles simple; with mesenteries in multiples of five or six.

Include three families — Malacodermata, Sclerobasica, Sclerodermata.

Note that the Millepores and Tabulata are referred by Agassiz to Hydroida.

2. Alcyonaria.—Type, Alcyonium. Tentacles, eight flattened, pinnate; with mesenteries, in multiples of four; canal-system of cænosarc. Families: Alcyonidæ, Tubiporidæ, Pennatulidæ (including Virgularia, Pennatula, Renilla), Gorgonidæ.

3. Rugosa, parts in multiples of four. These are mostly referred to Hydroida by Agassiz.

4. Ctenophora.—Type, Beroe or Cydippe.

Transparent, free-swimming forms, without any skeleton, swimming by means of rows of tiny paddles (coalesced cilia). These are to be compared with Actiniæ, in which the mesenteries may be supposed to have become enormously swollen and transparent, leaving only eight canals to represent the loculi—one corresponding to each line of paddles,—which canals are joined by radiating channels to an axial and paraxial system of canals, representing stomach and somatic cavity. Tentacles present or not.—In some cases highly organized. Parts evidently in multiples of four.

SUB-KINGDOM, ANNULOSA.—Includes Classes—

Insecta	Bees and Butterflies.
Arachnida	Spiders and Mites
Crustacea	Lobster, Crab, Barnacle.
Myriapoda	Centipede and Julus.
Annelida	Worms, not parasitic.
Scolecida	Worms, mostly parasitic.
Echinodermata	Starfishes.

These, as before noticed, are collected into two groups: a higher, Articulata, including the first four classes; a lower, Annuloida, including the remaining three.

Articulata.—Body composed of distinct segments, with well-marked lateral appendages; in all, the nervous system forms a longitudinal chain of ganglia, perforated anteriorly by the alimentary canal; all possess a dorsal contractile chamber (heart) connected with the distribution of the fluid of the perivisceral cavity—the true blood. No ciliation of external surface.

Annuloida.—No true heart; all have a set of vessels carrying a fluid distinct from that of the perivisceral cavity; distinction of segments often lost; appendages mostly imperfect where developed, and altogether wanting in a large part of the group. There may be no trace of nervous system, and even the alimentary canal may be wanting. Ciliation common.

Begin with Annuloida: Annelida taken as a sort of central class, with definite outgoings in the direction of Scolecida and Echinodermata respectively.

Cl. ANNELIDA.—Includes five orders :—

Orders : 1.	Annelida	Errantia	Marine Annelida, or A. proper.
2.	,,	Tubicola	
3.	,,	Terricola.	
4.	,,	Suctoria	(Hirudinidæ.)
5.	,,	Gephyrea, or	

ıke an errant or locomotive Marine Annelid, such as ereis, or Aphrodite, as first type.

Body elongated, worm-shaped; divided by transverse nstrictions into a number of segments, each similar and uivalent to each, but with varying development of formal ements in different parts of the body, particularly in the o ends as compared with the middle portion.

Segments generally called "*somites*." Take a somite from iddle of chain.

ırts : Dorsal and ventral arch. Each arch ends on each side in a conical eminence constituting, with its appendages, a locomotive organ (dorsal and ventral "*oars*" of Cuvier; "*Notopodium*" and "*Neuropodium*" of Huxley.)

Appendages of oars. 1. Bristles and spikes (*setæ* and *acicula)* imbedded, and moved by muscles. 2. Proximal, (as regards median line) a soft process, which may be either slender and subarticulated, with a swollen pigmented base (*cirrhus*), or may be expanded, membranous, and more or less stalked (*elytron*). Elytra found on dorsal surface alternating with cirrhi, or on alternating segments (Aphrodite), and having a protective relation to the breathing organs.

On dorsal arch, proximal to cirrhus or elytron, the breathing organ—a surface, cone, or tree.

On ventral arch, in corresponding position the reproductive prominence.

Internally, each somite typically contains a marked segment of alimentary canal, a pair of nervous ganglia, a definite division of circulatory system, a proper set of muscles, and distinct reproductive organs.

Anterior somites; cirrhi developed, and acquire title of tentacula; setæ and acicula dwarfed or lost. First few somites more or less fused to form a head; the mouth placed on the inferior aspect of 2nd, 3rd, or 4th.

Posteriorly similar but less pronounced changes. Anus opens usually on inferior surface of last somite but one.

Muscular system.—Muscles connected with external skeleton and oars, numerous, and regularly arranged.

Alimentary Canal.—Usually runs through the body in one straight line without flexure or convolutions. Usually exhibits a dilatation corresponding to each somite, and linked to its walls by delicate mesenteries. These segmental dilatations often also send off branching diverticula. (Aphrodite.)

At commencement of alimentary canal often a proboscis, formed by a very muscular evertible pharynx; supporting hooks or teeth; teeth (sometimes called "jaws") are placed on each side of the mouth, and work in horizontal plane.

Salivary glands (?) of Nereis.

Hepatic function (?) of cæcal diverticula.

Blood, and perivisceral cavity.—Fluid, filled with small oat-shaped corpuscles; surface ciliated: no heart; distribution of fluid by cilia and by movements of body; all the tissues bathed in this fluid.

Pseudo-hæmal system.—A system of closed contractile vessels, usually much convoluted and exhibiting many dilatations—so-called hearts—which have, however, no extra thickness of wall. They contain a non-corpusculated, transparent fluid, variously coloured, and propelled by peristalsis of the walls of the vessels. This system appears very late in development; it is not a blood-system, but rather to be compared to tracheal system of insects. The system always much connected with respiration, and always throws fluid coming from respiratory organs towards head. Arrangement of the vessels often very complicated, but general principle is that there is a dorsal stream towards head, and a ventral back-flowing stream.

Respiration.—Primarily through the skin. Chief activity in certain dorsal spots, which are in many forms, *e.g.*, Arenicola, projected into arborescent processes filled with plexuses of pseudo-hæmal system, covered by the thinnest possible skin, and shrinking almost to disappearance when the vessels contract, while in other forms they are supported by cartilage. In some cases, the elytra seem to aid in the function; in others, there are merely plexuses under the skin without projection. In some cases there are projections containing fluid of perivisceral cavity instead of pseudo-hæmal vessels. Here an important difference;—if pseudo-hæmal, external surface not ciliated; if perivisceral, surface ciliated.

Nervous system.—Ganglia of chain, in pairs corresponding to somites; ganglia of each pair united by long or short transverse commissural cords, or fused into one.

Ganglia of somites anterior to mouth, gathered usually into one supra-œsophageal mass, giving off branches to smaller ganglia appropriated to sense organs and pharynx.

Eyes, vary in development; in lower stages merely an expansion of nerve covered by pigment; but lens, and even a sort of cornea may be added. Ears, doubtful.

Reproduction.—Genital organs. A parallel series of saccular bodies, a pair to each segment. When sexual elements developed, the sacs burst and discharge their contents into the perivisceral cavity. These worms unisexual;

congress occurs; products emitted by genital pores already noticed. Complete knowledge wanting.

Ova, after fecundation, developed either within the body, or in pouches attached to the body, or beneath the elytra.

Development (Terebella).—Embryo first a ciliated sphere; next the sphere elongated to a cylinder, and the cilia lost except at three circlets, two anterior surrounding the future head, one posterior. The mouth opens between the two anterior circlets, one of which is, therefore, prestomial; the other circlets embracing the alimentary canal. Fresh segments are formed in the bald space just in front of the posterior circlet, not by growth beyond the last circlet; and it will be generally observed, in all Annulosa, that growth is most active in the region of the ante-penultimate or penultimate segment, not of the terminal.

In Nereis prolifera, this portion so active that a complete animal is formed, and eventually thrown off as a bud from the parent, the process being repeated several times, and not infrequently going on at once in several stages. The parent, however, does not form true sexual organs during the process, and the worms thus budded off are often little more than reproductive zooids, having hardly other contents than sexual organs.

Compare other forms.

Tubicola.—Type, Terebella, or Sabella.—Fixed; body contained in tube. Setæ, &c., dwarfed to mere organs of attachment. Respiratory processes surround head, taking two forms: 1. Long, unbranched, flexible, ciliated tentacles, containing perivisceral fluid; 2. Branched, more fixed, often stiffened, not ciliated processes, containing pseudo-hæmal vessels. No proboscis or teeth. Congress of the sexes being impossible, these worms are gregarious, and fertilization goes on much as in diœcious plants.

From the stand-point of the Marine Annelid we look down

three avenues leading respectively by easy steps to the Echinodermata, to the round, and to the flat worms among the Scolecida. The Gephyrea form so decided a transition between the Annelida and Echinodermata, that it is hard to say which class has the better claim to include them. Through the Terricola (Lumbricina) we approach the nematoid worms; and through the Suctoria (Hirudinidæ, or Discophora) we find easy transition to turbellarians, flukes, and tapeworms in succession.

First in *Lumbricina*, the external form shows far less distinction between somites; setæ reduced in numbers, regularity, and importance; some of the Naids in both respects forming transitions between the higher Annelids and the Earthworm. In the Earthworm, the muscles, instead of taking segmental distribution, form cylinders, one within the other, running the whole length of the body; constituting three layers, external circular, internal longitudinal, middle of decussating oblique fibres. Alimentary canal, straight, not much complicated by processes. Pharynx often evertible in Naids, not in Earthworm, in which the mouth is a single terminal orifice, leading by a long pharynx to a sort of gizzard, placed one-fifth down the body, and followed by a simple intestine, the outer wall of which is surrounded by a glandular structure of bright yellow colour.

Perivisceral cavity smaller than in Annelids proper.

Pseudo-hæmal system well developed.

No external respiratory organs, but subcutaneous processes very rich. Ciliated tubes, however, are found in the Naids particularly, constituting inverted respiratory organs, establishing a possible communication between the perivisceral cavity and the surrounding medium, and surrounded by special plexuses of the pseudo-hæmal system.

Some respire by means of the posterior part of the alimentary canal, which is ciliated.

Nervous chain in earthworm a long thread with scarcely any trace of ganglionic enlargements; ring round œsophagus.

Earthworm hermaphrodite; ova and spermatozoa developed in sacs surrounding pharynx, apparently communicating with each other internally, and opening externally by small orifices in the thickened banded portion of the body. Copulation; ova discharged into perivisceral cavity; make exit by apertures at posterior part of body; nidamental capsules.

In Naids, certain of the respiratory tubes are turned into special reproductive organs.

Suctoria, Leech.

No distinct segmentation; no setæ; muscular system much as in earthworm, expanded into two hollow cones, round mouth and anus.

Alimentary canal; three dental ridges on sides of oval cone, radiating from mouth. Canal much sacculated, but not otherwise differentiated.

Perivisceral cavity encroached upon almost to obliteration by great bulk of alimentary canal.

Pseudo-hæmal system well developed.

Respiratory organs as in Naids.

Nervous system; thread-like cord.

Eye-spots on margin of anterior sucker, each with a nervous twig from œsophageal collar.

Reproduction much as in earthworm.

Gephyrea, Sipunculus.

Worm-formed animals, with only traces of segmentation, and having integument hardened by horny as opposed to calcareous deposit. They have a convoluted alimentary canal, and a system of vessels resembling the main trunks of the "ambulacral system" of the Echinodermata, but without any ambulacra. Diœcious, with curious developmental metamorphoses, as for instance in Actinotrocha and Phoronis, larval and adult forms of one Sipunculid.

These linking-forms are of doubtful position, and though in conformity with received usage they are here placed among the Annelida, approach possibly more closely to the Echinodermata.

Cl. Scolecida. Far from compact, the included orders being linked together by the possession of a water-vascular system, but otherwise exhibiting great differences among themselves. The orders, in fact, are so different that it is not possible to find any central type, and they must be taken in detail.

Orders.—	1. Turbellaria.	Planaria, Nemertes
	2. Trematoda.	Flukes.
	3. Tæniada (Cestodea).	Tapeworms.
	4. Acanthocephala.	Echinorhynchus.
	5. Nematoidea.	Ascaris.
	6. Gordiacea.	Gordius, Mermis.
	7. Rotifera.	Wheel-animalcules.

Order 1. *Turbellaria*, round or flat worms with little or no segmentation, usually flattened shape, and ciliated integument, found in both fresh and sea-water, and in damp places on land. Planaria may be taken as a type.

Body flat, leech-like in shape, ciliated on surface with feeble transverse striation; at anterior part a pair of eyes. Ill made-out muscles beneath skin. Mouth placed on inferior aspect of body, usually about middle; an extensive net-like proboscis; a globular pharynx, and a ramified alimentary canal, ending at all points blindly, without any anus. Cæca dilated, with dark pigment. Perivisceral space with characteristic fluid. No projecting respiratory organs. Water-vascular system; a set of branching tubes, sometimes ciliated within, sometimes not, communicating externally with the surrounding medium, but not with the perivisceral cavity; contents, structureless fluid.

Nervous system: a large bilobed ganglion in anterior part of body, sending threads backwards. Branches to eye-spots. Eye-spots sometimes pigment only, sometimes a lens with pigment on the side of the nerve.

Reproduction; hermaphrodite; organs much complicated. Male orifice in Planaria on ventral aspect, behind mouth; leads to an open sac lodging a cylindrical intromittent organ; testes, two long, bent, tubular organs with ducts leading to a sort of vesicula seminalis placed at the base of the penis.

Ovaries not distinct, but ova are found distributed through the body in the interspaces of organs. Two dilated oviducts, possibly branching after the fashion of the alimentary canal, can be traced on each side of the body; they unite to form a large cavity (spermotheca ?) from which a copulatory tube (vagina) runs to an orifice placed just behind the male orifice. Vitellarium sometimes to be detected; and germigéne (?) also, both probably opening into oviduct near spermotheca (cf. Trematoda).

Compare with leech as to form, and alimentary canal, with Annelid embryo as to ciliation of surface. But there are forms of Turbellaria which have a perfect alimentary canal, as well as others having a stem of canal without cæcal diverticula. And there are both hermaphrodite and diœcious Turbellarians. Thread-cells in some forms.

Hence classification.

Hermaphrodite—	Aprocta (without anus)	Dendrocœla— Planaria. Rhabdocœla.
Chiefly unisexual; long-vermiform	Proctucha (having anus)	Arhynchia. Rhynchocæla—Nemertes.

The Nemertidæ approach very closely to the Annelida in form, in the water-vascular system, which, in the adult at least (Huxley), is closed, and composed of contractile vessels, and in the arrangement of the reproductive organs; proboscis, however, distinct from alimentary canal.

Order 2. *Trematoda*, mostly flat, parasitic worms, resembling Turbellarians in form, but not ciliated on surface. Aproctous. Type, Distoma Hepaticum; excessively flattened, somewhat oval in outline, presenting two suckers, one at the anterior extremity of the oval, perforated by the mouth, the other on the ventral surface at no great distance behind the former, imperforate. Length about one inch.

Skin delicate, transparent, chitinous, little if at all marked with transverse striæ. Muscles of no very regular distribution within.

Mouth leads to a goblet-shaped muscular pharynx; beyond this the alimentary canal runs as a simple tube to a point corresponding with the edge of the ventral sucker, and there divides into two branches, at first divergent, afterwards parallel, ending cæcally near the posterior end of the body; each gives off from its outer side a number of dendritic branches ending in cæcal dilatations; there is no anus. This alimentary canal supported in a distinct perivisceral cavity by mesenteries.

Water-vascular system. From a minute pore placed at the posterior end of the body a saccular vessel starts forward and divides shortly into two large sinuous branches ending near the mouth cæcally; they are not ciliated, but contractile, and contain, as well as fluid, minute highly refractile corpuscles; they give off branches which ramify, are in places ciliated, and are not contractile; the fluid is not corpusculated in the branches. This apparatus is by some supposed to have a urinary function (Van Beneden); by others a respiratory function. Nervous system very imperfectly known. Two threads, running one each side of the body, and communicating between the suckers, are described, and supposed to be nerves. The life of the creature renders any high organization of nervous system unnecessary.

On the other hand, the reproductive system is much developed, and occupies a large part of the body. Animal hermaphrodite.

Female organs: 1. Ovary (*germigéne*) with duct; 2. Two *vitellaria* (yelk-supplying organs); 3. Uterus; 4. Vagina. Ovary, subglobular, near median line just behind ventral sucker. Contains a transparent material with imbedded nucleated vesicles, most advanced at commencement of duct; duct joined by yelk-tubes, by internal vas deferens, and then expands into a convoluted tubular oviduct (uterus) occupying a considerable space in front of the ventral sucker; vagina opens into a common vestibulum just behind the oval sucker. The germ-cells invested by yelk, and impregnated shortly after leaving the ovary; then in the convolutions of the uterus they acquire their shell.

The vitellaria occupy the lateral region of the body on each side; they consist of delicate racemose vessels, communicating on each side with one long trunk running parallel to the margin, and internal to the vesicles; this trunk, blind at both extremities, sends from its middle a transverse branch to join the oviduct.

Male Organs: 1. Testis; 2. Internal vas deferens; 3. A pair of external vasa deferentia; 4. Penis and sac. Testis, a convoluted tube, with numerous lateral cæca, occupying a space behind the ovary, between the branches of the alimentary canal; from this one short duct runs into the oviduct close to the entrance of the vitellarian duct, and two long ducts lead to the sac of the penis. Penis contained within a sac; when everted, spiral and armed with dense spines; placed side by side with vaginal orifice, having a common vestibulum.

Mature eggs consist of a thick transparent shell, with

brown, semi-transparent contents, not quite filling the shell. *Varieties of Trematoda.*

Body may be flat, cylindrical, or irregular. Suckers, one or many. Skin smooth, or transversely striated, or armed with minute hooks or recurved spines attached to the transverse ridges. Mouth varies in position; alimentary canal usually bifurcated, but division often proceeds no further. In no instance does anus exist. Nervous system better developed in some forms. Most are hermaphrodite; note, however, Bilharzia hæmatobia.

Development.—In some cases no metamorphosis, but usually a long and interesting history, which from many observations and descriptions may be built up in the following way:—

1. From egg issues a ciliated embryo, which is capable of locomotion, more naturally in water, may be furnished with eye-spots (Monostomum), and has its interior in great part occupied by a long, cylindrical, cyst-like body.

2. Embryo becomes stationary, loses its skin, and sets free the contained body (*cercaria-cyst, redia, or sporo-cyst*), which is commonly mobile, and provided with two symmetrical lateral appendages, and a sort of tail. In some, at the anterior part of the body, is a sucker-like mouth leading to a short cæcal digestive canal. Behind this the cavity of the body filled with little caudate worms (*cercariæ*), which are budded off from the walls of the body. Such cysts often found in breathing organs of fresh-water snails.

3. *Cercariæ* set free by rupture of cyst; variously provided with suckers; body oval, pointed anteriorly; a flexible tail, used in swimming. Oral sucker anterior, with usually one or more boring spikes appended; alimentary canal simply once branched; rudimentary water-vascular system; but no reproductive organs. This creature swims about till it finds

a resting-place in the body of snail or soft-bodied aquatic insect-larva, burrowing into the interior by means of its barbs, and when fairly entered casting away its tail; afterwards encysted.

4. When such an encysted larva finds its way into the alimentary canal of a vertebrate animal, it is set free, and grows to adult fluke form, acquiring sexual organs.

The embryonic and larval forms are usually found free, or in the interior of Invertebrata; the adult forms mostly in the alimentary canal and its off-shoots in Vertebrata, but may be found also in the blood-vessels, and even in the vitreous humour.

The gentle transition from these two orders to the leech-tribe may again be noticed, particularly in respect of form, suckers, and ramifications of alimentary canal encroaching upon perivisceral cavity.

Order *Tæniada* (Cestodea), Tapeworms.

The mature worm, flattened, elongated, ribbon-like, divided into well-defined segments, each perfect in itself, and capable of maintaining a short separate existence. Whole worm—*strobila*; segment—*proglottis.*

The worm is found thus perfectly segmented only towards one extremity; at the other it thins away to a narrow thread-like neck, and ends in a round head about the size of the head of a pin. The neck near the head is smooth and non-segmented, but as it widens towards the body, it begins to be marked by transverse striæ, at first closely placed, then gradually drawn apart, till at length the segments which they mark off are often three or four times as long as broad.

Parts of Head:—

1. Terminal proboscis, often retractile within a muscular sac—usually single; four in Tetrarhynchus.

2. Circlet of hooks, on proboscis, or, if proboscis absent, on anterior part of head.

3. Suckers; mere shallow pits (Bothriocephalus), or projecting suckers with thick fleshy lips (Tænia).

Hooks, partly free, partly imbedded; homologues of setæ of Annelids. Neck, below the suckers, in some armed with hooks.

Mature Proglottis. (Tænia solium).—Of elongated oblong form; whitish colour, opaque.

Chitinous epiderm; longitudinal fibres beneath this, and beneath them transverse fibres; through these scattered bright (microscopic) spherical bodies, calcareous, with concentric lamination.

No digestive system, unless the proboscis, with its muscular sac, be a rudiment.

Water-vascular System.—A pair of vessels running down one on each side of each proglottis, communicating with one another by a transverse branch across the posterior part of each proglottis, close to the margin. These vessels form a continuous structure in the strobila—a sort of ladder; they form convolutions in the head, and therein communicate; and when the worm is perfect, the transverse branch of the last segment opens externally by a pore in the median line; the main trunks give off many lateral offsets which branch freely. The branches are said to be ciliated internally.

Nervous System.—Mr. Huxley has described a structure possibly of nervous nature as existing in the middle of the head of the tapeworm.

Reproduction.—All hermaphrodite.

In Tænia solium the genital apertures are placed together on small cupped eminences on one lateral margin of a segment, the side alternating in adjoining segments.

The lower or posterior aperture is that of the vagina, a narrow tube, curved inwards and backwards toward the middle of the posterior margin of the proglottis, and there dilated into a pyriform vesicle (spermotheca ?), beyond which it appears to be joined by the ducts from the ovary and vitellarium, and then expands into a ramified " uterus."

Ovary.—An expanded, lobed, leafy organ, occupying the posterior sixth of the body, and containing only germ-vesicles.

Vitellaria.—Longitudinal sacculated glands, placed on each side of the body, close to the longitudinal canals of the water-vascular system ; their ducts not clearly traceable.

Uterus, a long central tube running forward from the posterior end of the spermotheca, with lateral ramifying offsets, ending cæcally, like the alimentary canal in Distomum. Male Organs—

Testes are little vesicles placed in the intervals of the ramification of the uterus ; their efferent ducts not traceable, but the termination of the spermatic duct is seen as a densely convoluted tube running close to the commencement of the vagina, but more perpendicular to the lateral margin ; on the one side it opens out, and is lost toward the median line of the body, on the other it ends in a sac containing a hook-beset evertible penis.—Compare Bothriocephalus ; genital openings in median line of segments, towards posterior margin. Ligula, no distinct segmentation, but "brood-places."

Ovum, evidently retained until the proglottis dies or is digested ; shape oval, about $\frac{1}{800}$th by $\frac{1}{1100}$th in. ; shell dense, hard, smooth, or beset with asperities ; contents gelatinous, with numerous bright granules.

Embryo, when set free from egg, oval ; supports six small hooks or boring spicula, in pairs, symmetrical on each side of medial vertical plane, which passes through the middle pair. Embryo has power of locomotion, and of boring by means of hooks.

This embryo undergoes further development on entering into the tissues of animals; becoming encysted, and expanding by imbibition of fluid to a vesicular form, the hooks remaining, however, still very close together.

At one point in the wall of the vesicle, near the hooks, a deposit of germinal matter takes place, projecting into the cavity of the vesicle. This knob is next hollowed out by a pit or indent running in from the outer surface, and is turned into a flask with a small neck and narrow external opening; at the bottom of the flask a cellular projection rises like the "kick" of a wine-bottle, presently developing into a tænia-head with the appendages proper to the particular species, and a tænia-neck with often very definite segmentation, but no development of organs. This tænia-head, with its neck, is therefore budded off from the embryo. It is now called *scolex*, and the rest of the embryo *receptaculum scolecis.*

When such a compound body is introduced into the alimentary canal of a vertebrate animal, the scolex becomes detached from the receptaculum, and commences independent existence, growing rapidly to the rank of mature sexually-perfect strobila. This strobila comparable to Hydra Tuba, with sexually-perfect segments. Note also, however, the relation of the cercaria-cyst to the embryo in Monostomum as paralleled by the relation of the scolex to the receptaculum.

Variations.—Embryo much the same in all Tæniadæ. Larva (or scolex and receptaculum) varies; a single scolex with a dropsical receptaculum constitutes a Cysticercus, a form found encysted in the liver, peritoneum, connective tissue, and many other parts of animals, Vertebrate and Invertebrate.

A receptaculum may bud off many scoleces from its surface, Cœnurus.

In other cases the scoleces are found within the receptaculum—Echinococcus,— and here often we find cyst within cyst, containing scoleces—pill-box hydatids.

The Echinococcus, Cœnurus, and Cysticercus, formerly called Cystic Entozoa, and, their relation of larva to adult tapeworm form not being known, were considered as a separate group.

Detail of experiments upon which those statements are founded: Leuckart, Stein, Siebold, Cobbold.

Rabbits, &c., fed with tænia-eggs, become filled with scoleces. Dogs and predaceous animals fed with scoleces develope tapeworms.

Particular animals infested by particular kinds of tapeworm larva and strobila respectively.

Tapeworms infesting man, belong to two genera, Tænia and Bothriocephalus. Tæniæ prevalent in England and France; Bothriocephali in Russia, and Europe beyond the Rhine.

Tænia serrata of dog and cat in relation to Cysticercus pisiformis of rabbit.

Similar relations in cystic form infesting stickleback, and strobila lodging in predaceous aquatic birds, salmon, and pike, &c.

Relations of such facts to public health: Raw meat and unwashed vegetables dangerous; danger from evacuations of domestic animals.

Order *Acanthocephala.*—Type, Echinorhynchus. A small order. Round-bodied worms, not segmented; no alimentary canal; a large, retractile, thickly-hooked proboscis. Unisexual. Budding within. Water-vascular system fairly developed. Lemniscus. Intermediate between Tænidæ and Gordiacea.

Order *Gordiacea.*—Long, round worms, with alimentary canal, but no anus. Gordius, and Mermis, hair-worms, parasitic during part of their life, but free at breeding time —worm-showers.

Order *Nematoidea.*—Round worms, free or parasitic. Type, Ascaris Lumbricoïdes. In shape and size much resembling a large earthworm. Diœcious. Female, five to eight inches long; male, three inches long. Integument marked by fine closely-set transverse striations; thin, transparent, divisible into several layers, viz.:—1. An outer structureless chitinous epidermis. 2. Several layers of decussating fibres (Siebold), or of lamellæ with markings (Bastian). 3. A deep "cellulo-granular" layer. According to Bastian, the granular layer is secretory of the layers outside, which are again in succession so many stages of the formation of the investing chitinous layer. Moults. Median and lateral lines, projections of the inner layer ("*Enderon*" of Bastian). Cephalic papillæ. Integumental pores and channels, leading to deep cellular layer; and again, within this, four longitudinal (muscular ?) bands, two ventral, two dorsal, separated from each other by the lateral and median lines. Mouth at anterior end of body; three fleshy lips, no armature; long muscular pharynx; straight intestine, ending in anus, short of the posterior termination of the body. Intestine has very delicate walls, surrounded by a soft glandular structure (*appendices nourriciers* of Cloquet; glandular portions of muscles, Bastian); mesenteries abundant in anterior half of body, few in posterior.

Water-vascular System.—Two lateral longitudinal canals with transverse communication in anterior part of body, said to communicate externally. (Von Siebold). Bastian, confirming this, places the canals in lateral thickenings of the deep cellular layer of the integument.

Nervous System variously represented.—A ring of nerve-fibre surrounds, according to Bastian, the œsophagus, and has ganglionic masses connected with it in front and behind;

branches run forwards to mouth, cephalic lobes, and lateral muscles; the backward branches not well traced.

Reproduction. Female.—External orifice a minute pore at the middle of the body on its ventral aspect; from this a single tube (vagina) half an inch long; bifurcating into two tubes each some two to three feet long, divisible into several tracts, viz., uterus, oviduct, vitellarium, and ovary. These tubes coiled in an intricate way round posterior half of alimentary canal.

Ova commence as germinal vesicles at the cæcal end of each tube; this part of tube about three inches long or more, very fine and transparent; passing into the next part, which is white and opaque, they become successively imbedded in yelk, and the yelk becomes segmented around each in polygonal masses; from the vitellarium these compound masses pass singly, and in oval form, through a constriction into a thick-walled oviduct, where they meet with the spermatozoa, and are afterwards invested by a gelatinous coat (*chorion*) presently hardening to a shell.

Male.—Orifice near posterior end of body. Internal organ. A single convoluted tube, two to three feet long; divisible into testis, vas deferens, vesicula seminalis, and ductus ejaculatorius, just within the external orifice—a contractile sac with two extrusible copulatory spicules.

The spermatozoa (Nelson) attain by the time that they are emitted a vesicular form, and undergo further development into a flask with open mouth, as they make their way along the female tube to the commencement of the oviduct.

Development without Metamorphosis.—This worm inhabits small intestine of man.

Other forms infesting man:—

Tricocephalus dispar; lower part of small, and upper part of largeintestine.

Oxyuris vermicularis; "threadworm;" rectum.

Strongylus (Eustrongylus) gigas; liver, lungs, kidneys.

Ancylostomum duodenale; found only on the other side of the Alps.

Filaria medinensis; Guinea-worm; subcutaneous tissue.

Trichina spiralis; encysted larval form in muscles; sexual form in alimentary canal.

In development of many Nematoids there is an alternation of free and parasitic habit.

Order *Rotifera.* In Ascaris we have come back in many points to the Annelidan type; and in the Rotifera we are carried in some respects even further toward the Crustacea, at the same time that we are carried by downgoing characters towards the Infusoria.

Rotifera.—Microscopic. Elongated body, divided very distinctly into segments, which may be nine or ten in number. Integument chitinous; transverse muscles. Anterior part of body presents a ciliated disc, in the middle or on the lower aspect of which is the mouth. Arrangements of disc very various. Posterior end of body attenuated; last segment often supports two little appendages, forming a sort of foot, and acting like forceps. Some Rotifers swim freely; some are fixed, and protected by various kinds of house. Some have a sort of carapace made out of the anterior segments of the body; others hardly show any traces even of segmentation.

Mouth leads to a muscular pharynx, with powerful masticatory apparatus, often like grindstones; œsophagus short; stomach oval, internally ciliated, with investing hepatic (?) cæca; short intestine; valvular cloaca; salivary glands (?) at end of œsophagus.

Water-vascular System.—First, a large contractile sac, with thin, transparent, homogeneous walls, communicating with cloaca. Second, two delicate wavy tubes, of uniform calibre, non-contractile, starting from the sac and running forward;

to sides of tubes attached little hollow pear-shaped bodies, each with a long cilium playing internally, fixed to the distal end of the cavity ; these appear to communicate with the perivisceral cavity. Sac contracts rhythmically, without causing change in calibre of tubes.

Nervous System.—A single ganglion on lower aspect of œsophagus. Eye-spots, calcaria (antenniform processes).

Reproduction.—Unisexual. Females much larger than males.

Ovary an elongated pear-shaped body adjoining the cloaca, into which it is said to open. After copulation, spermatozoa are found in the perivsceral cavity of the female, and the embryo undergoes a considerable degree of development therein.

Male often contains only a testis and vas deferens. Penis, perforate, retractile.

No metamorphosis.

Compare briefly, Melicerta, Stephanoceros, Floscularia. Quasi-parasitic habit of some Rotifers. Resuscitation after dying.

Cl. Echinodermata.—Having certain characters in common with Annuloida, are in many respects so unlike them and all other animals that it becomes a question whether they should not form a sub-kingdom by themselves. They will be best understood by the minute analysis of a central form. We note, therefore, that there are about five recognised orders :—

1. Crinoidea.	Comatula (Antedon), Feather Stars.
2. Ophiuridea.	Snake Stars.
3. Asteridea.	Asterias—Starfish.
4. Echinidea.	Sea Urchins.
5. Holuthuridea.	Sea Cucumbers.

And we take a common form from the middle order, the Asteridea.

Type, Asterias; common starfish.

Form, a depressed spheroidal body, extended in the horizontal plane into five or more radial angles or arms, which are arranged with great regularity round a central vertical axis, but exhibit also, with the body, a bilateral symmetry on each side of a vertical plane corresponding to a line joining the mouth and a dorsal appendage (*madreporic tubercle*) placed on the body opposite the retiring angle between two arms (*inter-radial space*). The whole structure has two surfaces, dorsal and ventral. The mouth is placed in the middle of the ventral surface, and on the same aspect of the arms are found the locomotive suckers peculiar to the class (ambulacra). This surface (and its homologue through the class) is called the "ambulacral;" the dorsal (or remaining portion of) surface the "antambulacral."

Ambulacral structures.—On lower surface of any starfish, the ambulacra are to be seen running in parallel series along causeways radiating from the mouth along the middle of each arm, the structures being in each arm symmetrical on each side of the median line of the arm.

The ambulacra are soft cylindrical sacs, permanently projecting from the surface, but varying in the amount of their extension. Their free extremity is flattened and hollowed to form a sucker, often with the addition of an earthy disc; their attached extremity perforates the integument by two hollow roots, by which it is brought into communication with a vessel placed within the wall of the arm running along the median line. Such a vessel is common to all the feet of its arm, and besides this, has also a number of little hollow vesicles connected with it, each corresponding with a foot or ambulacrum, and apparently intended by its contraction or dilatation to regulate the amount of protrusion of the foot. Each median (ambulacral) vessel runs to join a circular vessel surrounding the œsophagus; with this circlet are connected a number of free-hanging sacs (*Polian vesicles*), and one vessel running to the madreporic tubercle. This vessel is generally called the madreporic vessel or duct; it has earthy matter in its walls, and was formerly called the "*sand canal*," a filtering process being attributed to it in conjunction with the porous madreporic tubercle.

Integument, tough, thick, contractile. Earthy matter deposited in it in a reticulate form, and aggregated in Asterias into a sort of skeleton. On the dorsal surface the skeleton is irregular and reticulated. On the ventral surface, particularly in the arms, the skeleton consists of a number of plates placed at right angles to the axis of arms built up into segments, and moving upon one another after the fashion of vertebræ. The central plates (a pair) are called "*ambulacral*" ossicles, those adjoining on each side "*adambulacral*," and any additional lateral plates "*intermediate*." The ambulacral vessel runs beneath the integument along the under surface of the ambulacral ossicles, which form a groove for it.

Appendages of Skin:—

1. *Spines.* Irregular multifid processes (*paxillæ*) arranged mostly irregularly, and not provided with any distinct joint at the base.

2. Soft ciliate processes of skin, containing offsets of perivisceral cavity, on dorsal region.

3. *Pedicellariæ.* Curious structures, consisting of a column supporting a sort of forceps having two or three short blades, moved by muscular tissues. Probably modifications of spines.

Digestive System.—Mouth circular, protrusile to a very considerable extent (Forbes's drawing); no oval skeleton; stomach shaped like a tomato, sending a pair of racemose cæcal processes into each arm, where they lie above the ambulacral ossicles. Anus present or not; if present, rarely, if ever, functional.

Circulation.—Starfishes possess a system of vessels distinct from the ambulacral system, apparently corresponding to the pseudo-hæmal system of the Annelida. It appears to consist of a circlet surrounding the œsophagus, and another surrounding the intestine above the stomach; the two connected by one or two tumid vessels or "hearts." Intermediate branches go to alimentary canal, and from the œsophageal circlet a vessel radiates along the floor of each arm. The pseudo-hæmal circlet internal to the ambulacral.

Nervous system.—A circular collar surrounding the œsophagus, external to the ambulacral circlet; branches to viscera, and one main thread to each arm, running along the median line of the arm, and ending in eye-spots at the tip of the arm. Eye-spots often protected by a sort of calcareous lid. The nerve runs superficial to the ambulacral vessel.

Genital organs.—Mostly diœcious. In each ray two bunches of cæca (testes or ovaria). The adjoining bunches of adjoining rays connected together by one excretory duct opening at a point corresponding to the interval or angle between two rays or arms not far from the mouth.

Development.—Embryo, in first stage, ciliated.

Second stage, convex dorsally, concave ventrally; a flexuous ciliated fringe encircles the margin of the concavity, in which is placed the mouth; cilia elsewhere disappear; well-marked stomach and intestine; anus opens on convexity. The fringe, therefore, encircles the body between mouth and anus. Another circlet in front of the mouth. Such a larva called a *Bipinnaria*, from the regular and symmetrical arrangement of the fin-like bends of the ciliated band on each side of the body.

Third stage. The future starfish developed within this larva; an indent from the dorsal surface behind the band assumes a tubular form, and, bifurcating, encircles the œsophagus—this the rudiment of the ambulacral system, the madreporic canal and tubercle being the remains of the first tube. Around this germinal matter deposited, and presently shaped to the form of starfish, which includes the stomach and parts of the œsophagus and intestine of the larva. Eventually the starfish breaks away, leaving the larva to die. The resemblance of this embryo in early stages to the embryo of Annelida, is well pointed out by Mr. Huxley. From the Asterid form we work first through Ophiuridea to Crinoidea.

Order *Ophiuridea.* Snake stars. Arms elongated, and devoted to locomotion only, the digestive and reproductive cæca being withdrawn into the central sub-globular body.

Arms; supported internally by an axis of jointed discs, representing apparently the fused ambulacral ossicles of starfish; protected externally by an armour of imbricated plates, from between which, without the formation of an ambulacral causeway, the suckers protrude. No vesicles at base of suckers.

Body also protected by imbricating, or at least not ankylosed, plates.

Alimentary canal, a few earthy plates around œsophagus. No anus.

Madreporic vessel ends in one of five large plates surrounding the mouth inter-radially; the plate not perforated.

Genital organs open by vertical slits at junction of arms with body.

Reproduction much as in Echinus, to be presently described.

Through Euryalidæ we pass on to—

Order *Crinoidea.*—Mostly fossil; three existing forms—Rhizocrinus, representing fossil Encrinites; Pentacrinus, representing fossil Pentacrinites; Pentacrinus Europæus, a fixed form in its early life, afterwards becomes a free feather star, Comatula or Antedon.

Brief note of general anatomy:—

Comatula consists of central rounded body, and arms. Body supported by dense, suture-joined, immovable dermal plates, constituting together a "*calyx*" open on the oral aspect; fixed during early life by a column of discs continued from a basial disc situated on the middle of the aboral (apical) surface. The plates in the body arranged with great regularity in five radial series. Arms, five, each dividing into two branches; flexible, supported by articulating discs; with lateral processes (*pinnules*) given off at regular intervals, corresponding to discs of support; ambulacral processes ranged in median sulcus tentacularis of arms and pinnules; their function here respiratory rather than locomotive; on apical aspect of calyx, a number of jointed processes, hooked at the end (cirrhi).

Alimentary canal complete; anus opening inter-radially near mouth; the canal said to send branches into arms, but this denied by Carpenter.

Reproductive organs external, in sacs developed on pinnules near base of arms.

In development, the embryo buds off the future Crinoid without giving up its alimentary canal. The young Crinoid has a peduncle of attachment, permanent in Pentacrinus, not in Comatula.

Again, from Asterid form we work through Echinidea to Holothuridea.

Order *Echinidea.*—Type, Echinus. Body globular, without arms, which are, as it were, altogether retracted and fused with the ambulacral surface of the body.

Integument supported by earthy matter in the form of a globular shell, with a perforation at each pole for mouth and anus. This shell composed of a number of pentagonal plates firmly joined together. The plates run in rows from pole to pole; there are twenty rows arranged in ten pairs of rows; five pairs presenting orifices for ambulacral suckers, five, alternating with them, imperforate. At the anal pole are found only ten plates, corresponding to ambulacral and inter-ambulacral (inter-radial) rows respectively. The five corresponding to ambulacral rows, excavated by pits for supposed eye-spots; the other five by ducts of genital organs, one of them being enlarged to form a porous madreporic tubercle. Thus nearly the whole surface ambulacral, the apical region being represented only by the ten plates.

Integument tough; contractile; supports—1. Spines, long calcareous processes, with expanded concave base articulated to a corresponding convex tubercle on outer aspect of shell, and moved by the muscular integument fixed round the base. Spines vary in size; the larger ones regular in their arrangement. 2. Around mouth, where the shell is deficient, branched soft hollow organs, corresponding in position to inter-ambulacral rows, and probably equivalent to the dorsal cæca of Asterias. 3. Pedicellariæ, largest around mouth, usually three-bladed.

Alimentary canal. Mouth in centre of ambulacral surface; circular; exposes ends of five teeth. Teeth and jaws form a mass about one-seventh of the size of the whole animal—the "lantern" of Aristotle. Each tooth a long, slightly curved, three-sided rod, lodged in a hollow wedge-shaped alveolus; the five alveoli bound together into a pyramid, with apex pointed to mouth, base inwards; adjoining alveoli joined together at base by five broad radiating pieces (*rotulæ*); to these again joined five slender arched pieces (*radii*), overhanging the sides of the pyramid, and linked to the mouth of the shell by a pair of diverging muscles.

In correspondence with the lantern, five bridges of bone are developed along the lip of the shell on its inner aspect, each spanning an ambulacral causeway at its commencement, and each bearing homologically the same relation to the ambulacral vessel that is held by the pair of ambulacral ossicles in the Asterias. The bridges are called *auriculæ*, and give origin to retractor muscles of the lantern.

Œsophagus short; intestine spiral; mesenteries; anus apical.

Perivisceral cavity large; walls ciliated; extends into branching cæca round mouth.

Ambulacral and pseudo-hæmal systems differ only in detail from the same in Asterias.

Radial nerve, and vessels run within shell, under auricula to anal extremity; the nerves terminating in the eye-spots.

Reproduction: Diœcious. Five genital glands with ducts opening through apical inter-ambulacral plates.

Development:

Larva called *Pluteus*. Body sub-conical; hollow beneath; margin prolonged into four angles; ciliated fringe round margin of hollow; mouth in a fifth process; anus on convexity; the ciliated fringe surrounds the mouth, and a second ring of cilia runs above and behind anus. Body and angles supported by calcareous rods. Within this an Echinus formed as in the case of the Asterid; indent occurs between the circlets; Echinus appropriates stomach, &c., of larva, and builds its skeleton at the expense of the calcareous rods.

Holothuridea—Sea-cucumbers. Type-form, Holothuria.

Echinus-form drawn out in the direction of its inter-polar axis, and without a continuous skeleton.

Integument tough, muscular, containing spicules; and supporting in some cases very curious spines; around mouth branched tentacula (respiratory) of great size and beauty in some, hardly detectable in others. Ambulacra in some still in five rows along body, but often restricted to neighbourhood of mouth, or arranged irregularly or unsymmetrically.

Five strong longitudinal muscular bands within the integument correspond to the ambulacra. The internal ambulacral system well developed in all; madreporic canal hangs freely from circlet, so that madreporic tubercle is contained within the perivisceral cavity.

Alimentary canal; plates round mouth still represent lantern or auriculæ. Canal bent; enters a muscular cloaca. From the cloaca sprouts a curious system of much-branched yellow vessels ending cæcally, forming a sort of double (so-called) respiratory tree projecting into the interior of the body, and having a close relation with plexuses of the pseudo-hæmal system. It is asserted that the ultimate twigs of the tree communicate with the perivisceral cavity.

Reproduction: Genital organs, five ramified cæca opening by a single common orifice on the back of the animal near the head. Diœcious, excepting Synaptæ.

Development: Process not well made out. In some cases a larva not unlike the Bipinnaria is formed, and is called Auricularia (Müller), the Echinus-zooid uniting with the rest of the larva to form the entire Holothuria (Müller, Huxley). In some cases there is less noticeable metamorphosis (Kowalevsky).

(Note curious powers of reproducing lost parts in the whole class. Luidia (Forbes), Ophiuridea, self-evisceration of Holothuria, economical self-amputations of Synapta.)

The Gephyrea, with their long vermiform bodies, tentaculate head, and convoluted canal, resemble the Holothurids very much, but differ importantly in not having an ambulacral system. Yet the several gradations of this system towards abortion in the Holothurida, particularly in the Synaptid group, render the passage through the Gephyrea to the Annelida easy and natural.

Group Articulata.

Of the four classes included in the Annulosa proper,

Articulata, or Arthropoda, the Myriapoda in general form are nearest to the Annelida; but as they approach in many important respects to the Insecta, so that some authors include them as a sub-class of that class, they will be considered as a stepping-stone to the Insecta, and postponed to the Crustacea in order of description.

Cl. CRUSTACEA.—In their total anatomy, these creatures must be regarded as inferior to the Arachnida and Insecta; an inferiority due most probably to the fact that they live an aquatic or semi-aquatic life. In aquatic life the relations to surroundings are simpler than in the terrestrial or aërial life; and as we see fishes among Vertebrata, so we see Crustacea among Arthropoda less highly organized than land animals of the same type. Among Vertebrata, too, the Reptile and the Bird will be found to illustrate the same principle. A few of the more important determining conditions are, the specific gravity of the surrounding medium, greater uniformity of temperature, different conducting power of surrounding medium, limitations of vision, &c. The most highly organized Crustacea are to a certain degree fitted for temporary terrestrial existence, in certain cases even to the extent of being able to climb trees; and one order, the Isopoda, includes a number of terrestrial forms.

The class includes several orders, and is differently divided by almost every authority upon the subject.

Crustacea, a class of Arthropoda constructed for life in the water, and therefore breathing by gills.

	Orders.	
Podophthalmia	Decapoda	Brachyura—Crab.
		Macrura—Lobster.
		Anomura—Hermit-crab.
	Stomapoda	Squilla, Mysis.
Edriophthalmia	Amphipoda	Sand-hopper.
	Isopoda	Wood-louse.
	Læmodipoda	Whale-louse; Caprella.

Entomostraca	Branchipoda	Phyllopoda	Branchipus
		Cladocera	Daphnia
		Ostracoda	Cypris
		Copepoda	Cyclops
	Siphonostoma	Lernaæ	
	Xiphosura	King-crab (Limulus)	
Cirrhipedia		Barnacles	

Begin with one of the Macrura—the Lobster. But note first that there are very important differences in the form and development of the various animals included in the class. Taking the Macrura as a high type, we shall find numerous shortcomings as we go down the list; and in the Siphonostoma and Cirrhipedia we shall find forms only to be recognised as Crustacea after the study of their embryonic history. It is, in fact, by such study only that the affinities of Crustaceans can be properly determined.

Lobster.

Body divisible into two parts, cephalo-thorax, covered by carapace, and tail. But on examining the under surface and appendages we find that it includes twenty-one segments or somites, divisible into three sets of seven, belonging to head, thorax, and tail, respectively. Somite-value of last segment or "telson" disputed. In the cephalo-thorax various parts of adjoining somites are fused together, and the appendages variously altered for particular purposes. But in the tail the segments are distinct, and no parts are developed in excess of the rest.

Examine third or fourth caudal segment. Each consists of dorsal arch and ventral arch, and appendages.

Dorsal arch, "tergum" originally of two pieces, ankylosed at the median line; prolonged at its two ends into angles overlapping the ends of the ventral arch (*Pleura*).

Ventral arch, consists of—1. Two middle pieces meeting

and fusing at the median line (*sterna*); 2. Two lateral pieces joining the pleura (*epimera*); 3. Two intermediate pieces (*episterna*).

Appendages, articulated; supported at junction of sternum and episternum. Here consist of basial portion containing two or three joints (*basipodite*), and two many-jointed processes attached to its terminal joint, *endopodite and exopodite*. Examination of other segments shows that we must add *epipodite*, a third appendage, fixed to outer side of basial joint, and *apodemata*, internal processes, projecting inwards, at junctions of elements of arches.

(Note, Mr. Huxley chiefly followed here.)

In Mr. Spence Bates's nomenclature, the segments 1-7 are called "Cephalon," 8-14 Pereion, 15-21 Pleon; appendages 5-9 Siagonopods, 10-14 Pereiopods, 15-19 Pleopods, 20 Uropods; the number of these last varying according to the constitution of the tail.

Analyze by aid of appendages and apodemes the constitution of segments.

1. Eyes; two joints; eye compound.
2. Antennules; basi-, endo-, exopodite.
3. Antennæ, do. (Note flexure.)
4. Mandibles; horny basipodite with palp (endopodite).
5.–6. } Maxillæ — 5 Epi- and exopodite undeveloped. 6 Basipodite masticatory; endopodite holds food; exo- and epipodite form *scaphognathite*, a baling valve for branchial chamber.
7.–9. } Maxillipedes or Foot-jaws. — All four parts. Epipodite here a flabrum or branchial organ.

10. 11. 12. 13. 14.	Ambulatory limbs.	Basipodite and endopodite form limbs. Seven joints—1, *coxopodite*, 2 *basipodite*, 3, *ischiopodite*, 4, *meropodite*, 5 *carpopodite*, 6, *propodite*, 7, *dactylopodite*; 10-13 have epipodite.
15.	Modified for sexual purposes	basi endopodite; much dwarfed and altered.
16.	in male.	basi-, endo-, exopodite.
17. 18. 19.	Natatory limbs.	
20.	Tail fin limb	broadly expanded endopodite and exopodite.
21.	Telson	no appendages.

(Note—1-6 ventral arches ankylosed.
7-13 do.
14 and onwards free.)

Carapace apparently formed by coalescence of terga of first 14 somites; groove corresponding to interval between 6th and 7th. (Huxley.)

Apodemata in head and thorax form an arrangement of cells and processes for lodgment of viscera and attachment of muscles.

(Note process of moult.)

Alimentary canal. Œsophagus and stomach lined by a sort of chitinous layer, thrown off with the shell at moult.

Stomach large, with special bony supports, teeth, and bristles.

Intestine; two divisions.

Salivary glands; large liver, composed of cœcal tubes opening into pyloric portion of stomach.

Blood, nearly colourless; oat-shaped corpuscles.

Heart in posterior part of thorax behind stomach, pentagonal in shape, enclosed in a pericardial sinus; gives off ophthalmic, antennary, hepatic and ventral or sternal arteries. From their subdivisions the blood passes into the perivisceral cavity, and interstitial prolongations thereof; thence to a set of large venous sinuses at the roots of branchiæ, through branchiæ, and on by branchio-cardiac sinuses to heart.

Branchiæ, hollow processes of the external surface, branched and in lashes or *flabra;* partly on basipodites of thoracic limbs (epipodites), partly from walls of branchial chamber. The epimera of the cephalo-thorax are membranous and much inverted, while the pleuræ are very long, and bent inwards at their margin so as to fit closely along the basial joints of the legs; so on each side of the body a large chamber is formed distinct from the body cavity, and communicating at the ends with the surrounding medium.

This is the branchial chamber; it contains the branchiæ, and acurrent is maintained through it by the scaphognathite.

Nervous System:

1. Supra-œsophageal ganglia, suppying organs of sense, &c.—cephalic.

2. Chain of twelve ganglia; six thoracic, joined together by double cords, six abdominal smaller, joined by single cord; one small ganglion intermediate; last ganglion seemingly composed of two fused together.

3. Special visceral ganglia, connected by cords to supra or sub-œsophageal ganglia.

Organs of Sense:

Eyes; compound; square corneal facets; tubes, membranous, pigmented; diaphragm; nerve-ganglion; retina with bacilli. Ears, in basial joint of antennules, sac, otolithes, hairs; orifice in shell—auditory hairs of Hensen.

Reproduction:

Female organs. Ovary; on each side of body a pair of thick tubes, situated in the thorax, and uniting to form a single oviductal tube of same structure, opening externally through the basial joint of the 3rd ambulatory leg; corresponding tubes of opposite sides join across median line.

Male organs: Testes in thorax, each of anterior and posterior portion communicating with fellow across median line; the vas deferens of each side ends in a membrano-muscular penis, which can be everted through an orifice in the basial joint of the last thoracic limb; curious modification of 1st and 2nd abdominal limbs, which are partly exciting organs, partly guide the copulatory organ.

Development: Many moults, the segments supporting antennæ, and mandibles, eyes, and following anterior segments immediately behind mouth being successively developed before the posterior segments.

Here, then, is a median type of stalk-eyed Crustacean of the Decapod order, having twenty-one segments, a cephalo-thoracic carapace, and thoracic branchiæ contained in a special branchial chamber.

In *Brachura;* cephalo-thorax much developed; tail dwarfed and curled under the body. Broad carapace, overshadowing eyes and antennæ. Branchiæ few, not more than nine on each side. Nerves concentrated below œsophagus into one ganglion. Sixth abdominal somite has no appendage. Metamorphosis of much complication.

Anomura; intermediate; sixth abdominal somite has appendages.

Order *Stomapoda.* Type, Squilla.

Antennary and ophthalmic somites free, and in same line with rest. Carapace connected solely with cephalic somites, though overlapping anterior thoracic. Branchiæ plumose, abdominal. Heart multilocular, extending into abdomen.

Sub-Cl. Edriophthalmia. Sessile-eyed Crustacea. Take Talitrus or sand-hopper as a type.

Twenty-one segments (a number never exceeded, though not always reached). Eyes compound, sessile; their segment coalesces with succeeding segments to form a compact head. Branchiæ attached to thoracic legs except 1st; no branchial chamber. Heart elongated, many chambered. Tail of four segments instead of two.

Divisions:

1. Order *Amphipoda.* Still Talitrus. (Latreille). Has both swimming and walking legs, a distinction from Isopoda, which have only walking legs. Form compressed. Three portions of body well defined.

Appendages: First part of foot-jaws conceal masticatory apparatus; 2nd and 3rd pair prehensile. Legs; all have coxa expanded to protect branchiæ, &c.; vesicular branchiæ attached to 1st joint of all but the first; oöstegites to 1st joint of four anterior pairs in female.

Abdominal legs, 1, 2, 3, swimming; 4, 5, 6, stiff for walking or leaping.

2. Order *Isopoda.* Wood-louse. Body depressed; thoracic limbs and somites equal; oöstegites, but no branchiæ. Limbs slender, hooked.

Abdominal limbs, 1-5 support curious branchial (air-breathing) plates; in some a swimming tail.

3. Order *Lœmodipoda,* intermediate; abdomen rudimentary. Not recognised by Spence Bates, who distributes its contents between the Amphipoda and Isopoda.

Sub-Cl. Branchipoda. With head-arrangements much as in foregoing orders. Distinguished by thoracic limbs, which are foliaceous, membranous, and almost entirely devoted to respiratory purposes. These thoracic limbs generally consist of basipodite, endopodite, exopodite, and epipodite, all lamellar.

Order *Phyllopoda.* (Branchipus, Apus.) Body of great

number of segments (Apus has twenty-six behind the head), all carrying foliaceous feet. With carapace (Apus) or not (Branchipus). (Note, here is probable position of Trilobites, unless, as recently suggested, they were Isopoda.)

Order *Cladocera.* (Daphnia.) Head distinct, with large compound eye, small antennules, oar-like antennæ, a pair of mandibles, and a pair of maxillæ. Thoracic feet, only four or five pairs; abdomen little more than rudimentary, with two terminal bristly appendages. Ephippial egg.

Order *Ostracoda.* (Cypris.) Bivalve shell, with hinge; and adductor muscles. Segmentation of body very imperfect; eyes single or double. Antennæ and antennules ambulatory; mandibles; two pair maxillæ, the second with large flabellum. Thoracic limbs round, few (two or three pairs), not foliaceous. Abdomen rudimentary. No heart; singularly large copulatory apparatus. No metamorphosis. (Many affinities with Cirrhipedia.)

Order *Copepoda.* (Cyclops.) Body very distinctly segmented; distinct head with a carapace; three, four, or five posterior thoracic somites free; four abdominal somites. Eye single or double. Antennules form a large pair of oars; mandibles; one or two pairs of maxillæ; two or three pairs foot-jaws; four pairs of swimming limbs. No heart; no special branchial organs. Ovisacs of female attached to last thoracic somite. Abdomen terminated by a pair of bristled processes constituting a tail fin.

Order *Siphonostoma* (Epizoa). This order often called Epizoa, though many other forms are parasitic, particularly among the Edriophthalmia. Form varies very much. Usually a piercing and suctorial mouth, and various kinds of modifications of limbs for permanent or temporary attachment to host. Range, from Argulus, very perfect in cephalo-thorax, to Lernea, little more than a long bag with rudimentary prehensile appendages, and long ovisacs.

Order *Xiphosura.* (King-crab)—1. Large cephalo-thorax with overhanging carapace ; 2. Abdomen, of six compressed and fused somites, wedged between posterior prolongation of carapace ; 3. Long sword-shaped telson.

Cephalo-thorax. On anterior part of carapace two simple eyes. On lateral aspect of ridge on each side a large compound eye.

Appendages, six pairs ; all ambulatory.

Abdomen, six pairs of appendages ; first pair expanded, opercular to the rest ; the rest lamellar branchial processes.

Heart, eight-chambered.

Order *Cirrhipedia.* Embraces pedunculate forms, such as Lepas, sessile forms such as Balanus, and apodal forms such as Sacculira.

Take Lepas—Consists of peduncle and capitulum.

Peduncle round, soft, fleshy ; capitulum a sort of head, formed by a carapace enclosing body and limbs. Carapace of five pieces—1, carina, median, inferior ; 2, 3, scuta—a pair—proximal ; 4, 5, terga—a pair—distal. Within capitulum body found attached by its back to carina, with mouth, mandibles, and two pairs of maxillæ ; lying therefore on its back. Parts : 1st, prosoma ; 2nd, six thoracic segments ; 3rd, rudimentary abdomen, prolonged into a penis, with two caudal appendages ; 4th, ovigerous frænum projecting on each side between body and capitulum. Peduncle being detached from the object to which it is fixed, presents on rostral aspect of surface of adhesion two rudimentary sucker-like antennæ. No eyes. No heart. Hermaphrodite.

The Crustacean nature of the animal proved by its development, which has several stages.

1st. Three-limbed, locomotive larva, with single eye, and two pairs of rudimentary antennæ.

2nd. Two eyes, antennæ large, prehensile ; three pairs of limbs behind mouth.

3rd. Compressed larva, something like a Cyprid; with large carapace hiding limbs, and forward flexure of head. Two large compound eyes; mouth existing with proper appendages, but imperforate. Becomes fixed by antennæ and cement.

4th. Body and head thrown into one line, eyes and antennary apodeme being cast off. The peduncle then formed by growth of anterior (antennary) somites.

Hermaphrodism. Impregnation possible by reason of gregarious habits. Accessory males of imperfect development found within the carapace in certain species. (Note, that with regard to the homologies of the Cirrhipedia, Mr. Darwin finds seventeen out of the typical twenty-one segments, all but the last three abdominal and telson.)

Brief note of sessile forms.

Cl. MYRIAPODA, compact; two forms, Centipede and Julus. Many-jointed Articulata, with many limbs, air breathers, wingless.

Centipede. Type of sub-order, *Chilopoda.* A head sup porting eyes, antennæ, and jaws, followed by twenty-one distinct segments, each supporting a pair of five-jointed legs terminating in claws. The mandibles are a pair of sharp, hooked fangs working with their points to each other, perforated at the end, and provided with poison-gland and duct opening through the perforation.

Integument tough, and horny.

Alimentary canal; œsophagus, stomach, intestine; termination of stomach marked by attachment of hepatic cæca; salivary glands; this sub-order carnivorous.

Blood corpusculated; large perivisceral cavity.

Heart, dorsal, of fifteen to twenty chambers. These distinctly muscular, having both longitudinal and transverse fibres; between them are efficient valves directing the blood-stream forwards. Intrinsic muscles produce contraction of chambers; dilatation by lateral muscles attached to the walls of the body; each chamber receives blood from chamber behind, and from perivisceral cavity by a pair of lateral valve-guarded orifices. Anterior chamber gives off three vessels; 1st, cephalic, 2nd and 3rd sternal, uniting below œsophagus to form a single trunk running backwards with the ganglionic chain; arteries, after branching, at length open into spaces of perivisceral cavity.

Respiration: Each segment has a pair of lateral apertures for admission of air to a system of tracheal vessels, consisting of air-containing tubes and sacculi kept permanently open by closely twisted spiral elastic filaments in their walls. The large vessel starting from each spiracle speedily branches to very fine ramifications, and adjoining systems freely communicate; the air pumped in and out by movements of the walls of the body. All parts of the body, to the smallest fragments of tissue, found permeated by the fine vessels of the tracheal system, most abundantly in the most active organs and tissues.

Nervous System: 1st, supra-œsophageal mass. 2nd, gangliated ventral chain joined by branches round œsophagus to 1; and consisting of as many ganglia (double) as the body has somites, except that the ganglia of the two last somites are usually joined into one. 3. Visceral ganglia, connected with œsophagus and stomach

Eyes simple (see Insecta), scattered in patches on the head.

Antennæ tactile; auditory (?).

Reproduction: Male. Seven fusiform testes open by fourteen ducts into one convoluted excretory tube discharging near anus. Five glandular cœca also open into the same tube.

Female. A simple tube without appendages.

Development: No metamorphosis. Growth effected by a succession of moults, in each of which segments are added to the body between the last segment but one, and the segment in front of it

Compare Julus, Sub-order *Chilognatha*.

Vegetable feeder. Segments much more numerous, forty

to sixty; each, excepting one or two at each end, supporting two pairs of fully-jointed legs. The seeming anomaly explained by the fact that each segment consists of two original segments fused together; evidence of permanent transverse groove. First three segments and two last have but one pair of legs each. Head has a pair of stout, horny jaws, and a pair of seven-jointed antennæ. Integument brittle.

Heart. Chambers equal to segments, with imperfect valves. Tracheal system imperfectly developed.

Generative organs, in both sexes, a pair of simple tubes with a series of cæcal appendages, opening in the seventh segment.

Cl. INSECTA.—In this class we find structures much resembling those of the preceding class, but compacted, localised, and specially developed in relation with special needs; great centralization as opposed to individuality of segments. Insects are Arthropoda, breathing air, having six thoracic legs, and four, two, or no wings; the body being distinctly divided into head, thorax, and abdomen. Briefly,—head supports a pair of compound eyes, a pair of antennæ, of mandibles, and of maxillæ; thorax, legs and wings; abdomen, in great part without external organs, contains organic viscera, and supports, terminally, apparatus of offence, copulation, or oviposition, rarely, as in Podura, of locomotion. Integument characteristically chitinous, firm, elastic, very indifferent to re-agents.

For form, take a large Beetle, and examine external skeleton.

1. *Head.*—Consists, at first sight, of one segment, but in reality of four, or perhaps six.

Obvious divisions: *epicranium, clypei, anterior and posterior, gula and mentum.*

Appendages—1st. Pair *antennæ*, many (usually nine to

eleven) jointed, on dorsal surface. 2nd. Posterior and external to antennæ, the *eyes*, large convex bodies, each composed of a multitude of minute *ocelli*; other simple eyes (*stemmata*) are placed on the top of the head, or on the forehead between the antennæ; usually three in number. 3rd. Parts about mouth; (*a*) *labrum*, a moveable horny plate; (*b*) pair of *mandibles*, short, stout, serrate, single-jointed processes, without appendages; (*c*) pair of *maxillæ*, complicated, consisting of a basial joint (*cardo*), supporting an internal few-jointed process, of expanded form (*lacinia*), and an external four-jointed process (*palpus*); lacinia calculated to hold food while being masticated by mandible; (*d*) *labium*, or posterior lip, supported upon a transverse plate (gula). The labium consists, at its base, of a single transverse plate (*mentum*), supporting at its end a tongue (*ligula*), and laterally a pair of *palpi*. Tongue of three parts, one central (*glossa*), two lateral (*paraglossæ*).

2. *Thorax*, devoted to locomotion. Divisible into, at least, three segments, *prothorax*, *mesothorax*, and *metathorax*. These are probably each again ultimately composed of about three segments (Audouin, Newport); but this cannot here be worked out.

Each of the three recognised segments is a complete ring, consisting of a dorsal arch and ventral arch. The middle of the ventral arch prolonged into a strong prominent ridge, separable with the adjoining part of the arch on each side as a distinct piece (*sternum*); *episternum* and *epimeron*, complete lower arch on each side; dorsal arch divisible into two pieces (*terga*).

Legs, always six—two to each segment; each composed of a linear series of joints, named in order, *coxa*, *trochanter*, *femur*, *tibia*, *tarsus*; the last embracing two to six, usually five, little joints, and terminated by claws.

Wings.—Not regarded as modifications of parts already

existing in other segments, or other Arthropoda (though possibly homologous with *Elytra* of Annelids), but are double membranous expansions of the integument supported by thicker portions (nervures), corresponding to tracheæ. The wings are four in number, and are attached to dorsal surface of metathorax and mesothorax; they are, of course, not always present, and are sometimes deciduous. The mesothorax and metathorax usually possess spiracles.

Abdomen.—Of about nine segments, each composed of a dorsal and ventral arch, united at the side by membrane; each segment has a pair of spiracles. The last one or two segments support appendages usually modified for other purposes than locomotion. (Note, however, Podura and allies.)

Here discuss Classification.—For class-purposes, a classification which depends upon easily-observed external characters, is, perhaps, the best. There are now extant, and much used, systems in which the developmental history, and the relative degrees of organization, and perfection of structure and form are recognised. But until these are more perfect and more uniform, the older arrangement is more useful for beginners.

According to this, there will be fourteen orders, seven more or less mandibulate, or having biting mouths, seven more or less haustellate, or having suctorial mouths.—(Newport and others).

MANDIBULATA.

1. Coleoptera	Beetles, Weevils.
2. Dermaptera	Earwigs.
3. Orthoptera	Crickets, Grasshoppers, Locusts.
4. Neuroptera	Dragon-flies, White Ants.
5. Trichoptera	Caddis-flies.
6. Hymenoptera	Bees, Wasps, Ants.
7. Strepsiptera	Stylops.

Haustellata.

8. Lepidoptera	Moths and Butterflies.
9. Diptera	Flies and Gnats.
10. Homaloptera	Forest-flies.
11. Aphaniptera	Fleas.
12. Aptera	Lice.
13. Hemiptera	Bugs, Water-scorpions, Boatmen.
14. Homoptera	Aphides, Cicadæ.

It will be well, however, to compare, at least, one of the more recent arrangements,—that, namely, which is adopted by M. Dallas, in "Record of Zoological Literature."

Orders 1. Coleoptera (including Strepsiptera of list above).
2. Hymenoptera.
3. Lepidoptera.
4. Diptera (including Aphaniptera, Homaloptera.)
5. Neuroptera (excluding Dragon-flies, &c.; including Ant-lions, Scorpion-flies and Trichoptera.)
6. Orthoptera (including Thysanura, Mallophaga (part of Aptera), Pseudo-neuroptera—White Ants, Dragon-flies, May-flies —and Dermaptera.)
7. Rhynchota (including Hemiptera (or Heteroptera), Homoptera, and Anoplura, (part of Aptera).)

Order *Coleoptera*—Includes Beetles, Glowworms, Weevils, Ladybirds, Cantharidæ.

Wings, two pairs. First pair (elytra) hard, horny, fitting together to cover over second pair when at rest.

Second pair membranous, with usually a distinct joint, at base, with a sharp-pointed horny apex, and folding up with appearance of irregularity.

Jaws markedly mandibulate.

Metamorphosis complete.

Order *Dermaptera* (Euplexiptera). — Earwigs ; joined by some authors to Orthoptera.

Wings, two pairs. First, elytra, insufficient to cover second completely when at rest. Second, membranous, beautifully folded longitudinally and transversely, like a fan. Anus armed with large movable forceps.

Metamorphosis incomplete, the larva closely resembling the perfect insect.

Order *Orthoptera.* — Includes Locusts, house and mole Crickets, Mantidæ or praying insects, and Blattidæ, or destructive Cockroaches.

Wings, two pair ; first, dense, coriaceous, reticulated, decussating at points ; second, partly coriaceous, partly membranous ; folding longitudinally when at rest.

Legs ; third pair in one sub-division strengthened and lengthened for leaping.

Jaws much as in Coleoptera.

Metamorphosis not complete ; larva, except in having no wings, resembling adult.

Order *Neuroptera.*—Includes May-flies, Dragon-flies, White Ants, Ant-lions, Scorpion-flies.

Wings, two pairs ; both membranous, transparent, elongated, finely reticulated ; nearly equal, not overlapping, usually not folded in repose, but second pair exceptionally folded in some forms.

Jaws usually very powerful.

Body elongated, and soft ; eyes very large.

Metamorphosis not complete; degree of change variable.

Order *Trichoptera.* — Caddis-flies. Placed as a sub-order of Neuroptera by many authors.

Wings, two pairs; hairy, with branched nervures; second pair folded in repose.

Jaws, in adult rudimentary, in larva well-formed.

Metamorphosis not perfect.

Order *Hymenoptera.*—Includes Bees, Wasps, Ants, Cynips, Ichneumon-flies.

Wings, two pairs, membranous, with large open expansions between the nervures. Posterior pair smaller than anterior. Locking of wings.

Jaws; interesting as showing a transitional character.

Labrum well marked.

Mandibles strong, usually much dentated.

Maxillæ drawn out, so as to form together a long double-bladed sheath, applied upon the equally lengthened labium and appendages. Sheath formed of lacinia.

Mentum and labium have all their joints lengthened.

Labial palpi elongated in second joint, so as to equal maxilla.

Paraglossa long, pointed.

Female has abdomen armed with sting or boring apparatus.

Metamorphosis complete.

Order, *Strepsiptera.*—A small group of parasitic insects infesting bees and wasps. In many respects they approach the Coleoptera, and are, indeed, placed with them by some entomologists. Genus, Stylops. The males are winged; anterior pair of wings turned into curious curled processes, whence the name of the order; posterior pair proportionally large, membranous, folding.

Order *Lepidoptera.*—Includes Moths and Butterflies.

Wings, two pairs; membranous; covered with a dust of fine scales. Mouth no longer biting, but soft and suctorial. Labrum small, almost lost; mandibles reduced to functionless plates applied to the base of the maxillæ.

Maxillæ developed at the expense of all the other parts of the mouth. They take each the form of a half cylinder, and the two unite to form one long hollow, ringed, flexible, suctorial proboscis. The two halves of the cylinder are the laciniæ, and besides fitting with great accuracy, they are curiously fastened together by tiny hooklets. At the base of the structure, the remaining parts of the maxillæ can be detected by careful examination. The labium is almost as much dwarfed as the labrum, but still supports a pair of large palpi, which are seen sweeping round from beneath to the front of the head, partly encircling the root of the proboscis.

Metamorphosis typically perfect; larva, caterpillar, long, worm-like; head of one piece, with biting jaws, and spinneret or labium, eyes single; behind head twelve joints; first three each support a pair of horny jointed legs, equivalent to legs of perfect insect; a varying number of terminal joints support pairs of soft cylindrical processes, called pro-legs; pupa, chrysalis, fixed, enclosed in horny case by moult; imago, perfect butterfly or moth.

Order *Diptera.*—Includes Flies and Gnats.

Wings, one pair, membranous, naked, or with few scales, corresponding to anterior pair of wings of other insects; posterior pair rudimentary, consisting of little knobs supported upon a short thin stem; these structures called "halteres" or "poisers."

Mesothorax very large in relation to wings.

Head rounded; eyes prominent; mouth variously constructed. In some, as in common fly, the form of simple proboscis is found, built up of the labium, with sometimes part of the maxillæ, and enclosing small bristles formed of the other parts of the mouth; in the gnats six long, sharp, lancet-shaped bristles are enclosed in a very long proboscis. A piercing and suctorial mouth.

Metamorphosis complete.

Order *Homaloptera* closely allied to, if not properly included under Diptera. Forest-flies.

Wings two, head sunk into abdomen; singular piercing and suctorial mouth, in several respects reminding us of sucking Crustaceans. Habits parasitic.

Order *Aphaniptera.* Fleas.

Wings, two pairs, rudimentary, Eyes simple, orbicular. Mouth piercing, suctorial; piercing organs, mandibles, and labrum, enclosed by three-jointed labial palpi; labium and maxillæ small.

Body oval, compressed. Hind legs particularly strong.

Order *Aptera.* Lice.

Wingless. Eyes simple. Mouth suctorial or biting.

Body depressed. No metamorphosis.

Order *Hemiptera.* Bugs. (Heteroptera).

Wings four; first pair partly membranous, partly leathery; decussating at apex; second pair membranous. Mouth rostriform, composed of elongated jointed setæ, capable in many cases of inflicting severe wounds. Compound eyes.

Metamorphosis incomplete.

Order *Homoptera*; includes Coccus family, Aphides, tree-hoppers and Cicadæ. Wings four; first pair homogeneous, either membranous or coriaceous. Mouth turned backwards; rostrum applied against ventral surface of body.

Now return to the general anatomy of insects.

Muscles. Numerous; of striped kind, arranged in regular

fasciculi without sarcolemma. Lyonnet describes nearly 1,800 muscles in the larva of the goat moth.

Digestive system—

Mouth already described.

Alimentary canal, three coats, peritoneal, muscular, and mucous.

Parts—1. Pharynx; 2. Œsophagus; 3. Crop (in Lepid., Hymen., Dipt.); 4. Proventriculus or gizzard; 5. Ventriculus or digestive stomach; 6. Small intestine; 7. Colon; 8. Rectum.

Isthmus between crop and proventriculus corresponds to point of communication between thorax and abdomen.

Gizzard muscular, with ridges, often armed with bristles internally.

Stomach, covered with a mass of small glandular cæca.

Colon, usually of great comparative calibre; receives at upper part openings of glandular appendages.

Glands—

1. Salivary, 2, 4, or 6; tubular (Lepidoptera) or racemose (Hymenoptera).

2 Malpighian, or biliary tubes, 2-100 in number opening at pylorus.

3. So-called uriniferous organs, tubular, simple, or branched, opening into rectum on each side of anus.

Alimentary canal often surrounded by delicate fatty tissue.

Circulation. Abdominal dorsal vessel or heart; eight chambers, separated by very complete valves; each receiving blood from a pericardial chamber by a pair of lateral valve-guarded orifices; current always forwards; contraction and dilatation of chambers effected as in Myriopoda; from anterior chamber one vessel runs into thorax, and divides into three branches, which cannot be traced very far. The blood thus poured into the head and thorax flows backwards along the venter and sides of the body, and then to the pericardial chamber. This circulation takes place in the perivisceral cavity.

The blood-corpuscles in transparent larvæ can be seen penetrating into all the interstices of tissues, and every minutest branch of the tracheal system is invested by a sheath prolonged from the perivisceral cavity, in which blood circulates on its way to the heart.

Respiration, by tracheæ as in Myriopoda.

On sides of body are spiracles or breathing apparatus; generally about nine on each side, a pair to each segment of abdomen except last; and a varying number on thorax. Each spiracle a horny ring, with two successive sphincters within. Tracheæ start from spiracles, branch, and anastomose, often dilating into large reservoirs; every part of all tissues minutely interpenetrated by their ultimate ramifications.

Mechanism of respiration.

Spiracles at end of body in aquatic insects, plumose or lamellar branchial processes with tracheæ within in many aquatic larvæ.

Nervous system—

In long-bodied larvæ still very much resembles in arrangement the nervous system of Myriapoda and higher Annelida.

But in perfect insect much centralization. In the Coleoptera, by shortening of commissures and soldering of ganglia we find all the abdominal ganglia drawn forward into the thorax and fused with the thoracic masses.

In higher insects the supra-œsophageal ganglia are much developed, and are exceedingly compact. Their chief branches to compound and simple eyes, antennæ, œsophagus (called often glosso-pharyngeal) to pharyngeal ganglia (vagi), mandibles, and mouth generally. Thoracic ganglia two or three in number in Coleoptera; the nerves from the last radiating as a cauda equina into the abdomen. Branches given off both from the ganglia, and from the inter-ganglionic cords. Special visceral ganglia connected with pharynx.

Sense organs—

1. *Eyes*, of two kinds, simple and compound.

Compound Eyes. Two; one on each side of head, behind antennæ. Each has its surface divided into a varying number of minute hexagonal facets, each the cornea of a distinct ocellus. Each cornea is found on section to be deeper than broad, forming in fact the base of a cone whose apex is in contact with the retina. Cornea mostly plano-convex, resting internally upon a pyramid of clear refractile matter, "vitreous humour" imbedded in pigment, and as it were plunged into a little terminal expansion of the optic nerve, from which a pigment-bedded filament passes back to a primary expansion of the entire nerve. In this retinal structure elements in some respects corresponding to the cones of the human retina exist. Each little eye is completely shut away from its neighbours by a wall of pigment, and the pigment intrudes also to a certain extent between the cornea and the pyramid, so as to leave a sort of tiny pupillary opening.

Simple Eyes, or stemmata; one, two, or three in number; placed on epicranium; resemble eyes of Arachnida, to be presently described.

2. *Ears*. Organ of hearing possibly contained in basial joint of antennæ. No demonstrative evidence. Certainly, however, in anterior legs of some Orthoptera.

Reproduction. All insects diœcious.

Agamic reproduction in Aphis and many bees, consisting in gemmation from interior of body.

In Aphis, for example, the form which buds off others is larval in its organization, wingless, and without sexual organs; after several generations of this kind will come at last a generation which acquires wings and sexual organs, and proceeds to lay eggs, from which a fresh series of larval gemmation-forms are produced.

Male organs, open at the last segment. Trace backwards.

(1.) Conical penis enclosed between one or two plates developed from the last segment of the abdomen, perforated by the termination of (2), the ductus ejaculatorius, which being traced backwards, is found to be formed by the junction of (3), two vasa deferentia with each of which, (4), a vesicula seminalis is connected. The vas deferens leads with many convolutions to (5), a testis which may be simple or composed of several little subglobular bodies, each with its efferent duct. The ultimate constitution of testis, though the detail varies enormously, is tubular.

Female organs; connected with external orifice are appendages homologous with those of the male, forming either an ovipositor, or implements used in processes preliminary to oviposition—sawing, boring or piercing organs, or a sting.

The vaginal orifice placed between the plates leads to a dilatation (uterus) with the base of which a spermotheca is connected. The uterus also receives the two oviducts, and these connect it with the ovaries.

The ovaries consist of a varying number of conical tubes, resting with open base on the oviducts, and attached to the abdominal walls by filiform mesovarium running from the attenuated imperforate apex. Each tube contains ova in various stages of development.

Insects pass through several distinct stages of development.

In the complete metamorphosis of Lepidoptera, Coleoptera, &c., three stages.

1. Larva (caterpillar), sexless.
2. Pupa (chrysalis), sexual organs showing, but having no function.
3. Imago (winged, sexual insect).

Larva ; varies much in form ; usually worm-like, with or without legs. Taking caterpillar of Lepidoptera we find the body composed of thirteen segments, including the head; head with jaws, and simple eyes; behind head first three segments have each a pair of jointed horny legs; then follow five or six segments without appendages; the one or two last again provided with soft, non-articulated locomotive processes, or pro-legs.

Chrysalis.—In this stage, the insect begins to form wings, and sexual organs, and during this process is usually quiescent. In the third stage the wings and sexual organs assume their distinctive functions shortly after the process of moulting. But the stages are not always clearly defined, and the larval form more closely resembles the adult form.

Cl. ARACHNIDA.—In most respects resemble Crustacea, but are fitted for air-breathing, and have internal organs of respiration, not branchiæ.

Further, the body consists, in the higher form, of twenty-one somites; the locomotive limbs are four on each side, and there are no wings. The eyes are sessile and simple.

The Arachnida, like the Crustacea, have a great variety of form, and many degrees of perfection, so that, low down in the list, it is not easy to define an Arachnidan from a Crustacean; *e.g.* Pycnogonon. They are divided into two great groups, according to the nature of their respiratory apparatus, viz., the Pulmonaria, which breathe by pulmonary sacs, and the Trachearia, which have a tracheal system like that of insects. The further divisions are as follows:—

CLASS ARACHNIDA.

1. Sub-class,		Pulmonaria.	
Orders,	1.	Araneidæ	Spiders.
	2.	Pedipalpi	Scorpions.
2. Sub-class,		Trachearia.	
Orders,	3.	Adelarthrosomata	Harvest spiders, &c.
	4.	Acarina	Mites.
	5.	Podosomata	(Marine and doubtfully Arachnidan) Pycnogonon.

Taking one of the Pulmonaria, we find the body divisible into two regions, cephalo-thorax and abdomen. From the anatomy of the scorpions, it appears probable that the so-called cephalo-thorax only includes certain of the anterior of the proper thoracic segments; the rest being free, as in scorpion, or fused with abdominal segments, as in common spider. The abdominal segments are distinct and hard-walled in scorpions, soft-walled and confluent in spiders. So-called post-abdomen of scorpion.

In the cephalo-thorax, a transverse groove is easily recognised, whereby the head (consisting, according to Professor Huxley, of six fused segments) is defined from the thorax.

This head supports several sessile simple eyes; a single pair of antennæ, much modified, so as to form a sort of mandible, with a perforated claw at the end, and a contained poison-gland; a pair of maxillæ, supporting palpi, and a sternal labrum without palpi. The thoracic portion supports four pairs of locomotive legs, presenting the same parts as the legs of insects. It is right to observe that certain of the anterior of these legs,—the first pair very probably,—may, without much stretch of homology, be supposed to represent the maxillæ of Crustacea.

Digestive organs. Arachnida feed chiefly by suction, imbibing the juices of their prey. Throughout the class, therefore, the mouth is piercing and suctorial; and the alimentary canal is short and straight.

In the spiders, œsophagus short, terminating in four sacs, supposed homologues of gizzard of insects; beyond this the canal forms a spindle-shaped dilatation, and then again another dilatation ending in the rectum. The biliary vessels join it close to the rectum. In scorpions, the biliary vessels are inserted much higher, and from the canal above are given off five tubes ramifying in fatty masses surrounding the intestine.

Respiration. The pulmonary pouches are bags containing laminæ, closely packed together like the leaves of a book, with the surfaces of which air admitted by stigmata comes in contact.

The stigmata are in four pairs in scorpions, and are placed on the lower surface of the abdomen; in spiders, there are four, six, or eight pairs.

Circulation. A dorsal vessel, abdominal, of four or five not very distinct chambers; arrangement of vessels much as in higher Crustacea.

Nerves—In spiders: (1.) Supra-œsophageal ganglion, united by œsophageal collar with (2), a thoracic mass of four pairs of ganglia fused into one; (3), in abdomen, a single ganglion joined to the thoracic by a double cord.

In scorpion: (1.) Supra-œsophageal ganglion, supplying limbs, (2), (3), and (4) abdominal (thoracic ?), (5), (6), (7), (8) post-abdomen.

Eyes; six or eight in number. Comprise cornea, lens, vitreous body, aqueous chamber, choroid and retina.

Ears unknown.

In *scorpions*, the last segment of the abdomen (telson)

prolonged into a sharp, hooked process, perforated near its end by a canal leading to a poison-bag.

In spiders, a varying number of little mammillated projections, the spinnerets, are found on the posterior part of the abdomen; of glandular internal structure; perforated on surface by infinite minute pores; delicate microscopic threads spun out through the pores uniting to form the visible threads of web.

Reproduction. In male spiders, testes open on inferior aspect of abdomen, just where it joins thorax. The semen emitted from these orifices is received by the maxillary palpi, which have a special modification of their penultimate joints, and is by the palps applied to the vulva of the female.

Female. Oviducts open on base of abdomen, the orifices being covered by little opercula.

In the Trachearia, the stigmata are two or four in number, the eyes two or four, and the whole group is of lower type than the Pulmonary group.

The Adelarthrosomata include the harvest-spiders, which approach the common spider in form, though with, at first sight, little demarcation between cephalo-thorax and abdomen, and the chelifers, which rather resemble scorpions, but have no tail.

In the Acarina, the body has lost its annulation, and, as is usual with parasitic animals, is degraded in various ways; but the respiration is distinctly tracheal.

The Podosomata have no respiratory organs; have very curious processes of the alimentary canal, extending even into the limbs; are marine, and are often included among the Crustacea, under the head of Crustacea Suctoria, or Araneiformia.

SUB-KINGDOM—MOLLUSCA.

In the comparison and classification of the Mollusca we have fewer opportunities of tracing homologies of parts than in the other sub-kingdoms. There is no much subdivided external or internal skeleton with much subdivided appendages, to be followed through various modifications; no division of the body into segments with serially equivalent parts. There are, without doubt, some regular relations of the soft parts to one another, relations possibly of as great morphological value as are exhibited among themselves by the bones of a vertebrate, or the ambulatory appendages of an articulate animal. But with a high amount of physiological development the Mollusca have only a feeble development of structures of support. If there be any external structure of support it takes the form of shell,—of a calcareous or horny deposit following the outline of a certain part of the body,—if there be internal structure of support, it is placed for convenience, either to give some sort of coherence to the otherwise unwieldy mass, for the attachment of certain muscles, or for the protection of certain organs. The indications of homologies among the soft parts have been studied in this country by Huxley, Allman, Rolleston, Hancock, and others, with results which, though not to be held as final, have added much clearness to our conceptions of the class, and its natural subdivisions.

A mollusc may be described as a bag of highly wrought organs of nutrition and reproduction; one part of the bag, specially protruded and more differentiated, constituting the mantle, in connection with which the shell is developed. As before noted, the whole animal exhibits bilateral symmetry on each side of a median curved line. The alimentary canal is always well developed, is rarely straight, but usually bent so that its termination is brought near to the mouth. An anal opening generally exists, and in no case is there any communication between the alimentary canal, and the perivisceral cavity. A hepatic organ is always present. In all but the lowest class (Polyzoa), and some exceptional forms among other classes, the blood circulates partly in definite channels, and is propelled by a heart. A renal organ is generally present. The nervous system does not form a longitudinal chain of pairs of ganglia, but the position of the ganglia is determined by the position of the organs with which they are related.

The sub-kingdom includes the following classes :—

Cephalopoda.
Pulmo-gasteropoda.
Branchio-gasteropoda.
Pteropoda.
Lamellibranchiata.

Brachiopoda.
Ascidioidea or Tunicata.
Polyzoa or Bryozoa.

The classes above the line usually joined to form a group of Mollusca proper; the classes below the line are called Molluscoidea.

The Mollusca proper have generally a median muscular organ or foot; have a complete alimentary canal; have a heart with two cavities, auricle and ventricle; have three pairs of ganglia, supra-œsophageal (sensory), parieto-splanchnic, and pedal. The Molluscoidea have no foot; have a single-chambered heart or none at all; have a less developed nervous system; and reproduce themselves largely by gemmation, forming large compound animals or societies. Most are hermaphrodite.

Cl. Polyzoa.—Placed by Cuvier among the Polypes;

to-day by Gegenbaur among the Annuloidea (Vermes). They differ, however, fundamentally from the Cœlenterata in the superior development of their alimentary canal. All minute; all aquatic; all form composite structures, almost always fixed.

Plumatella repens, a fresh-water species, taken as type, and compared with others as description proceeds. Composite; consists of a number of individuals joined into a common mass; mass called *polypary* or *cœnœcium* (Allman); individual, *polypide*. Mass here branched, tree-fashion. Each polypide retractile within a cell formed by the wall of the proximal part of its body hardened with horny matter; each, in fact, a tube, attached by base to the rest of the polypary, the mouth opening at the free distal extremity, which is crowned with a circlet of *tentacles* supported by a disc (*lophophore*). In the fresh-water forms the disc is horseshoe-shaped, and supports a double row of tentacles (*Hippocrepian* form); in the marine (Pedicellina an exception) the lophophore is circular, and the row of tentacles single; but the horseshoe is only the circle folded in on the anal aspect, and the mouth is, in both cases, encircled by tentacles.

Cœnœcium, composed of two membranes.

1. Outer, *ectocyst*, tough, brown, horny, strengthened often by siliceous or earthy particles.
2. *Endocyst*, lining ectocyst; soft, transparent, and contractile, projecting beyond ectocyst to form the evertible part of the body.

Digestive system; mouth, a slit guarded by a valve (*epistome*) on the anal aspect. This peculiar to fresh-water forms, hence called Phylactolæmatous as opposed to marine, Gymnolæmatous. Tentacles, crescentic lophophore, and epistome hollow, their cavities communicating with perivisceral cavity. Both surfaces ciliated. The crescent of tentacles surrounded in lower third by a delicate cup of membrane attached to the back of each tentacle (*calyx*). This peculiar to fresh-water form.

Œsophagus ciliated internally. *Stomach* not ciliated, cæcal, the œsophageal and intestinal openings being placed close to each other. In marine forms a distinct *gizzard*. Intestine leads without further bend to *anus*, placed at a point just below the tentacular ring opposite the concave side of the lophophore.

Brown cells, possibly *hepatic*, in walls of stomach.

No heart or vessels; the fluid of perivisceral cavity must represent blood; colourless and crowded with irregularly-shaped particles; does not stagnate, but is constantly redistributed by the cilia lining the endocyst, and by changes in the position of the body-wall.

Respiration, partly by tentacles; partly by surface of endocyst; partly, in some cases, by the regular sucking-in and throwing-out of water by the œsophagus.

Nervous system, consists of one ganglion placed between commencement of œsophagus and rectum; therefore sub-œsophageal; giving off branches to all surrounding parts.

Reproduction by eggs, and by gemmation.

All Hermaphrodite. *Ovary* roundish, fixed to endocyst a little below lophophore. *Testis* irregular, lobed, formed upon a flexible cord attached by one end to the stomach, by the other to the floor of the cell. Spermatozoa formed in "vesicles of evolution." Ova, after fertilization, undergo much of their development within the body of the parent; mode of escape by rent, not by duct.

Process of development (Allman).

1. Mature ovum; yelk granular, enclosed in definite membrane, and including germinal vesicle and spot.

2. After fecundation, vesicle and spot vanish, yelk undergoes segmentation; "mulberry mass;" presently a roundish body, ciliated externally, hollow within.

3. Within the round body, still in the egg, a second bag formed, opening on the surface, and evertible.

4. In this protrusile portion, first one, and then two little polypides grow up by budding. Ovum now bursts.

5. Polypides and cœnœcium further differentiated, and give rise to fresh polypides by fresh acts of gemmation.

The muscles moving the parts of the body upon one another are to be noted as numerous and somewhat complicated.

In certain marine forms, curious appendages found, viz., *Avicularia*, *Vibracula*, and *Ovi-cells*.

Avicularium.—Like a bird's head, with a very moveable under jaw; when opened, exhibiting within a prominence studded with delicate bristly hairs; tactile? (Busk). Provided with striped muscles, and curious perforated tympanum. Resemblance in form to shell of Brachiopoda, suggested by Mr. Huxley, in connection with other relations between Polyzoa and Brachiopoda.

Vibraculum.—A long slender rod, fixed by one end in a cup, and swayed about by special muscles.

Query, in both cases, altered polypides?

Winter-eggs, *stato-blasts*, developed by gemmation in the cord fixed to the end of the stomach; double watch-glasses, face to face, with germinal matter included.

Cl. TUNICATA, or ASCIDIOIDEA.

A class of wider range of perfection than Polyzoa, including, 1, forms little superior to the Polyzoa, and constituting, like them, compound masses; and 2, solitary forms approaching in the complexity of their organization the Mollusca proper. All marine; fixed or free.

Take first one of the large solitary forms (Ascidia).

Habit, fixed; shape subglobular.

Invested externally by a tunic called the *test*—corresponding apparently to the ectocyst of the Polyzoa, and containing cellulose. *Test* sometimes transparent and flexible, sometimes opaque, tough, leathery, horny, or shelly, or strengthened by impaction of foreign bodies. Test perforated by two orifices, placed on what would be the upper aspect of the animal in its natural position. One orifice inhalant (oral), one exhalant (anal); the inhalant always on a higher level. The test lined by a muscular bag (*mantle*) connected with it at the orifices, generally free elsewhere, except for vessels running from one to the other; in some cases muscular bands also connect the two.

The inner bag perforated like the outer; its oral orifice leads to a large cavity, occupying often a great part of the body, called the *branchial* or *pharyngeal sac*, and presenting at its lower end the orifice of the alimentary canal. The sac presents often internally a circular row of tentacles hanging within the inhalant orifice, and also, on the anal aspect of the sac, a row of tentacles running from the inhalant to the œsophageal orifice (*languettes*); the inner surface of the sac is richly ciliated, and marked by transverse and longitudinal bars, corresponding to vessels, with depressions or perforations between them. The exhalant opening of the mantle also communicates with a cavity (*atrium* or *cloaca*) lined by a distinct membrane (3rd tunic of Huxley; accepted by Hancock). This atrial cavity comes into contact with the branchial sac on its anal aspect, and is very often reflected round it on each side, but never invests it completely, being stopped by a vertical fold of the pharyngeal sac on the hæmal aspect (distal to anal), connected with a large vessel (dorsal sinus); it also extends among the viscera. Besides these two cavities, the mantle contains a third, the *true perivisceral cavity*, much encroached upon by the others, and represented mainly by freely communicating channels occupying the spaces left between them and the viscera at various points. Where the atrium and the pharyngeal or branchial sac are in contact, they usually communicate by perforations between the bars of the sac, and the vessels in the bars may be looked upon as so many lines of perivisceral cavity included between the two elsewhere-adherent membranes. This, at least, would be the result of the views advocated by Carpenter, Huxley, and others, who consider that the atrium arises primarily in an inversion of the integument around the anal orifice, and that this inversion gradually insinuates itself among the internal organs, leaving only a very narrow external passage.

Professor Allman, on the other hand, sees in an Ascidian the homologue of a retracted Hippocrepian Polyzoon, with the lophophore (always tilted in retraction) turned into the dorsal vertical vessel or sinus, and the tentacles forming the transverse bars of the branchial sac; the epistome being represented by the languettes.

Mr. Hancock, who at first adopted Mr. Allman's ideas, has recently given a very careful analysis of the anatomy of the branchial chamber, upon which he founds conclusions tending to prove homology between the chamber, or, at least, parts of the chamber, and the gills of the Lamellibranchiata. He describes the true branchial organ as formed by two lateral plates or laminæ transversely and longitudinally barred, separated dorsally from each other by two longitudinal folds of the "lining membrane" (atrial tunic), between which the *endostyle* is found at the bottom of a deep groove; separated ventrally from each other by another longitudinal fold, forming the "*ventral lamina*," along which food runs, collected into strings, to the mouth (œsophageal orifice). Above and below—at lines of anterior and posterior "*collars*" or "*cords*"—the laminæ are firmly attached to the "lining membrane," but elsewhere, excepting at the two vertical lines just mentioned, are free, being linked to the lining membrane by muscular suspenders.

The "*branchial chamber*" is, therefore, only in part formed by the true branchial laminæ, and the circlet of tentacles within the inhalant orifice is unconnected with the laminæ. A projection (*languet*) between this circlet and the upper margin of the laminæ is called by Mr. Hancock the *branchial tubercle.* He is inclined to attribute to it a sensory function, as a sort of inspector of introduced food, a distinct nerve always going to it. The entrance of the *œsophagus* (mouth, oral orifice, Auct.), placed at the bottom of the branchial chamber, is a narrow slit, to which the food is brought along certain grooves, moulded into threads with mucus; œsophagus short; stomach simple; intestine makes its first turn in a dorsal (hæmal) direction—away from the anus, and towards endostyle—afterwards doubling back with perhaps a loop or two; and the rectum in part hangs free in the atrium or cloaca. The hepatic organ has been most carefully described by Mr. Hancock. It forms a thin coating over the walls of the intestine, and, in some cases, of the stomach, and consists of fine dichotomously dividing, sometimes anastomozing tubes ending in vesicular dilatations. One or more ducts from this structure can be traced to an opening in the stomach near the pylorus. Around this true liver is a gland-like matter, consisting of large vesicles, among which the adjoining viscera are packed and much hidden. Function unknown. The food of the Ascidia is derived from the minute particles of solid matter brought in by the respiratory currents, and collected in special grooves as already noted.

Circulation.—From the great dorsal vertical sinus, transverse vessels run round the branchial chamber and are collected by a ventral sinus. These and other vessels may be only partitions of the perivisceral cavity, though Mr. Hancock finds an inner tube in some of the great trunks. With the lower end of the great sinus is connected the heart, a simple fusiform muscular tube, without valves. It propels the blood by peristalses, which alternate regularly in their direction, sending the blood at one time into the branchial organ; at another time drawing it from the branchial organ. The "*muscular suspenders*" running between the branchial chamber and the wall of the body, act, according to Hancock, as accessory hearts in respect of insuring a flow of blood to and from large sinuses which are out of the direct line of the circulation.

Nervous system.—One ganglion, placed between the oral and anal orifices in a venous sinus supplied from the branchial organs. It supplies the two orifices, the languet, and certain structures supposed to be *eye-spots* found at the orifices of the mantle. Sub-œsophageal, as in Polyzoon.

Reproduction.—Ascidiæ all hermaphrodite. The ovary and testis, though probably distinct, are much interwoven with each other; from the ovary a duct leads into the cloaca, and a *vas deferens* can generally be made out. Fecundation cloacal or abdominal, of course without congress.

Development—

Embryo at early period pushes out at one end a sort of tail, and forms at the other three suckers and an eye-spot. Tail said by some recent observers to contain a structure like a chorda dorsalis, and the whole animal certainly bears a superficial resemblance to a tadpole. Quitting the egg in this form, the embryo swims freely for a time, then fixes itself by the suckers to some selected point, casts off the now useless eye and tail, and gradually assumes the Ascidian form.

Classification and comparison—

The *Ascidians* form the first group or order of the class; the other groups are the *Clavellinidæ*, *Botryllidæ*, *Pyrosomidæ*, *Salpidæ*, *Pelonaiadæ*. These are arranged, as follows, by Mr. J. D. Macdonald.

1. Sub-Cl. Tunicata Fixa. Types.
    1. Simple. Ascidia, Cynthia.
    2. Social. Clavellina.
    3. Compound. Botryllus.
2. Sub-Cl. Tunicata Pelagica (free).
    1. Simple. Doliolum (a rare form).
    2. Social. Salpa.
    3. Compound. Pyrosoma.

The *Clavellinidæ* are fixed, and form composite masses; the individuals being joined by a common tunic, in which the blood circulates, but being otherwise distinct.

Botryllidæ also fixed; composite; forming, by junction of swollen tests, a common mass in which the individuals are grouped in star-like systems, and are so far confused as to have in each system a common cloaca, with one exhalant orifice. They reproduce by ova and gemmæ.

Pyrosomidæ free, composite; tests confused, the individuals joined by their sides to form a tube with the inhalant orifices external, the exhalant internal; the interior of the tube forms a common cloaca as in Botryllus. Phosphorescent.

Salpidæ free; sometimes solitary, sometimes compound; no structural separation of tunics.

Solitary form. Animals transparent.—Quadrate or oval in form, with various processes in various species; test or ectocyst closely lined by mantle in which muscular bands are formed. At each end of body an orifice penetrates both tunics, communicating with a chamber occupying the greater part of the cavity of the mantle. The chamber is partly subdivided by a flat, obliquely-placed band into an oval and an atrial portion. The band extends from the "nucleus" or collection of viscera, placed in one angle of the cavity across to the opposite angle, and so is interposed between the orifices which occupy the alternate angles of the oblong; it is furrowed transversely and contains vessels; it is a double reflection of the walls of the cavity, and is considered by Mr. Hancock to be the homologue of the "oral or ventral" lamina found on the ventral aspect of the branchial chamber of the Ascidians.

Nerve-ganglion in the substance of the mantle near the exhalant orifice; several pigment spots with nerves ending in them are called eyes by some, ears by others.

Reproduction.—The solitary and aggregate Salpians are alternate forms, produced by gemmation and from egg respectively.

A. Single, produced from egg, buds off internal stolons supporting chains of little Salpæ; lays no egg.

B. Compound: individuals differing often much in shape and size from corresponding solitary form; aggregate in long chains produced by gemmation; lay eggs, but give off no stolons.

Tunicata, to sum up, are acephalous mollusca, invested by a test perforated by two orifices, and not bivalve; the branchial chamber may be regarded either as equivalent to lophophore and tentacles of Polyzoon retracted within adherent endocyst, or as the equivalent of the branchial chamber in the Lamellibranchs, when the valves are closed, with the mouth at the base; the latter view being now in more favour.

Cl. Brachiopoda.—Solitary Bivalves, in which the valves are dorsal and ventral like the two parts of a cabriolet in relation to the animal within, instead of lateral (wing-like), as in Lamellibranchs. Valves joined by hinge or not; never with elastic spring. When not hinged, the valves imperforate; when hinged, one, the larger, is perforate, for the transmission of an anchoring ligament; in the non-hinged, the ligament passes out between the valves.

The Class divided into two orders or sub-classes—the *Articulate* and *Inarticulate:* the Articulate, of which Terebratula is type, have usually curious shelly processes developed from the inner surface of the imperforate valve for the support of the arms, and have in the adult condition no anus; the Inarticulate, of which Lingula is type, have no arm-supporting processes, and have an anus.

Taking one of the Articulate forms, we find the valves unequal, and bearing such relation as to give the whole shell the appearance of a classical lamp.

The valves are formed in the outer layer of two reduplications of the mantle of the dorsal aspect of the body. The soft mantle lobes therefore line the valves, and project a little beyond them in the form of richly vascular fringes. Of the two valves the dorsal and smaller is imperforate, the ventral and larger perforate; when fixed by the ligament, the anatomically dorsal valve is inferior. Differences in structure of shell,—punctate or impunctate.

On separating the valves (or decalcifying), the cavity formed between the two large pallial lobes is found occupied in the two-thirds next the gape by two spirally-curled arms or tentacles (Eponyms of the class). They are attached to the body (which is restricted to the third next the hinge) on each side of the mouth. The mouth is a slit lying in a groove continuous with grooves running along the convexity of each arm, along which food is brought by ciliary action.

The arms are muscular and contractile, and joined across at their base by a transverse plate of membrane lying beneath the mouth. In these forms the arms are supported by calcareous loops springing from the imperforate valve. On their convex surface runs a cartilaginous ridge supporting a dense fringe of cirrhi; within their muscular substance is a membranous canal, with a basial cæcum appended to it.

The first turn of the alimentary canal is ventral, as in Polyzoa.

The stomach is invested by hepatic follicles.

The muscular structures are complicated, as in Polyzoa.

Heart, dorsal to intestine, simple.

On each side of the mouth are orifices leading to hollow fusiform organs (pseudo-hearts) from which branching prolongations make their way into the body among the viscera. Through these organs the generative products make their way outwards. At one time they were supposed to be hearts. The system is called "Atrial" by some authors, and compared to the organ of Bojanus in the Lamellibranchs by others.

The nervous system consists of a sub-œsophageal ganglion corresponding to that of the Tunica and Polyzoa, and of ganglia placed at the base of the arms, all united by threads forming a sort of collar round the œsophagus.

Reproduction: mostly diœcious; no remarkable metamorphoses, or alternations.

Their early forms much resemble the Polyzoa; it may be noted that the first turn of their intestine is neural, as in the Polyzoa; and their arms are suggested to be homologues of the two arms of the lophophore. Some authors incline to find a relation between the solitary Brachiopod and the compound Polyzoon equivalent to that existing between the solitary and compound Tunicates.

Cl. Lamellibranchiata.—Solitary, bivalved mollusca, having the valves lateral, and, with the exception of the hinge-part, symmetrical; having no arms like those of the Brachiopods, having parial lamellar branchiæ, and, mostly, a foot; of fixed or free habit. Types: Oyster, or Fresh-water Mussel (Unio). The two valves of the shell are lined and formed by two folds of the mantle projecting laterally from the median line of the dorsal region. On opening the valves and mantle lobes, the body of the mollusc is found occupying the anterior and dorsal part of the cavity; the laminar branchiæ (one or two on each side) being fixed in the posterior part of the cavity, in the re-entering angle between the body and the mantle fold of each side. Where the edges of the two mantle lobes are free and separable, as in the fresh-water mussel, they are in perfect contact during closure of the gape, except at two points posteriorly, where two orifices—one inhalant, one exhalant—exist; the lower of these communicates with the branchial chamber, the upper with a smaller cloacal chamber marked off by the line of attachment of branchia, and by a further special fold of mantle on each side. In many forms the margins of lobes cohere, and an evertible "siphon" is formed in connection with the two orifices; where a foot exists, a separation is left anteriorly—*e.g.*, Mya.

Shell—Usually equivalve (though oyster an exception); valves inequilateral, anterior part shorter than posterior: shell formed by successive calcifications of the outer layer of the mantle; growing therefore as the animal grows. Each valve is a modification of a bent cone, and the apex of the cone, the boss (*umbo*) of the valve, is formed by the first shell-layer of the mollusc, which thus carries, so to speak, its first smallclothes about with it.

The epiderm of the mantle sometimes remains still covering the outer aspect of the calcareous deposit, but is usually more or less rubbed away.

Parts of Shell—

1. *Umbo* or boss, projecting forwards.
2. *Lunule*, a crescentic depression in front of umbo.
3. *Hinge;* opposing surfaces fitted with interdigitating processes or *teeth*, with *ligament*, and with *spring*. *Ligament* fibrous, unyielding, fixed at the most dorsal edge of valves behind umbo; *spring*, indiarubber-like, within and below ligament, antagonistic to closing (*adductor*) muscles.
4. *Markings* on interior; indicate position of adductor muscles, mantle, siphon, and foot; foot-marking anterior, siphon posterior.

Mantle, forms shell externally, lined with ciliated epithelium internally; fimbriated at edges in branchial chamber. Various degrees of union of two lobes indicated already. The siphon before alluded to is a prolongation of the mantle, having the two orifices at its apex; it is simple, or has a diaphragm separating anal from branchial channel. In some cases this portion of the animal assumes overwhelming proportions, the shell being dwarfed into two little finger-nail-like appendages of one end of a large siphonal tube (Teredo; Aspergillum); the total form then reminding one much of the Ascidians.

Foot, absent in forms which are fixed by one valve, as Oyster; where present, a projection of the median inferior line of the body, behind the mouth; may be compared to the tongue of man, not having any internal or external hard substance, not being jointed, being composed of interlacing muscular fibres.

Uses various: ploughshare in fresh-water mussels; leaping-organ in cockle; burrowing-organ in razorshells, pholads, and shipworms. In other cases, as in marine mussels, it secretes the byssus or bunch of horny threads by which the animal is anchored, and fixes the threads to the requisite points.

Muscles.—Adductors of shell; single or double, when they are anterior and posterior (monomyary, Oyster; dimyary, Mussel); run horizontally between corresponding parts of valves. Protractors and retractors of foot.

Digestion.—*Mouth* at anterior inferior aspect of body; a vertical slit, without jaws or odontophore, surrounded by four fleshy lips, *labial tentacles*. Œsophagus short. *Stomach*, imbedded in liver, contains *crystalline style*; *intestine* forms several coils, but first turn neural; rectum usually traverses ventricle of heart, and ends in cloacal part of cavity of mantle. *Liver-ducts* open into stomach.

Circulation.—*Heart* has two auricles and one ventricle, contained in large pericardial sinus: *aorta* divides into two branches, the ramifications of which open into large lacunar intervisceral spaces, and into large sinuses running along the base of the branchia and the margins of the mantle; thence blood is collected by two branchio-cardiac vessels, which empty themselves into the auricles.

Respiration.—Lamellate gills, two or four in number, the external gills being variable. Each gill composed of two longitudinally and transversely barred plates, placed close together, and joined face to face by numerous short processes of union. Between the bars are lattice-work perforations, and through the intricate system of canals thus formed the water makes its way, impelled by cilia. The bars are supported by firm material, and contain vessels. In some Lamellibranchs (*e.g.*, *Anodon*), the interval between the laminæ of the outer gill is converted into a pouch, in which the ova undergo a part of their development.

Nervous System.—*Labial* (*supra-œsophageal*), *pedal*, and *branchial* (or *parieto-splanchnic*) *ganglia;* the labial united with each other by cord above œsophagus, and with the pedal and branchial ganglia respectively by lower cords. The branchial ganglion occupies the position of the single ganglion of the Tunicata and Polyzoa. Other smaller ganglia found in the border of the mantle in some forms.

Sense Organs.—Eye-spots upon the margin of the mantle lobes in Pecten and other free forms.

Auditory Vesicle connected with pedal ganglion. (Siebold.)

Renal Organ (?) carefully described by Rolleston; formerly much confounded with ovarian apparatus. Consists in each lateral half of body of two sacs—one simple, opening into branchial chambers, one secretory and lamellar, opening internally into the blood system through the pericardial sinus; with the outer portion of this structure (the details of which vary), the opening of a tree-like system of ovarian tubes is connected.

Reproduction.—Lamellibranchs mostly diœcious; the generative glands are formed along the course of the intestine, causing often projection inward of the wall of the lower portion. No external organs; no sexual congress.

Development in ovarian tube, in pouch of outer branchia, or in cloaca, or mantle cavity, or outside parent.

Young ovum early ciliated; rotatory movements; then developed in two halves, each forming a separate set of organs, symmetrical with those of the other half, which as growth proceeds gradually unite across; the two ventricles, in uniting to form one, enclose the rectum.

Temporary appendages.—*Velum; eye-spot; byssus; flagellum,* in different instances.

The Lamellibranchiata, although generally included among the Mollusca proper, retain many important affinities with the Molluscoidea, and are much inferior in organization to the Cephalopoda, Pteropoda, and Gasteropoda. These latter, which complete the sub-kingdom, are called the Cephalous Mollusca, and possess a head, with appended organs of sense, a remarkable apparatus of mastication (*odontophore*), and a variously-formed median foot.

Cl. Gasteropoda.—May be taken as the typical class of the Cephalous Mollusca. Includes two great sub-classes—the branchiate and the pulmonate Gasteropoda, having respectively the snail and the whelk as convenient types.

Sub-Cl. 1. Pulmogasteropoda (Huxley). Snail, slug.

Sub-Cl. 2. Branchiogasteropoda.

Orders:	1. Heteropoda.	Atlanta.
Order, Prosobranchiata. (M. Edw.)	2. Pectinibranchiata.	Whelk.
	3. Scutibranchiata.	Haliotis.
	4. Cyclobranchiata.	Limpet, Chiton.
	5. Tubulibranchiata.	Dentalium.

Order, Opisthobranchiata. (M. Edw.)	6. Tectibranchiata.	Aplysia.
	7. Inferobranchiata.	Phyllidia.
	8. Nudibranchiata.	Doris.

General characteristics of Gasteropoda. Cephalous mollusca with organs of locomotion posterior to mouth, under anterior part of abdomen.

External Configuration.—Mantle usually projected in a fold from the back of the neck. In a great proportion of gasteropods a shell, formed by calcification of outer surface of this projection. Shell univalve, or, if composed of more than one piece, has the segments arranged in linear series along the median line, one behind the other, never opposed. Head, placed at anterior part of body, supports tentacles and eyes. On the inferior surface of the body is the creeping disc or foot, which, by its position, gives name to the class.

Mantle, a fold with oblique position in relation to median line; draws into its cavity many of the organic viscera, so that, while the parts of the head and foot are symmetrical on each side of the median line, the other organs are distorted. Professor Huxley founds upon variations in the mode of asymmetry of the mantle fold certain generalizations with regard to the homologies of the several classes of the Mollusca which may be conveniently noticed here.

They are to this effect :—

1. Development always commences on the hæmal side of the embryo.

2. The axis is at first straight, with symmetry of parts on each side of a longitudinal vertical plane.

3. The subsequent bent, spiral, or other unsymmetrical arrangement is caused by the over-development of certain parts; the head and foot in no case involved, but only the whole or part of the hæmal surface.

4. To this part, and its projecting angles and ridges, Professor Huxley applies the term "mantle."

5. If the outgrowth be before the anus, an abdomen is formed, as in Polyzoa; if behind, a "post-abdomen," as in Tunicata.

6. The Pulmonate Gasteropoda and the Cephalopoda form an abdomen, and the intestine being drawn into this abdominal sac, makes its first curve in a neural direction; the Branchiate Gasteropoda have a post-abdomen and hæmal curve of intestine. Similarly, the Polyzoa, Brachiopods, and Lamellibranchs have a neural, the Tunicata a hæmal first turn of intestine.

Shell, an oblique cone; laterally symmetrical in Heteropods and Limpets; apex oblique and excentric, directed forwards in Limpet, backwards in other forms; the extension of obliquity and excentricity produces the spiral form of shell; apex first-formed part; spiral directed from apex downwards, mostly to the right, but in a few species to the left (dextral and sinistral spires.)

Parts of spiral shell:—

1. *Apex or nucleus.*

2. *Whorls.*

3. *Columella*, or axis around which whorls are coiled, formed by the inner part of the whorls; solid, or hollowed by a tubular cavity; the opening of the hollow, *umbilicus*.

4. *Shell-aperture*, bounded by an inner and outer lip; the former smooth, for movements of foot. In most of the pulmonate and vegetable-feeding Gasteropods this opening is entire; but in others it is variously interrupted; the inner lip being notched in carnivorous forms, and channels being formed at the anterior and posterior corners, or junctions of the lips; anterior siphonal in Pectinibranchs; posterior anal.

Operculum, valvular structure closing orifice of shell when the animal is retracted. Like the shell, horny, albuminous, or calcareous; not homologous with second valve of bivalves, but a median appendage of the foot, comparable with the byssus of the Mussel tribe, if with any structure in the Lamellibranchs.

The calcification is often not complete, leaving parts of the mantle free to form siphon as in Pectinibranchs, or to be folded backwards on the external surface of the shell.

Foot, a special development of the muscular fibres of the integument; fibres interlace in all directions, but are predominantly longitudinal and transverse. Ordinarily used as creeping disc; sucker in Limpets. Its best development in the Heteropoda, where it forms a swimming organ; here may be recognised three parts—

1. Anterior; swimming portion (*propodium*, Huxley).
2. Middle, with sucker attached (*mesopodium*).
3. Posterior, bearing operculum (*metapodium*).

Note in connection with the foot the alar organ, formed by a fringe of the mantle, running in development around the body on each side from the back of the neck to behind the foot (*epipodium*).

Muscles; special retractors and protrusors of head and foot.

Digestive system—

Mouth in lower surface of head; lips various; frequently a cutting edge formed by a crescent of horn in upper lip; within the mouth the so-called *buccal mass, glottidium*, or *odontophore*, consisting of a pair of vertically-placed compressed plates of cartilaginous stuff, lying face to face, and imbedded on their posterior and inferior aspect in muscle; occupying therefore in the buccal cavity very much the position of a short tongue. To the front and upper surface of this structure is applied a thin plate or strap of membrane, the lingual ribbon. This ribbon is made to glide backwards and forwards over the convexity of the cartilage by muscles attached to its ends, and is armed on its free aspect with very beautifully formed teeth, or recurved spines, arranged in many transverse rows, the teeth near the rhachis being smaller than the lateral teeth. The whole structure, therefore, constitutes a sort of rasp (*radula*), and can be easily seen operating as such in the aquatic forms The teeth are seen in their full development in the middle of the strap; anteriorly they become worn away, and posteriorly, where the strap is contained in a sac or dental canal, new teeth are as constantly formed. Connected with the mouth is a distinct pair of *salivary* glands with ducts. To the mouth succeeds a dilatable *œsophagus*, into which usually opens a gland of doubtful nature and great delicacy of structure; œsophagus often expanded into a crop just above the stomach. A distinct *stomach*, mostly siphonal in form, and often armed internally with teeth or bristles; the *intestine*, after making its first turn in a neural direction, is variously coiled before it ends at the anterior part of the body with hæmal relation to the mouth. Note of aproctous forms, with branching canal. The *liver* is large, and its duct or ducts open into the commencement of the intestine or into the stomach, or into both. In Doris one of the liver-ducts enters the rectum.

Circulation.—Heart dorsal, in close connection with breathing organ; always present, except in a few curious aberrant, chiefly parasitic, forms; consists, in typical forms, of one auricle, and one ventricle, with a definite valve between; the auricle receives blood from the breathing organ and sends it into the system through an aorta. The branches of the aorta appear generally to communicate with lacunar compartments of the perivisceral cavity, but this is much disputed. (Note Prof. Huxley on Firola, and Prof. Owen's comments.) The views which favour such communication here adopted.

Respiration.—Very varying.

Some few low forms (Apneusta) have no *respiratory organs.*

In the Branchiate Gasteropoda, the gills form external ciliated processes, sometimes free and exposed, usually more or less sheltered; in some cases so far as to be enclosed in distinct dorsal pallial chamber with siphonal orifice; the processes may be dendritic, lamellar, plumose, or pectinate.

In the Pulmonata, the breathing organ is a dorsal chamber, with muscular floor and richly-vascular roof. A wide opening on the right side of the body, at the neck, admits air.

The relation of the heart to the breathing organ is not always the same; in Pectinibranchiata (Whelk), Scutibranchiata (Haliotis), and Cyclobranchiata (Limpet), the branchiæ, pectinated, or plumed, are placed in advance of the heart, and the group is called Prosobranchiate; in Tectibranchiata, Inferobranchiata, and Nudibranchiata, the "arborescent or fasciculated" branchiæ are placed towards the hinder end of the body, behind the heart.

Renal organ, single, between heart and rectum; opening close to respiratory orifice.

Nervous System.—Average.

(a) *Two supra-œsophageal ganglia* (sensory), united by commissure above œsophagus, and connected by cords on each side with

(b) *Pedal ganglia,* double, and mostly separate, and with

(c) *Branchial ganglia* (parieto-splanchnic);

(d) *Stomato-gastric* ganglia; ganglia proper to cephalous Mollusca, chiefly connected with buccal apparatus.

Organs of Sense—

Eyes well developed; placed on tentacles in Snail and Slug.

Ear, a sac, with otoliths, connected with sub-œsophageal collar; pedal portion.

Doubtful organ of smell.

Note of special glandular organs.

1. "Aquiferous" many-orificed system of foot.

2. Colour-glands, between heart and liver.

3. Muciparous glands along medial line of foot, with common duct opening behind mouth.

Reproduction. In the hermaphrodite Pulmonata the organs are most complicated, consisting of much connected ovary and testis with spermatophorous sac attached to vas deferens, and spermotheca to termination of oviduct; with evertible penis, spiculum of excitement, and with copulatory sac. Congress with mutual impregnation. In diœcious forms copulatory apparatus variously developed; sometimes of much complexity, sometimes almost or entirely wanting.

The eggs are very often protected by a "nidamentum" or common sheltering structure, secreted by a special gland. (Whelk.)

In development; albumen in very large proportion, early rotation of embryo within; head and mantle early formed; a shell connected with mantle, even in forms which as adults are naked (Eolis); and a bilobed velum (*epipodium*) is formed on the neck, at the back of the head; auditory vesicle early seen.

Notes on orders of Gasteropoda: (*cf.* Woodward and Tate).

I. Prosobranchiata. Abdomen well developed, protected by shell; branchiæ almost always lodged in chamber of mantle; diœcious.

Orders. 1. Pectinibranchiata, shell spiral; aperture notched, or produced into siphonal canal; operculum horny; branchiæ comb-like. (Whelk.)

2. Scutibranchiata; shell spiral or conical, notched or perforated for anal siphon; branchiæ plumose (Haliotis; Fissurella); note, much bilateral symmetry.

3. Cyclobranchiata, shell conical (Limpet) or multivalve (Chiton); branchiæ plumed, in a circle between margin of foot and mantle.

4. Tubulibranchiata (Cirrhobranchiata), shell tubular, symmetrical, open at each end; branchiæ cirrhose; two; symmetrical.

II. Pulmonifera; shell usually spiral; foot broad, long; operculate or not. (Snail and Slug). Differing from the rest in hæmal turn of intestine.

III. Opisthobranchiata. Shell rudimentary or wanting; branchiæ arborescent or fasciculated, more or less completely exposed, on back or side of body. Monœcious.

Orders. 1. Tectibranchiata; have a shell; branchiæ covered by shell or mantle. (Aplysia, Bulla.)

2. Inferobranchiata; shell-less; branchiæ on both sides of body, below fold of mantle.

3. Nudibranchiata; shell-less; branchiæ exposed on back or side of body. (Doris, Eolis.)

IV. Heteropoda. (Nucleobranchiata.) Free swimmers; with shell (Atlanta), or without (Firola); visceral mass (nucleus) small in proportion to head and foot. Branchiæ present or not; diœcious; auditory vesicles connected with cephalic ganglia.

Cl. Pteropoda.—Cephalous Mollusca, with wing-like fins (Epipodia) projecting from the sides of the head or neck; small, free-swimming, marine. Types, Clio and Hyalæa.

External configuration.

Head small; sometimes marked off from body by a well-defined neck (Clio), sometimes not (Cleodora); fins spring from side of neck, or of head if neck absent.

Mantle in some little developed (Clio), in others forms a large cavity on the inferior aspect of the body (Cleodora).

Shell, present or absent (Gymnosomata, Clio; Thecosomata, Hyalæa); if present, very delicate and transparent. Its form may be a simple cone, a bent cone, or a spiral; the simple cone may be partially divided into dorsal and ventral plates by a transverse slit. (Hyalæa).

The head supports around the mouth tentacles varying in number, and armed with retractile suckers; on the upper aspect also retractile tentacles like those of Gasteropoda. On the inferior surface, behind the mouth, are organs which appear to be homologues of the second and third parts of the foot of Gasteropoda.

Digestion. An odontophore; a gizzard; first bend of intestine ventral.

Respiration. Branchial organs slightly developed, as ciliate, sometimes folded surfaces; often absent. *Heart* opisthobranchiate.

Renal organ connected with pericardial sinus, and opening externally.

Nervous system much as in Gasteropoda, but supra-œsophageal ganglia less developed.

Eyes tentacular in some; absent in others.

Auditory sac connected with pedal ganglion, which also supplies epipodia.

All hermaphrodite.

Mr. Huxley's table of oppositions of Pteropoda and Heteropoda.

Heteropod.	Pteropod.
Intestine bent dorsally; a post-abdomen;	Intestine bent ventrally; an abdomen;
Foot consists of pro-, meso-, and metapodium;	Foot consists of pro-, meso-, meta-, and epipodium;
Auditory organ connected with cephalic ganglia;	Auditory organ connected with pedal ganglia;
Diœcious.	Monœcious.

Note affinities with Cephalopoda, in sucker-bearing oral

tentacles, and anterior fold of mantle of Cleodora; with, on the other side, the Cirrhobranchiate Gasteropods.

Cl. CEPHALOPODA.—Cephalous Mollusca, with locomotive organs (modified foot) taking the form of tentacles radiating from the head, and surrounding the mouth. Free swimming or creeping; marine. Types, Nautilus and Cuttle-fish.

General appearance. Surrounding the mouth are prehensile arms, varying in number; the head, which supports these organs, contains also the organs of mastication and deglutition, and the organs of sense; it is well defined from the body or pallial division. On the front of the body the mantle is projected in front to form a fold enclosing the branchiæ; corresponding with the anterior margin of the fold—aperture of branchial chamber—is a large siphon or funnel, fitting by expanded portion or base into the mouth of the chamber. Shell various, external, concealed, or absent.

Classification. Two orders—1, Tetrabranchiata, including Nautilus; 2, Dibranchiata, including Squids, Cuttle-fishes, Poulpes and Argonaut.

Anatomy—

Shell.—In Tetrabranchiata, external, many-chambered; the chambers represent so many stages of growth, the chamber adjoining the opening of the shell being alone occupied. When the animal grows too large for a chamber, it is gradually walled off by a partition built inwards, from circumference to centre; at the centre a tubular perforation is left, through which a membranous tube (*siphuncle*) passes. This tube runs from an atrial cavity, through the successive compartments to the nucleus. The vacant chambers filled with air.

Among the Dibranchiates, Argonauta has a delicate external, single-chambered shell, much resembling the shell of some Heteropods (Carinariæ); the animal has no organic connection with the shell, which is secreted by two sail-like arms of the dorsal aspect, always found completely investing the outer surface of the shell. The other Dibranchiates have an internal calcareous or horny-shell, placed on the dorsal aspect of the body in a cavity of the mantle.

Locomotive organs—

Arms. The tentacles in the Tetrabranchiata are very numerous, and form two groups—1, *labial*, corresponding, as is suggested, to the buccal membrane of the calamaries; 2, *brachial*, a double series, very numerous, on each side of the head, retractile within sheaths; besides these, four *ocular* tentacles.

In the Dibranchiata, the arms are either eight or ten in number, whence a division into Octopods and Decapods.

In Octopods, a web of muscular membrane surrounds the mouth, and joins the bases of the arms; the arms are eight hollow cones of muscular tissue, deriving their origin from an internal cartilage surrounding the œsophagus; have suckers in series along their oral surface; suckers sessile, with fleshy piston and flexible margins.

The Decapods have two additional arms, which do not form part of the circle, but arise separately from the cartilage, near the eyes, and emerge between the third and fourth pair of arms on the ventral aspect. These arms or tentacles are much longer than the rest, and are expanded at their extremities. Suckers with horny ring; pedunculated; piston often hardened into a strong hook.

Hectocotylus, arm in male; altered to form spermatophore; and, detached in coitu, left attached within branchial chamber of female.

The *funnel* fixed in front of the orifice of the branchial chamber belongs to the list of locomotive organs. It is formed, according to the observations of Kölliker, by the

Epipodia of the embryo, uniting, beneath the head, behind the foot. In the Dibranchiata the funnel is a complete conical cylinder; in the Tetrabranchiata it is composed of two distinct but accurately fitting lateral halves. The base of the funnel is applied within the margin of the branchial chamber, so that when the chamber contracts, the branchial orifice is closed as by a valve, and the contents of the chamber are forced through the narrow funnel; in this way the animal drives itself backwards through the water.

Integument, provided with singular colour-cells in connection with power of changing the tints of the body; projected at the sides of the body in Decapods to form lateral fins. Internal cartilage, connected with attachment of muscles, protection of nerve-ganglia, of eyes, and of auditory organ, transmission of œsophagus. Other cartilages support funnel and lateral fins of Decapods.

Digestive system—

Mouth in nearly middle of circle of feet; often fringed by a soft papillated lip ("*oral sheath*," "*buccal membrane*"); within this a pair of stout mandibles working vertically, the upper within the lower, worked by powerful muscles, and provided with special protrusors and retractors.

Within these again the *glottidium* or odontophore, constructed much as in other cephalous Mollusca, but supporting, behind the tooth-strap, fleshy papillæ, probably of taste. Four *salivary* glands pour secretion into buccal cavity.

Œsophagus, after passing through cartilage, dilates into crop.

Stomach; cardiac and pyloric orifices close together; strong muscular walls; epithelial lining dense and rugged (gizzard-like).

Intestine short; first turn neural; ends at base of funnel.

Liver well marked; a curious laminated bag connected with duct.

Pancreas doubtful.

Ink-bag, present in Dibranchiates, not in Tetrabranchiates; its duct opens close to anus at base of funnel.

Branchiæ; parial, and symmetrical. In Dibranchiata, two, each consisting of a primary rod or stem with lateral pinnæ, and several degrees of pinnules, fixed in whole length to upper wall of branchial chamber. In Tetrabranchiata four, fixed only at the base. Branchiæ not ciliated; mantle-fold and siphon produce regular currents through chamber.

Circulation—

Heart, a systemic *ventricle* in middle of body, with striped muscular fibres; two *aortæ*, visceral and cephalic; both capillaries and lacunar spaces probably intervene between ends of arteries and veins; branchial hearts on great afferent branchial veins; two auricles at entry of *branchio-cardiac* veins into ventricle.

Renal organ, a thick spongy mass surrounding the two great afferent branchial veins (cavæ); appears to consist of a number of little glands opening internally by ducts into veins, externally by little orifices into a large cavity (pericardial sinus), enclosing the heart and large vessels, and communicating with the branchial chamber by pores. In Mr. Hancock's view a renal organ, purely excretory; called also atrium, with supposed aquiferous function.

Nervous system—

Supra-œsophageal ganglia, connecting with sub-œsophageal —*pedal anterior and parieto-splanchnic posterior*—by distinct pairs of cords. Also *stomato-gastric* and other visceral ganglia ("sympathetic"). The larger ganglia, with their commissures, form a collar round the œsophagus.

Eye, very perfect in higher forms; consists of cornea—modification of integument—sclerotic, post-corneal chamber, with aqueous humour, lens, vitreous humour, vascular choroid, retina; no iris.

Auditory sacs containing otoliths imbedded in posterior part of cephalic cartilage ; each receives a large nerve.

A supposed *olfactory* apparatus, placed close to the eyes, of laminated structure.

Reproduction. Diœcious.—Male has one of its arms altered in structure and appearance, and filled with a sac containing spermatozoa; this fixes itself by its suckers within the branchial chamber, and is detached from the body of the male and left adherent to the female. Female, ovary, oviduct, nidamental gland; opening in branchial chamber.

Eggs large, connected into bunches, grape-like, by nidamentum; the yelk, which escapes segmentation, very bulky in proportion to embryo-yelk. In development, first mantle and foot marked out; then the head in front; the arms appear as marginal processes of the foot, and the anterior pair gradually extend round and meet behind the head, so as to enclose the mouth; the epipodia appear as a ridge on each side between mantle and foot; their posterior ends presently unite to form the funnel; the alimentary canal is at first straight, afterwards curved in the way already noted, as the unsymmetrical growth of the mantle proceeds.

In summing up the Cephalopoda, note that the locomotive arms are still representatives of the foot, and that there is a great prevalence of bilateral symmetry among all parts of the body.

As regards distinction between the subordinate groups:

1. Tetrabranchiata; including existing Nautili, fossil Nautili, Orthoceratites, Ammonites, &c., characterized by external chambered shell with siphuncle, retracted head, calcareous mandibles, numerous arms, four branchiæ, split funnel, no ink-bag.

2. Dibranchiata; including Poulpes, Argonauts, Calamaries, Cuttle-fishes, and Spirulæ, with a great number of

fossil forms, such as Belemnites. Two branchiæ; whole funnel; few arms, eight or ten.

Divided into Octopoda and Decopoda, according to arms.

Octopoda—

1. Argonautidæ; dorsal arms of female form shell, which is free and unattached. Males small, shell-less.

2. Octopodidæ; arms similar; basial web; shell represented by two short styles imbedded in the substance of the mantle.

Decapoda—

1. Teuthidæ, Calamaries or Squids; elongated body, fins short and broad, shell internal, consisting of shaft and two wings.

2. Belemnitidæ, fossil; cone often chambered.

3. Sepiadæ; Cuttle-fishes, calcareous internal shell, laminated with posterior imperfectly chambered apex; tentacles (two additional arms) elongated, expanded terminally.

4. Spirulidæ; spiral internal shell, with siphuncle, the last chamber containing the ink-bag.

Sub-Kingdom Vertebrata.

Classes— Mammals.
Birds.
Reptiles.
Batrachians.
Fishes.

General characters of Vertebrata already stated. But some amplification now needed.

1. Skeleton; internal, living, subject to interstitial waste and repair, as opposed to skeleton of Invertebrata which for the most part is external, not living, and when inadequate to present need, either cast off in mass, or left attached to the new deposits.

Parts of the Skeleton.—Skull, spinal column, limbs.

Bases of determination of the several parts of skeleton. Vertebrate theory.—"Typical Vertebra," (Owen.) Not a type, but a diagrammatised conception. Take a vertebra from thorax of bird, neck of crocodile, neck of rabbit, neck of man.

Parts of Vertebra (after Owen): one *centrum;* with offshooting *dorsal* (neural) and *ventral* (hæmal) *arches.*

Neural arch, has three centres of ossification—two "*neurapophyses*" and one *neural spine.*

Hæmal arch in bird more complicated. Two roots:—1, *Diapophysis* (upper transverse process), a non-autogenous offshoot of neurapophysis; 2, *parapophysis* (lower transverse process), autogenous or not, sprouting from side of centrum. To these is suspended by a forked attachment the *pleurapophysis* (rib), enclosing with them on each side of the centrum a little canal, corresponding to the vertebral canal of the cervical vertebræ of man; the constitution of this being well seen in neck vertebræ of well-grown crocodile, where sutures still define the autogenous elements. Hæmal arch completed by *hæmapophyses* (sternal ribs or costal cartilages) and *hæmal spine* (sternum). But hæmal arch may be formed by these latter only, without intervention of ribs, as in tail of various animals.

Other parts:—*Zygapophyses* (articular processes), non-autogenous, two or four in number; *diverging appendages* attached to pleurapophysis, hæmapophysis, or even parapophysis.

In any vertebrate animal the trunk-skeleton can be resolved entirely into vertebræ and their appendages. The limbs and their arches of support, according to Owen, fall within the same category.

Skull.—Cranium, in part at least, divisible into segments comparable to upper arches and centra of vertebræ; face lower jaw, parts of temporal bone, hyoid arch, formed by downward processes in some sense comparable to hæmal arches of vertebræ ; scapular arch and anterior limb referred to the same system by Owen.

In comparison of a series of skulls, and of skull with vertebral column, determinations of homologies of bones founded upon,

1. Adult topography; relations of bones to each other, and to soft parts, particularly nerves, and muscles.
2. Development ; topographical or structural, the latter particularly in reference to origin of particular bones in cartilage or in membrane.

Taking a sheep's skull, a distinct segment can be separated posteriorly, consisting, 1st, of a bone continuing line of vertebral centra (*basi-occipital*); 2nd, of two lateral symmetrical bones continuing line of neurapophyses, and having similar relations to nerves (*ex-occipitals*); 3rd, of a single bone completing the ring or arch above, corresponding serially with neural spines (*supra-occipital*). Posteriorly, the basi-occipital joins by moveable articulation the centrum of the first vertebra (the articular surface in the fish exactly resembles those of vertebræ) ; anteriorly of course there is no such mobility.

The skull, in front of this, further divisible into three transverse segments, in which the parts of this *occipital* segment are serially repeated ; and which may be called *parietal*, *frontal*, and *nasal* (very doubtful) in succession from behind forwards.

In these the *basi-sphenoid* (posterior part of body of sphenoid, including sella turcica), the *pre-sphenoid* (rostral part), and *ethmo-vomerine plate*, continue the line of axial bones equivalent in position to centra of vertebræ. The basicranical axis argued by Huxley to end with pre-sphenoid, on grounds of development and of comparative anatomy.

Laterally, the neurapophysial series continued by *ali-sphenoids* (= greater wings of sphenoids, and always closely related with 5th pair of nerves), *orbito-sphenoids* (= lesser wings of sphenoid, and always related with optic nerves), and *pre-frontals* (= cribriform plate of ethnoid, always related with olfactory nerves).

Superiorly, the neural-spine series continued by *parietals* (often found (*e.g.*, in crocodile) united into one bone), *frontals* (do.), and *nasals* (according to Owen ; though other authors reject this view completely, chiefly on account of development) ; nasals united into one bone in fishes (*e.g.*, Cod).

Brain-case filled in with capsules of sense organs—1st, *turbinals*, submucous ossifications supporting olfactory mucous membrane. 2nd, *sclerotic*, a fibrous hardening of the equivalent of tissue deeper than submucous tissue, the eye being in part formed by an involution of the surface of the body. 3rd, *periotic capsule*, composed partly of bones comparable to alveoli of teeth, and developed out of the cartilage of the primordial skull, partly of thin bony layers immediately in contact with the labyrinth and its processes, possibly of submucous-tissue value. The periotic capsule wedged in between ex-occipitals behind and ali-sphenoids in front ; has always the 8th pair of nerves passing out behind its posterior edge, the 3rd division of 5th before its anterior edge. Demonstrated by Huxley to consist of three bones, viz. : *Epiotic* = mastoid, enclosing part of posterior semicircular canal ; *pro-otic*, = most of paro-petrosa, enclosing vestibule, anterior and external semicircular canals, and forming upper half of fenestra ovalis, and roof of tympanum ; *opisthotic*, enclosing cochlea and lower part of fenestra ovalis, and floor of tympanum.

Are the segments vertebræ ?

In development, after formation of primitive trace, neural canal and notochord, little masses of germinal tissue, each corresponding to a single vertebra (*proto-vertebræ*), are developed round the notochord, in the whole length of the spinal column; the skull, however, laid down as only one piece, not four, and the notochord, which, as far as appears, is continued posteriorly to the very end of the spinal column, ends anteriorly in a point where the sella turcica will afterwards be found. Development seems, therefore, in these respects to contradict the idea. On the other hand, we find in adult conditions almost as extreme modifications of terminal centra, *e.g.*, in bird and frog, as would be exhibited by ethno-vomerine bone, supposing it to be a centrum. The existence of these segments, a simple anatomical fact of great use in facilitating study of bones of head; their vertebral character not decisively proved or disproved.

Face. Composed of four bones on each side; *palatine*, *maxillary*, *pre-maxillary*, and *pterygoid*, regarded by Owen as respectively pleurapophysis, hæmapophysis, hæmal spine, and diverging appendage of first or nasal vertebræ. Development, not in detail supporting this view, still, in the fact that these bones are developed from certain rods of cartilage, suggests a general homology with ribs, or the structures of support which are found in the segments of ventral laminæ in the proper spinal region. Fronto-nasal process; maxillary process; visceral arches.

To these bones must be added the *jugal* or *malar* bone, link between maxilla and squamosal in Mammalia, between maxilla and quadrate (with intermediate *quadrato-jugal*) in bird; a second diverging appendage of the first vertebra, according to Owen, closely imitating the "diverging appendages" by which in a bird the ribs are bound to one another.

Lower jaw. In man and sheep a single bone on each side; equivalent to the terminal bone of a long series of bones on each side, when the bird, and fish, and Mammalian embryo are compared.

1. Developmental evidence as to identity of structures connecting lower jaw with cranium. (Goodsir and others.)

In human development three rods of cartilage sprout from the auditory region of the skull, within the first and second visceral arches.

1st rod; *Meckel's cartilage*, from which are formed the *incus*, and *malleus*, with the *dentary* bone (ramus of jaw) as a related membrane bone.

2nd rod gives rise to *stapes*, *stylohyoid cartilage, and ligament*, and *lesser cornua* of *hyoid* bone.

3rd rod gives rise to *body* and *greater cornua* of *hyoid*.

2. Evidence from adult anatomy.

Owen, going to fish, assumes that the line of structures joining the lower jaw (*dentary bone*) to the side of the skull will be the constituents of a hæmal arch belonging to second (frontal vertebræ), and divides them as follows :—

1. A single inverted Y-shaped bone, called generally the *hyo-mandibular*, from the fact that it is the link by which the mandibular and hyoid arches are suspended from the skull, is divided into two parts by an artificial vertical cut. (Note.—The "Hyo-mandibular" bone in the fish is now alleged by Professor Huxley to be the homologue of the incus.) It is then treated as one of four fragments of the "*tympanic*" bone, the four together constituting a divided pleurapophysis (*epi-, præ-, meso-, and hypotympanic*); the lowermost forming the articular surface for the lower mandible; the lower mandible consists of (1) the "*articular*" bone, which moves on the *hypotympanic*, and, with (2) an appended *surangular*, is called the hæmapophysis, and of (3) the "*dentary*" bone the hæmal spine. The bones of the gill-cover, "*operculars*," are called diverging appendage. Comparing this complicated arch with the developmental picture before drawn, we find

many reasons to identify the dentary bone of the fish with the half of the lower jaw of the Mammal; (note cartilage-rod in dentary bone of fish); the articular bone with the malleus (progressus gracilis still struggling to join dentary, though thrust aside by squamosal); hypotympanic, with incus; mesotympanic ("*symplectic*") with stapes, and pretympanic with orbicular. If this be accepted, the vertebral analysis must, of course, be rejected.

Note, that Professor Huxley has recently found reason to alter some of his determinations, and to identify the malleus with the os quadratum of the bird, and to banish all representation of the os articulare from the mandibular arch of the Mammal. Determinations of Peters.

Determination of tympanic bone. The bone which is called quadrate bone in the bird's head, and thus affords the articular surface for the lower mandible, was supposed by Cuvier to be the homologue of the tympanic bone of human anatomy, and certainly does in part support the membrana tympani. Owen has adopted this identification, and expanded it. But Goodsir's observations on development above referred to, the fact that the tympanic bone in man is a membrane bone and the so-called tympanic bone in the fish a cartilage bone, and the anatomical relations of the quadrate in fish and bird, lead first to the belief that the quadrate of the bird is the equivalent of the incus of man, next to the identification of the quadrate of the bird with the "hypotympanic" of the fish. And development shows that if the hyo-mandibular arches contain the elements of hæmal arches of vertebræ, three such arches at least must be recognised, and not two.

Elements of third hæmal (parietal) arch. (Owen.)

Styloid process and stylohyoid ligament = pleurapophysis.

Greater and lesser cornua of hyoid = hæmapophysis.

Basi-hyals (body of hyoid) = hæmal spine.

Branchiostegal rays = diverging appendages.

In the Owenian theory of the skull, the scapular arch is attributed as hæmal arch to the occipital vertebra, to which it is indeed attached in the fish. The elements of the arch are supra-scapular and scapular bones (pleurapophysis), coracoid bone (hæmapophysis) ; hæmal spine absent. Mr. Parker's analysis of the shoulder-girdle, hereafter noted, invalidates these determinations.

In the last three so-called vertebræ, bones are found on each side suspending the inferior arches, according to Owen, much as inferior transverse processes suspend hæmal arches in the posterior dorsal region. These would be then a series of parapophyses. In the fish, for example, these three are called by Owen par-occipital, mastoid, and post-frontal respectively. But here there is great reason to agree with Huxley in identifying the so-called "*par-occipital*" with true mastoid or epiotic; the so-called "mastoid" with the squamosal, a membrane bone; while the post-frontal does not find a representative in Mammalian anatomy.

Homologies of the *squamosal.* If the above determination be admitted, the bone called *squamosal* in the reptile and bird, and there used to join the quadrate bone (tympanic, Owen) to the jugal or malar bone, must find another name. It certainly holds the relation of the zygomatic process of the squamosal to the malar bone in human and Mammalian anatomy, and if it be not the squamosal, does not appear to correspond to any other bone. Meanwhile, the name *quadrato-jugal* seems appropriate, as involving no prejudice.

The *lacrymal* bone is a membrane bone, belonging to dermal structure.

Limbs.—1. *Scapular arch,* referred, as above, to occipital vertebræ by Owen. Its constant elements, a *scapular* portion dorsal to glenoid cavity, and entering into its formation, a *coracoid* portion ventral to glenoid cavity, and completing it. *Clavicular* element inconstant and variable, not entering into formation of glenoid cavity.

Mr. Parker recognises in the scapular and coracoid portions the essential lateral elements of the "shoulder-girdle" in connection with the medial sternal element; all these are, according to him, cartilage bones, and belong to the true internal skeleton. But the clavicle and inter-clavicle are membrane bones, of dermal origin, not belonging to the internal skeleton, but merely added splint-bones, assisting in retaining the other bones in their proper places. In the case of the fish, the bones joining the scapular arch to the skull (supra-scapula, and scapula, of Cuvier and Owen) are distinctly of dermal origin, and receive the names "post-temporal" and "supra-clavicle;" the so-called coracoid, also of the same nature, receives the name clavicle. The true scapular and coracoid are to be found in small cartilage-bones (radius and ulna of Owen), attached to the inner surface of the clavicle.

2. *Pelvic arch;* elements, *ilium* probably equivalent to *scapula; ischium* to *coracoid; pubic* bone to *clavicle.*

In digestive system; jaws work vertically; distinct stomach and liver; spleen, closely related with liver, constantly present.

Respiration; by lungs, or branchiæ, or by both together.

Heart (except in Lancelet) has at least two cavities—auricle and ventricle.

A lymphatic system in all; probably representative of blood-system of Invertebrata.

Nervous system; always comprehends brain, spinal cord, and sympathetic.

CLASS—PISCES.

Char. 1. Oviparous.
2. Always branchiate.
3. Heart with two cavities.
4. Cold-blooded.
5. Skin covered with scales.

The fish-form being generally familiar to the student, a description of a typical fish not given. The classification adopted is here briefly detailed, and the ordinal distinctions will be afterwards noted at the end of the general description of fish anatomy; but, as in this general description differences existing in the several orders will be alluded to, the list is inserted here in order that the student may, step by step, fill in the outline of the class-type, and the divergences of this type in secondary matters at the same time, and so be prepared for a comprehensive view upon which classification can be founded.

Classification of Fishes.

(From Dallas after Müller.)

Orders.	Sub-ord.—	Type.
1. Leptocardii (Branchiostomi; Cirrhostomi).		Lancelet.
2. Cyclostomi (Dermopteri).		Myxine. Lamprey.
3. Teleostei.	1. Physostomi.	Eel.
	2. Anacanthini.	Cod.
	3. Pharyngognathi.	Flying fish. Wrasse.
	4. Acanthopteri.	Perch. Mullet.
	5. Lophobranchii.	Pipe-fish.
	6. Plectognathi.	Sun-fish.
4. Ganoidei.	1. Holostei.	Bony-pike.
	2. Chondrostei.	Sturgeon.
5. Selachii.	1. Holocephali.	Chimæra.
	2. Plagiostomi.	Sharks. Rays.

External form.—Note the adaptations—No neck; no loin; body tapering to tail; fin-like form of locomotive appendages; and median fins having relation to balance in the water. Scaly skin. No eyelids or lacrymal glands. Note, in relation to many points, that fishes will be found less developed than the other classes, both in organs and tissues, apparently because their relations are simpler.

Skeleton.—See first in bony (Teleosteous) fish.

Bones more fibrous and less compact than in higher classes, and joining by much interdigitating surfaces.

Divided into skull, spinal column, and limbs.

Spinal column has only two regions, *trunk* and *tail.*

A *trunk* vertebræ comprehends, on an average—

1. *Centrum;* biconcave; subglobular masses of gelatinous matter (remains of *chorda dorsalis*) interposed between concavities of adjoining centra.

2. Two *neurapophyses.*

3. *Neural spine.*

4. Two *transverse processes.*

5. Two *ribs.*

6. Two *articular processes.*

The *ribs* end in free points, not joined to a bony sternum, though the position of sternum and sternal ribs is indicated by lines of fibrous tissue.

These ribs often support one or more diverging appendages.

In the *tail* there are no ribs, but a rigid and complete though small ventral arch is formed by two bones, which curve down from the sides of the centra, and meet in the median line; apparently *transverse processes.*

Limbs. 1. Anterior. Scapular arch or "shoulder-girdle." Consists, in Cod, of a linear series of three bones on each side, with the limb-bones sprouting from the inner surface of the third or lowest.—1st bone, forked above, attached by one branch to mastoid, by the other to the squamosal of Huxley (supra-scapula, Owen ; post-temporal, Parker) ; a membrane bone of dermal origin, Parker. 2nd bone, small, cylindrical (scapula, Owen ; supra-clavicle, Parker) ; also of dermal origin, according to Parker. 3rd bone (coracoid of Owen ; clavicle of Parker), large, flat, meeting its fellow in the median line. The two flat, sub-triangular bones attached to the inner surface of the third serial bone (coracoid or clavicle) are called by Parker scapula and coracoid, respectively, and support a glenoid cavity and four brachial bones, according to that author. It is evident that these interpretations completely alter our conceptions of the constitution of this arch, and it is certain that there are good grounds for accepting them; but it is also evident that the scapular arch here still tends to connect itself with the occipital region of the skull by some sort of bony union, as it does elsewhere by muscle. If in the complete idea of the vertebra are included muscles, ligaments, and fibrous processes with related vessels and nerves, such facts as the relations of the spinal-accessory nerve in man to the trapezius and sterno-mastoid muscles must still have an important bearing upon the question of the relation of the shoulder-girdle to the occipital region of the skull — a question which even Mr. Parker's noble monograph cannot be considered to have completely solved.

The digits in Cod are twenty in number, the lowermost, according to Owen, representing the thumb.

Posterior extremity.—Pelvic arch represented by a pair of symmetrical triangular bones joined to each other by articulation in the median line, but having no bony connection with any vertebræ. The fin-rays (digits) are connected to these without the intervention of other limb-bones. The position of hind limbs very variable—abdominal, pectoral, or sub-brachial.

Skull. Distinctive peculiarities—

1. *Axial bones;* basi-occipital bone joins 1st vertebra by a single concave surface exactly corresponding to a centrum; remaining bones usually cartilaginous, but kept together, and in part replaced by underlying ossification of notochord; the "para-sphenoid" of Huxley.

2. *Neurapophysial bones;* ex-occipitals perforated by 8th pair; no foramen for 9th.

3. Along side of cranium three bones wedged in between neurapophyses and neural spine (parapophyses of Owen), viz., (1) par-occipital (Owen) or mastoid (Huxley), (2) mastoid (Owen), squamosal (Huxley), and (3) post-frontal.

4. *Neural spines.*—Supra-occipital, frontal, and nasal single; parietal double, and the two halves thrust apart from each other.

5. Scapular arch attached to skull by furcate bone joining par-occipital and mastoid of Owen.

6. *Hyoid* and mandibular arches suspended from a common point of the skull; two bones apparently peculiar to fishes being here concerned—*hyo-mandibular*, and *symplectic*.

Hyoid arch, besides supporting tongue, has, as appendages, the *branchiostegal rays*, which are attached to epi- and cerato-hyals.

Mandibular arch, very complicated, consisting of a long series of ossicles, none as yet dwarfed to form bones of tympanic cavity; supports the opercular bones—flat ossicles constituting the gill-cover; four in number, viz., operculum, præ-operculum, inter-operculum, and sub-operculum; they join the hyo-mandibular and quadrate.

7. Maxillary bone generally toothless, and very moveable.

8. The periotic bones not united to each other, but tending to unite severally with surrounding bones. Pro-otic large, free.

In the non-bony *or cartilaginous* fishes the proper vertebral skeleton exhibits many gradations of structure.

In the Lancelet the chorda dorsalis occupies a relatively large space, retaining such proportion to the rest of the skeleton as might be originally seen in the embryo of an ordinary bony fish. It is enclosed in a membranous sheath, from which membranous processes, corresponding to neural arches, sprout to enclose the neural canal.

In the Lamprey, the chorda dorsalis takes the form of a long, semi-transparent column, enclosed by a series of delicate cartilaginous rings supporting fibrous neural and ventral arches.

In the Sturgeon, the cartilaginous ring encroaches very considerably on the chorda, and the neural arch is cartilaginous, consisting of neurapophysial and spinous elements. In the abdominal vertebræ the elements of hæmal arches appear in part in cartilaginous form.

In some of the Sharks, a beautiful series of concentric rings of bone, diminishing in length as they go centrewards, and joined into one bone by radiating bars, encroach still further on the chorda, and sketch out the typical biconcave centrum, leaving the chorda varicose, or consisting of a series of globular masses, connected by narrow isthmi.

In these cartilaginous fishes, confluence of adjoining vertebræ, in the whole or in part, is not uncommon.

The scapular and pelvic arches are moulded in cartilage, without segmentation, including, according to Parker, representatives of supra-scapula, scapula, coracoid, and epi-coracoid.

The tail-fin is of different form in the two groups : heterocercal or superficially unsymmetrical in cartilaginous ; homocercal or superficially symmetrical in osseous. In homocercal, symmetry attained by abortion of centra of terminal vertebræ ; in heterocercal, no abortion. Heterocercal tails, therefore, structurally symmetrical.

Skulls of cartilaginous fishes.—Three forms, according to Huxley :—

1. Where skull is formed of one mass of cartilage without a lower mandible. (Lamprey.)

2. A mandible directly joined to the skull. (Holocephali.)

3. A mandible joined to skull by a moveable suspensory cartilage. (Sharks and Rays.)

Lastly, it must be observed that in many lower fishes a large part of the skull remains permanently cartilaginous, and that a very long series of gradations connect the purely cartilaginous and the purely osseous types. In the Ganoids, the cartilaginous skull proper is strengthened in a supplementary way by strong superficial bony plates of dermal origin; and, according to Parker, bones of subcutaneous origin are similarly worked in among and around the endoskeletal elements of the shoulder-girdle. The scales of fishes indeed constitute a sort of dermal skeleton.

They assume four principal forms :—

1. Cycloid. Circular, or sub-circular scales, with entire margins, imbricating horny base, enamelled surface. (Carp, Salmon.)

2. Ctenoid. Scales with posterior margin pectinated, imbricating. (Perch.)

3. Placoid. Dense nodules or spiny plates, of various sizes, variously distributed over the integument, consisting of an almost crystalline enamel, supported upon bony matter. Shagreen. (Sharks.)

4. Ganoid. Large, flat, closely fitting, mostly not imbricating, plates of hard bone, invested by enamel of great density, and often beautiful arrangement. These are borne by few living fishes, but were characteristic of a great number of extinct fishes. It may be noticed that for the most part the ossification of the internal

vertebral skeleton bears an inverse ratio to the development of this dermal skeleton.

Lateral line and *mucous canal.*

Muscular system typically consists of segments corresponding to vertebræ; modified freely for local needs.

Digestive system.—Food for digestion and water for respiration enter the mouth together; water passes out by lateral vertical slits into branchial chamber on each side, food retained in mouth; sieve-like bristles guarding branchial slits.

Teeth.—At anterior part of mouth, retentive, laniary, or cutting; at posterior part, masticatory.

Forms of Teeth. Derived from simple cone; which may be curved backwards, and pointed as in Cod, or thinned out to bristle-shape, as in the velvet-like pile of the Chætodon, or widened at the base, and flattened, as in Sharks, or depressed and rounded, or flattened, as in Catfish, or in Rays.

Attachment by ligament, or by ankylosis; in shallow pits, or on flat surface, or on pediment. Sometimes moveable, as in Lophius; not so in Sharks.

The following bones bear teeth in various fishes:—Premaxillary, maxillary (rather rarely), palatine, pterygoids, mandibular, vomer, pre-sphenoid, basi-sphenoid, basi-occipital hyoid bones, pharyngeal arches, nasals, and rostrum.

Constitution. Chiefly of dentine, taking various degrees of hardness, and exhibiting many transitions towards simple bone structure, viz., vitreodentine, dentine, vasodentine, osteodentine (Owen). Enamel not commonly present. Enamel probably never formed unless during development the tooth shall have been enclosed in a sac. This is not the rule in fishes. Nevertheless, in some fishes, *e.g.*, Scarus, and many Plectognatha, the teeth have enamel.

When the body of a fish is opened, it is found to present two cavities; one anteriorly covered by the junction of the coracoid bones; the other posterior, and larger; the anterior contains the heart, the posterior the alimentary canal and appendages, and genito-urinary organs. The cavities are divided by a transverse membranous septum, and each cavity has its special serous membrane; severally pericardium and peritoneum. These, however, often communicate either by perforations of septum or short dorsally-placed canal.

Alimentary Canal, divisible into œsophagus, stomach, small and large intestine. Stomach divided from intestine by a pyloric sphincter; commencement of small intestine receives ducts of liver, and appendices pyloricæ. Posterior part of œsophagus and stomach contained in abdomen.

Stomach, siphonal or cæcal; gizzard-like in a few fishes—Mullets, Mackerel, and Gillaroo Trout—but has no great variety of form. Mucous coat, usually smooth, rarely reticulate, more rarely papillose. Gastric juice possesses great activity.

Intestine. Has peritoneal, muscular, and mucous tunics. Muscular tunic, of two layers; external longitudinal, internal circular. Mucous coat, smooth, as in Cod; rugose, Turbot, Salmon; reticulate, Wolf-fish; or villose. Forms a spiral valve in the large intestine in Ganoids and Selachii—*e.g.*, Sturgeon and Shark.

Anus; varies in position, following, to a great extent, the ventral fin.

Liver; well developed in ordinary fishes, but only a cæcal offshoot of the intestine in lowest forms. Colour varies; consistence, soft; attached in the fore part of the abdomen to an aponeurotic partition, which limits posteriorly the pericardial chamber; extending back in variously shaped lobes, further on the left than on the right. Gall bladder rarely absent, situate at front part of abdomen, attached to right portion of liver.

Pyloric cæca, blind tubes opening into commencement of intestine, and most probably the homologues of the pancreas; at all events, analogues. They exhibit a very interesting series of ascent. Dermopteri have none; Sand-launce, 1; Turbot, 2; Perch, 3; Cottus, 4–9; Gurnard, 5–9; in these cases each tube communicates with intestine by a separate orifice. When, however, the number of tubes increases, the orifices are fewer in proportion: in Pilchard, 50 cæca have 30 inlets; in Tunny, numerous cæca, 5 orifices; Swordfish, 2 orifices; Sturgeon, 1 orifice; finally, in Plagiostomi the cæca are bound together by connective tissue, and are surrounded by many vessels, so that a compact gland is formed, with one duct. (Owen.) But in some Ganoids, besides the tubular cæca, a small distinct glandular body exists in the position which a true pancreas would hold, and may, after all, be the homologue.

Lacteals and lymphatics.—Form plexuses, but not glands; have no valves; chief lymphatic trunk of tail possesses contractility, and pulsates with some regularity.

Respiration.—By *gills;* vascular ciliated pectinated processes, supported in series on bony arches, and lodged in a chamber on each side of fauces. *The branchial arches* are five in number, on each side, attached beneath to a median chain of bones prolonged backwards from the hyoid bone, and suspended above by ligamentous structure from the sides of the skull. Each arch of course concave internally, and armed with bristles or other processes; convex externally, and presenting two ridges with an intervening groove. To the ridges attached the branchial processes, which are simple or branched, and are arranged in a regular series like the teeth of a comb; two series to each arch. Each process is supported by bone or cartilage within, and invested by mucous membrane extremely rich in capillaries.

Of the five arches, the first four support gills ; the last, called also the *pharyngeal arch*, supports teeth, and guards the entry to the gullet.

The gills in an ordinary osseous fish contained in one chamber, to which the water finds access from the mouth through slits between the branchial arches, and after passing through the chamber, finds exit by one large slit, guarded by a membranous valve suppported by *branchiostegal rays.* The *operculum* (composed of the bones alluded to above) forms the outer wall of the chamber, with its posterior edge forming the anterior margin of the slit; it is moved by muscles, and has a bellows action in determining the flow of water from the mouth through and out of the branchial chamber.

In the Cyclostomi, and in the Selachii, there is no operculum, and the branchial chamber is split up into five (usually), six, or seven little chambers, each corresponding to a branchial slit, and each opening externally by a distinct orifice. Each little chamber contains a pair of laminæ, the opposed laminæ of two adjoining arches ; not the pair of one arch. This general description, however, is subject to great varieties of detail—*e.g.*, branchial sacs of Myxine ; single orifice of Chimæra, &c. The capillaries extract oxygen from the water which flows through the chamber.

Circulation.—Blood with oval nucleated red corpuscles (Lamprey exceptional), and white corpuscles. *Heart* placed under and behind the gills, in the cavity of the body already noted. It receives blood from a large *venous sinus*, sometimes contained within the pericardium, sometimes between layers of the aponeurotic septum. From this the blood flows through an *auricle*, a *ventricle*, and an *arterial bulb* in succession. These form a single series—not a double series, as in man—and transmit only *venous blood.*

The *auriculo-ventricular* orifice guarded by two semilunar valves (Teleostei), or by musculo-membranous valves, with tendinous chords (Selachii); *ventricle* strongly muscular, pyramidal in shape, tapering from behind forwards to arterial bulb; *arterial bulb* membranous in Teleostei, with two semilunar valves in one row guarding its communication with the ventricle; muscular in Ganoids and Selachii, with many rows of valves placed at various intervals within its cavity. The blood brought by the bulb applied upon the branchiæ by successive pairs of arteries, running along the groove of each branchial arch; these arteries break up into capillaries in which the blood undergoes oxidation; from the capillaries veins arise and continue the line of arteries upwards until they meet in a dorsally placed *aorta*, above the branchial arches; from the veins of the first arch the arterialized blood is sent pure to the head; in the last arch there are no branchiæ, so the artery, with its venous blood, goes on direct to the aorta. The aorta, therefore, running straight backwards underneath the spinal column, carries into the visceral region of the body and trunk-muscles blood only in part arterialized. Note that the aorta has no special propelling organ connected with its starting-point.

The veins from the digestive and generative organs and from the tail form large trunks, running to the liver and kidneys, wherein they break into capillary systems (*portal* and *reno-portal*); thence the blood goes by large hepatic and renal veins to a cava, or direct to the great præcardial venous sinus. In lower fishes, some of the veins have pulsating muscular thickenings of their walls at certain points; Lancelet, branchial, portal, and caval hearts; Myxine (Cyclostome), portal heart; Eel, a sort of heart at commencement of caudal vein; though this last supposed to be lymphatic by good observers.

Atmospheric respiration—

Air-bladder: an elastic bag filled with gas, lying in the dorsal and anterior part of the abdomen, under the spinal column.

Shape; bifurcate, Diodon; divided by constriction; transversely in Cyprinidæ (Carp tribe); longitudinally in Polypterus; notched, with many lateral processes, Cod.

Structure. Fibrous, shining, contractile, elastic; lined by a mucous membrane with pavement epithelium; cavity sometimes subdivided by partially complete septa, or completely severed in two (Gymnotus).

In most fishes it has a duct, patent, or closed and rudimentary, opening usually by dorsal aperture into the œsophagus or pharynx.

Internal surface vascular; vessels aggregated into tufts (vaso-ganglia), which are supposed to secrete air.

Contents gaseous; chiefly nitrogen; little oxygen, except in deep-sea fishes.

Air-bladder, the homologue of lungs of higher Vertebrata; transitional conditions in some Ganoids.

Absent in Cyclostomi, Holocephali, and Plagiostomi.

Urinary organs—

Kidneys; consist of a tube running longitudinally on each side of the spine, and giving off at right angles tufts of cæcal tubules; at the end of each cæcal tube is a body resembling a Malpighian tuft of the human kidney (vaso-ganglion).

Note simple form as seen in Cyclostomi.

The kidneys of the fish are the homologues of the Wolffian bodies of the Mammalian embryo.

Ureters single or double; generally unite to form a common sinus or bladder, which opens *behind* the vulva.

Nervous System—

Spinal cord; long and uniform in thickness in snake-like fishes; in heterocercal fishes it tapers to a point; in homocercal it ends in an enlargement; in some fishes it exhibits distinct enlargements at the attachments of nerves connected with parts of great functional activity—*e.g.*, in Gurnard.

In relation to the rest of the nervous system and the bulk of the body, the spinal cord is smaller in the fish than in higher Vertebrata, and seems, as Van der Kolk suggests, to be small in proportion to the limited variety of movements commonly performed by the animal. Compare Sturgeon and Frog.

The cord is obscurely divided into anterior, lateral, and posterior columns, with included grey matter in each half.

Medulla oblongata. Two structures peculiar to fishes:—

1. Vagal lobes; laterally.

2. Nodulus, in floor of fourth ventricle.

Encephalon above medulla comprehends in succession cerebellum, optic lobes, hemispheres, olfactory lobes.

Cerebellum. Single; median; relatively larger in the fish than in any other Vertebrates. Corresponds to middle lobe only of man, and has no pons Varolii. Usually covers fourth ventricle.

Restiform bodies—inferior crura cerebelli—appear to give off, on antero-lateral aspect of the medulla, the great trigeminal nerves (fifth pair of man); and great ganglia are in many fishes (chiefly in cartilaginous) connected with the roots. The ganglion enormous in Torpedo, whose electrical apparatus is supplied by the trigeminal. Auditory ganglia are also large.

Optic lobes consist of two parts: (1) upper, the equivalent of the corpora quadrigemina of man; (2) lower, enclosing third ventricle, and joined across by a commissure. With the ventricle are connected the pineal gland above, the pituitary below, constituting always very important landmarks.

3. Cerebral lobes; vary in size, being sometimes smaller and sometimes larger than the optic lobes. Pinkish, and furrowed externally. Solid in most osseous fishes, but in the higher cartilaginous fishes have each an enclosed ventricle (lateral). The part above the ventricle will then correspond with the hemisphere of man, the part below with the corpora striata (?); while the lower part of the optic lobes would correspond to the thalami optici.

4. Olfactory lobes often placed at a distance from the rest of the encephalon, following the position of the nasal organ.

Cranial nerves—

1st pair. Olfactory filaments go direct to nasal mucous membrane.

2nd pair. Optic. In cartilaginous fishes no decussation, but a well-marked commissure; origin from optic lobes.

In osseous a commissure before decussation, no interchange of fibres occurring at the crossing; apparent origin various; from optic lobes, wall of third ventricle and cerebellum.

5th pair. Trigeminal. Proportionally large in all fishes; origin from restiform columns, or angle between restiform and olivary bodies. Branches to face, including representative of portio dura, and to fins, lateral muscles of body, and mucous canal of side (lateral nerves).

8th pair. Vagus. Two roots; 1st, ganglionic, to branchiæ and stomach; 2nd, non-ganglionic, supra-temporal, glosso-pharyngeal, and "lateral."

Sense organs—

1. Smell.—A sac on each side of face, lined by mucous membrane; with one or two usually valve-guarded external orifices, and rarely communicating with the mouth; if communicating, never traversed by respiratory medium. Epithelium ciliated; surface often increased by folds.

2. Sight.—In well-developed fishes the eye exhibits the following peculiarities:—

Retina formed by fan-like unfolding of optic nerve into a plate bent round into the form of a rounded cone, leaving a fissure where the free borders meet; through the fissure penetrates a process of the choroid, which traverses the vitreous humour, and constitutes the suspensory ligament of the lens.

Lens; large, firm, dense at centre; nearly spherical.

Choroid consists of three layers; 1, external, membrana argentea; 2, middle, vascular; 3, internal, pigmentary.

Iris; consists of three membranes of choroid prolonged.

Additional pendent curtain in Skate.

Sclerotic; strengthened by cartilage; often of different shape from the true eyeball, with adipose or areolar tissue interposed.

Cornea; modified corium fixed into anterior aperture of *sclerotic;* always very flat.

Choroid gland; a vaso-ganglion lying between the silvery and vascular layers of the choroid at the back of the eye, around entrance of optic nerve.

Few fishes have eyelids.

Muscles of eye; four recti; two oblique.

No lacrymal gland.

3. Hearing.—In lowest fishes a simple membranous bag, containing otoliths, and receiving the distribution of the auditory nerve, is lodged in the walls of the skull without any external communication. To this first one, then two, then three semicircular canals are added, three being the number in all above the Cyclostomi. The vestibular portion consists always of a sacculus and utriculus, containing otoliths, andcommunicating with varying degrees of freedom.

No tympanum or cochlea; but the cranial walls usually found thinned over the organ.

The air-bladder found in some fishes (Cyprinidæ) sending processes to come in contact directly, or by a chain of bones, with the vestibule.

Electric organs.—Note that there are at least seven species of electric fishes.

Reproduction. *Male organs.*—1. May be, as in Lamprey, formed of a single gland, attached to the median line of the abdomen, under the spine, between the kidneys; this discharges spermatozoa, by rupture of cells, into abdominal cavity, from which they escape by orifices near the vent.

2. In most osseous fishes the testis is contained in a fibrous capsule, and has a distinct duct or vas deferens opening into the urethra. If there be two separate testes, their vasa deferentia unite into one. The arrangement subject to many minor variations.

3. In Plagiostomes, testes distinct; compact; proper capsule; proper peritonæal investment. Vas deferens forms an epididymis, and then, much contorted, runs to near cloaca, where it forms a reservoir; finally joins end of ureter and opens on a rudimentary cloacal penis. Claspers.

Female.—1. In Lamprey, single, longitudinal, flat gland without duct; ovules escape by rupture into peritoneum, and thence escape by proper orifices. 2. In other fishes where vasa deferentia are absent in the male, oviducts are absent in the female; but the converse does not necessarily obtain. Oviducts commonly open behind anus, and before urethra.

Viviparous fishes have dilatation of end of oviduct, containing abundant albuminous secretion; no attachment of embryo.

3. Cartilaginous fishes, no true oviducts. Ripe ova escape into abdominal cavity, and are there received into open mouths of tubular offsets from the ureters.

In Plagiostomes, these ducts are distinct from the ureters

and open externally to them. Here ovaries more compact; ova fewer; tubes divisible into three parts; (1), with thin muscular tunics; (2), with thicker, glandular; (3), with expanded "uterine" cavity. Inverse proportion of glandular and uterine portions.

In development, the details of which cannot be entered on, fishes are distinguished by forming neither amnion nor allantois.

Ordinal divisions of Fishes—

1. Leptocardii. Represented by but one form, the Lancelet, in which the heart is not subdivided.

2. Cyclostomi. Lamprey and Hag; snake-like, no lateral fins; median fins membranous (whence named also Dermopteri); skeleton partly membranous, partly cartilaginous; no lower jaw, no ribs; respiratory sacs; curious branchial skeleton.

3. Teleostei. Skeleton bony; skull complicated; gills placed upon free arches in one chamber with one outlet; mouth with proper jaws. Arterial bulb not muscular; two semilunar valves. Scales chiefly cycloid or ctenoid, a few ganoid.

Sub-orders—1. Physostomi—Eel, Carp, Herring, Salmon, Pike.

Air-bladder has a duct.

Fins rayed; rays soft, except first dorsal, anal, and pectoral, which may be spinous.

Scales, if present, cycloid.

2. Anacanthini; Cod, Sole, Sand-launce.

Air-bladder closed; duct usually quite gone.

Fins rayed; rays all soft.

Ventral fins on chest or throat.

Inferior pharyngeal bones always separated.

The Pleuronectidæ exhibit curious deformity, the eyes being brought to one side of the head, and the fish swimming always on one side. The eyes originally symmetrical in development, but change position during growth.

3. Pharyngognathi.—Flying-fish, Wrasse.

Inferior pharyngeal bones coalesced.

Rays of either kind. Fins of all attachments.

Scales ctenoid or cycloid.

Air-bladder closed.

4. Acanthopteri.—Gurnard, Perch, Weever, Mullet, Goby, Blenny, Mackerel.

Rays of first dorsal fin always spinous; membrane often deficient.

Ventral fins on breast or throat.

Air-bladder closed.

Pharyngeal bones separate.

5. Lophobranchii.—Pipe-fish, Hippocampus.

Gills in tufts, not laminæ; operculum comparatively fixed; no branchiostegal rays.

Face drawn out into a long snout.

Fins imperfect.

Bony plates in skin.

Marsupial pouch of male.

6. Plectognathi.—Trunk-fish, Diodon, Sunfish.

Firm fixature of bones of face to skull.

Bones of head well ossified; of body cartilagious.

Skin strengthened by scattered earthy points, or plates.

Air-bladder large; no pyloric cæca.

Order 4. Ganoidei.—Scales in form of smooth bony plates covered with enamel.

Great variations in ossification of skeleton—1, fossil forms; 2, Sturgeon; 3, Lepidosteus.

Caudal fin heterocercal.

Bulbus arteriosus muscular, with many semilunar valves.

Air-bladder freely communicating with alimentary canal.

Spiral valve in intestine.

No decussation of optic nerves.

Sub-order 1. Holostei. Entire surface covered with scales or bony plates. Head never covered with dermal bones. Lepidosteus.

2. Chondrostei.—Skeleton cartilaginous. Bony plates of dermal origin invest head, but only scattered loosely on body. Sturgeon and fossil fishes, *e.g.*, Pterichthys.

Order 5. Selachii ; scales placoid.

Skeleton variously ossified.

Skull without dermal plates.

Branchiæ in sacs, without operculum.

Arterial bulb as in Ganoidei.

In development external filamentous branchiæ.

Altogether more highly organized than Ganoidei.

Sub-order 1. Holocephali. Chimæra.

One branchial orifice, five sacs.

Suspensorium of lower jaw connate with head.

2. Plagiostomi.—Sharks and Rays.

Five, six, or seven orifices to as many branchial sacs.

Suspensorium distinct.

Cl. Batrachia, or Amphibia.

Characters.
1. Oviparous.
2. Branchiate in embryonic state, lungs being always added in conjunction with or to the exclusion of branchiæ.
3. Heart with two auricles.
4. Cold-blooded.
5. Skin mostly naked.
6. In development have no amnion and but a rudimentary allantois.

The orders of Batrachia are—

1. Anura	Frog.
2. Urodela	Newt.
3. Perennibranchiata	Axolotl, Siren.
4. Apoda	Cæcilia.

The Frog exhibits the highest development of the type. But it may be observed that, much as the Frog in many respects approaches the Reptile, the resemblances are teleological and of the surface, rather than original and of the type. In some Ganoid fishes, and especially in Lepidosiren, we see a high fish-form commencing an adaptation of its organism to some sort of air-breathing. And in the Frog we seem to see the furthest progress hitherto obtained by the Piscine type in this direction. The water-dweller has become also an air-dweller, and has a wider horizon of life-relations.

External form.—Head and trunk confluent without neck.

Locomotive limbs distinctly divisible into several joints; *e.g.*, in fore-limb we recognise arm, forearm, wrist, and hand.

Skin, naked, glandular, with pigment.

Skeleton.—Bone-structure, much more firm and calcified than in fish. *Vertebræ*, only eight in number, with a long, curved coccygeal appendage posteriorly. Their centra are concavo-convex, and their processes are few. The first vertebra has no transverse process. The rest have strong and well-formed transverse processes, the last, or sacral vertebra, supporting by these the pelvic arch. As there are no ribs, the column cannot be divided into neck, trunk, and loin regions.

Extremities. 1. Anterior. Scapula divided into an upper and lower piece (supra-scapula and scapula), the upper partly bony, partly cartilaginous; joined to sternum by stout coracoid (and epi-coracoid in cartilage, Parker). The coracoid and scapula together form the glenoid cavity. In front of coracoid a thin splint of bone runs from the scapula to a projection of the sternum (episternum, Auct; omosternum, Parker). This bone is sometimes called clavicle; but, as originating in cartilage, is called pre-coracoid by Parker, who regards it as the homologue of the os pubis in the pelvis. The sternum is distinctly segmented, consisting of omo-sternum, sternum, and xiphi-sternum (Parker). Limb. Long humerus; radius and ulna united; carpus of two rows of four bones each; and five digits; the thumb rudimentary, having only a metacarpal bone without phalanges.

2. Posterior. Pelvic arch. Iliac bones very long; extended backwards from extremity of sacral transverse processes, and besides forming the upper part of the acetabulum, uniting with each other in the median line. The arch completed by two stout bones forming the acetabulum and main part of the key; they are usually called ischia. No representatives of pubic bones exist. Limb. Long femur; tibia and fibula united; os calcis and astragalus much elongated, and united to each other at their ends; navicular and cuboid united; three cuneiform bones; five digits, composed of metatarsal bones and phalanges.

Skull. In certain important points, the skull of Batrachia approaches most closely to the Piscine type.

Under the still cartilaginous representatives of the axial bones of the skull runs a notochordal ossification, like the para-sphenoid of the fish ("basi-occipito-sphenoidal plate," Owen). The hyoidean arch is connected with the skull by a suspensorium common to it and the mandibular arch.

Peculiarities—

1. Basi-occipital being cartilaginous, skull articulates with first vertebra by means of zygapophyses developed on bony ex-occipitals.

2. "Os en ceinture," or girdle-bone, an ossification in

cartilage at front part of axial region of skull; as interpreted by Professor Huxley, the representative of five bones, ethmoid, pre-frontals, orbito-sphenoids; by Professor Owen, of two, the pre-frontals.

Differences from fish. In tympanum fenestra ovalis, with columella (homologue of stapes) attached; tympanic ring for membrana-tympani. Appearance of quadrato-jugal bone. No branchiostegal rays, and no opercular bones, unless the temporo-mastoid (masto-tympanic (?) Owen) represent the pre-operculum.

Digestive system—

Teeth, numerous, small, simple, conical; of dentine and cement; fixed to maxillaries, pre-maxillaries, and vomer; not to lower jaw.

Tongue fixed to back of symphysis of lower jaw, and, in repose, folded back along the floor of the mouth; evertible, and then found to be bifid; substance muscular, with investing mucous membrane, supporting an epithelium of mucus-forming ciliated chalice-cells. The epithelium of the mouth and fauces is also ciliated.

Œsophagus dilatable; stomach siphonal; small intestine, long; colon, wide and short; cloaca.

No distinct salivary glands.

Liver, large, bilobed; gall-bladder; common duct, opening into duodenum.

Pancreas, distinct, with one duct.

Circulation—

Blood with red and white corpuscles: red large, oval, bi-convex; usually said to be nucleated; but this denied by Savory, as affects fresh condition. Heart; two auricles, one ventricle, ending in a bulbus arteriosus, which is partially subdivided longitudinally by anterior and posterior folds.

Arteries; two pairs given off from bulb; first pair give

off carotids and brachials; then curve round œsophagus, unite, and form aorta. (Carotids sometimes regarded as a third pair, as indeed by development they are.) Second pair pulmonary. Both pairs give off subordinate branches not noticed here.

Veins. Few valves. Striped muscular fibres in coats (Flourens). The larger veins have power of rhythmical pulsation. Part of the venous blood from the hind limb, and the blood from the genital organs, is collected by a reno-portal vein, and circulates through a capillary system in the kidney, which thus derives its secretion mainly from venous blood. The two auricles are respectively pulmonic and systemic; the ventricle, therefore, receives and transmits a mingled stream.

Respiration; in adult by lungs only. These are a pair of sacs placed one on each side of the body, towards the dorsal aspect; not in any separate cavity. They receive air, each through a bronchus, which ends abruptly as it enters the sac; from the bronchial cartilage extends an areolated frame-work all round the walls of the lung sac, from which anastomosing processes are sent a short distance into the cavity, so as to form a superficial cellular system communicating with the large central cavity. Over this scaffolding is spread the vascular respiratory membrane, continuous with the bronchial mucous membrane. The bronchi unite and open into the floor of the mouth through a well-formed larynx, provided with vocal chords and accessory resonance-sacs. In the absence of bellows arrangements in the trunk, air is pumped into the lungs by a bellows arrangement in the mouth, which is kept shut while air is first drawn in chiefly by movements of the hyoid bone, through the nostrils, and then forced into the lungs through the glottis, the nostrils being closed by internal valvular flaps, and by the tongue applied against their palatal openings.

Absorbent system. The Frog has both lacteal and lymphatic vessels; there are no glands, and the vessels are unprovided with valves; on the back, connected with large plexuses of lymphatic vessels, are four "lymph-hearts," muscular sacs, acting with rhythm of their own, and pumping lymph into the veins. The anterior pair are placed in front of the scapulæ, the posterior on each side of the coccyx.

The spleen is well developed in the Frog.

Nervous system—

Spinal cord; large in proportion to size of body; presents distinct enlargements at points of junction of nerves of the two extremities.

Encephalon. The cerebellum is exceedingly small; the olfactory lobes sessile.

Sympathetic system has large prævertebral ganglia.

Organs of sense—

Nasal organs; little more than passages for air into mouth, without increase of surface by irregularity.

Eyes large, well developed, prominent; choroid tunic iridescent externally. A third eyelid or membrana nictitans. Lacrymal glands.

Ear. To apparatus of fish is added a tympanum, with drum externally, and Eustachian tube internally; one ossiculum auditus, the columella (stapes), running from membrana tympani to fenestra ovalis. But careful dissection makes it doubtful whether there be not a subdivision of this into a larger internal bony and smaller external cartilaginous style (orbicular ?).

Kidneys. Flat, compact, in dorsal part of posterior third of body. Malpighian bodies well developed; commencement of tubes ciliated (Bowman). Ureters open into cloaca. Cloaca the common outlet for all secretions; receives rectum above, with but slight demarcation, allantois in front; behind rectum are orifices of urino-seminal ducts, in male; of oviducts first, ureters next in female.

Note that the kidneys are not equivalent to those of fish, but to those of higher Vertebrates. Allantois, a remnant of development; not an urinary bladder, but a reservoir for fluid.

Supra-renal capsules are present in the Frog, and at the upper end of the kidneys are large relics of Wolffian bodies.

Genital organs—

Male. Testes, oval, white bodies, placed in front of kidneys, consist of cæcal tubules; have each six efferent ducts, which enter successively a longitudinally-placed canal. This canal (urino-seminal) receives also the ducts from the kidney, and opens at length into the cloaca, as before stated. No intromittent organ.

Female. Ovary, a much-folded sac placed close to the median line. Oviduct, with peritoneal opening near liver; cloacal opening as above; much convoluted; much dilated towards lower end.

Fecundation of the ova is effected in the Frog at the moment of their extrusion. The male fixes himself for this purpose to the back of the female, grasping her firmly with his forelegs just behind the head. The union lasts many days, and in connection with the prolonged clasp, the rudimentary thumb is found much increased in size and vascularity. Most probably the increased sensitiveness of its papillary structures gives rise to continuous reflex spasm in the arm-flexors.

Development—

1. In first stage the embryo (tadpole) is essentially piscine in structure, having branched gills developed upon the branchial arches, very vascular, with ciliated surfaces; between the arches are slits communicating with the pharynx. The body is fish-like in form, with a long com-

pressed tail, and legs only represented by little tubercles. The mouth is round, projecting, comparatively small, and placed under the snout, as in the higher fishes. The lips are armed with a horny beak.

2. As growth proceeds, and the trunk undergoes development, the branchiæ wither away, the tail withers, and the mouth widens and comes forward. Internally, the circulation, which was at first that of a fish, changes in a corresponding way. While the gills are in full play there start from the bulbus arteriosus three branchial arteries on each side; these ramify in the gills, and from their capillaries branchial veins arise and unite to form an aorta, the first branchial veins supplying the head directly. Each branchial vein, however, communicates on the inner aspect of the gill with the corresponding artery by a small direct vessel. As the branchiæ wither, the lungs are, of course, in process of development, and from the last of the three vessels a branch goes to the growing organ on each side. In proportion as the circulation through the branchiæ diminishes, the communicating vessels grow in size, and the little pulmonary branch finally absorbs the whole of the stream of the third vessel. So the middle pair run round direct to the aorta, and the first pair are reduced to appendages of them going to the head. The branchial arches, attached to the hyoid bone, wither like the branchiæ, leaving only traces of their existence in little processes of the permanent hyoid. Finally, the last traces of gills are lost, the tail is absorbed, the limbs grow and are jointed, and the horny beak is replaced by tooth-bearing jaws.

Noteworthy differences in other Batrachia.

In *external form*, the Urodela and Perennibranchiata approach much more closely to the fish. Many of them have vertical median fins on back and tail; but these fins are never supported by bones.

The development of the limbs is diminished as the tail

persists. The Apoda (Ophiomorphæ) are altogether snake-like in form, but are included with the Batrachia because in their early life they have gills and pharyngeal clefts.

Skin generally naked, but scaly in Cæcilia.

Skeleton. The Urodela and Perennibranchiata exhibit successive stages towards Piscine type. Vertebræ increase in number;—Siren has between eighty and ninety trunk vertebræ; the centra are bi-concave (except in land Salamanders); the trunk vertebræ have floating ribs; the tail vertebræ a hæmal canal formed by coalescing transverse processes.

Digestive system—

Teeth. Toads have none. In the Urodela and Perennibranchiata, besides the upper jawbones, the dentary and splenial bones of the lower jaw, and the palatine, pterygoid and sphenoid bones support teeth. Cœcilia has a double row of teeth at the anterior part of the lower jaw. (Owen.)

Respiratory organs. Where the branchiæ persist, the lungs never attain such development as in the Frog. They are smaller, less vascular and cellular, and their bronchial tubes and larynx reduced to membranous tubes, with only rudiments of cartilaginous rings.

Nervous system—

Spinal cord elongated and uniform in thickness in fish-like forms.

Eye often rudimentary (*e.g.*, Proteus).

Ear has tympanic apparatus only imperfect in aquatic forms.

Class Reptilia.

Distinguishing characters—

1. Oviparous.
2. Heart with two auricles; one ventricle.

3. Cold-blooded.
4. At no time in their existence provided with branchiæ ; breathing always air.
5. Skin covered with scales or scutes.
6. In early development both amnion and allantois fully formed.

Classification—

Orders.

1. Ophidia Snakes and Serpents	}	Squamata (Günther).
2. Lacertilia (Sauria) Lizards	}	
3. Crocodilia (Loricata) Crocodiles.		
3b. Rhynchocephalia. (Günther.)		
4. Chelonia. Tortoises and Turtles	{	Cataphracta (Günther).

To these must be added a number of extinct forms, comprehending probably three or four ordinal centres :—

Enaliosauria	Ichthyosaur, Plesiosaur.
Dinosauria	Iguanodon.
Pterosauria	Pterodactyle.
Anomodontia	Dicynodon.

Taking as a central form one of the Crocodilia, we find that, as regards *external shape*, the demarcation between head, neck, trunk, loin, and tail is well pronounced.

Skin covered with scutes ; ossifications of the derm.

Skeleton ; five regions of vertebræ.

1. Cervical, with small ribs, and incomplete hæmal arch, usually seven.
2. Dorsal, with ribs, and complete hæmal arch.
3. Lumbar, ribless, intervening between dorsal and sacral.
4. Sacral, supporting pelvis.
5. Caudal, behind sacrum.

Note that bone-structure more compact than in fish ;

remarkable persistence of sutures, associated apparently with low temperature of body.

Parts of vertebræ. Centra concavo-convex, the sub-spherical soft mass intervening between the bi-concave vertebra of the fish being here ossified and ankylosed to the posterior surfaces of centra.

Neural arches well formed, except towards end of tail; sutures between neurapophyses and centra long persisting. The other parts differently arranged in different regions.

Neck. Short bifid pleurapophyses unite by upper process with diapophyses (upper transverse process), by lower with parapophyses (lower transverse process), enclosing thereby a canal (vertebral) on each side of the centrum. Under the atlas are suspended two long, loose, sword-shaped bones.

Trunk. The shaft of ribs here lengthened, and bent round in a large sweep to meet sternal ribs (hæmapophyses); sternal ribs join sternum (hæmal spine). Sternum, where supporting ribs, compacted; an anterior free piece (epi-sternum) for coracoid. The sternum extends far back along the median line of the abdomen, where it must correspond to lumbar vertebræ, and actually sends short sternal ribs on their way to meet them.

The pleurapophyses attached in the fore part of the dorsal region to both diapophyses and parapophyses; gradually, however, towards the hinder part of the dorsal region, the diapophyses are much lengthened, and at last carry the ribs away from their parapophysial attachments.

Loin. To the diapophyses are still attached little floating ribs—floating only in name, as their junction is by firm and long-persistent suture.

Sacrum, of two vertebræ.

Tail. Vertebræ numerous. Tiny ribs still tip for some distance the diapophyses. Under the vertebræ hang V-shaped bones (chevron) with loose ligamentous connection. They are probably coalesced hæmapophyses, and form with the under surface of the centra a hæmal canal. Degradation of vertebræ at end of tail.

Extremities—

Anterior. Scapular arch consists of two bones on each side, scapula (divisible into supra- and infra-scapular bones) and coracoid. Both enter into formation of glenoid cavity, and coracoid joins below a central piece fitted on to the front of the sternum. (Epi-sternum of Owen; præ-sternum and inter-clavicle, Parker.) The sternal line of ossification is divided into inter-clavicle, a "subcutaneous derm-bone" (Parker), expanded præ-sternum, long narrow meso-sternum, and two-horned xiphi-sternum posteriorly. The abdominal "sternal ribs" of Owen are called by Parker "subcutaneous splints"—"the abdominal plates of the Chelonia broken up." No clavicles, unless, as suggested by Owen, the pair of bones under-hanging atlas are they. Limb. Humerus; radius and ulna distinct; three carpal bones; five digits.

Posterior. The transverse processes of the sacral vertebræ are stout and short, presenting a square articular surface, to which is joined a sub-cubical bone; the ilium is supported on each side by these bones, and the arch is completed below by the ischia, to which are appended in front two other bones (pubic). The ischium here, like the coracoid in the anterior extremity, forms a part of the articular cavity for the first bone of the limb, to the exclusion of the pubis. The pubis stretches from the anterior upper aspect of the ischium to the side of the posterior end of the abdominal sternum, which acts as its hæmal spine.

Scheme after Owen—Comparison of the two arches:—

Pleurapophysis	Supra-scapula	sub-cubical bone.
	Infra-scapula	ilium.
Hæmapophyses	Coracoid	ischium.
	Clavicle	pubis.
Hæmal spine	Epi-sternum.	
		End of abdominal sternum.

The ilium then regarded, not as coalesced ribs of several vertebræ, but as distal portion of pleurapophysis of 1st sacral vertebra extended backwards. The first caudal vertebra has a strong process projecting towards ilium.

Skull—

1. Axial bones ossified and distinct.
2. Articulation with atlas by a simple central condyle, formed by basi-occipital and ex-occipitals.
3. Ex-occipitals fused with par-occipitals (Owen). Ali-sphenoid much disputed; orbito-sphenoid, small; pre-frontal and post-frontal not disputed.
4. Supra-occipital, parietal, and frontal bones single; nasals divided.
5. Hyoid and mandibular arches not suspended by common attachment.
6. Hyoid arch; ligamentous stylo-hyal, bony epi-, and cerato hyals; cartilaginous basi-hyals.
7. Mandibular arch consists of—1st, quadrate (tympanic of Cuvier, Owen, and Peters), probably homologue of incus; 2nd, articular (malleus); 3rd, dentary, with several accessory splint bones.

The quadrate is firmly fixed to the skull, joining the squamosal (mastoid, Owen), post-frontal, and pro-otic above, and the pterygoid internally and inferiorly.

8. Maxillary arch. The palatine, maxillary, pre-maxillary, and pterygoid bones firmly united to one another and to the fore-part of the skull; the malar or jugal linking again the maxilla to the outer aspect of the os quadratum by intervention of quadrato-jugal (squamosal, Owen).

The two tympanic cavities communicate with one another by special canal, and with the pharynx by one common Eustachian tube, which receives two tubes from each tympanum.

Special bone, "Os transversum" of Cuvier, "Ecto-pterygoid"

of Owen, who regards it as a diverging appendage of the maxillary arch.

As is noted above, the homology of the ali-sphenoid is much disputed. According to Professor Huxley, we are to regard the ali-sphenoid of Professor Owen as in reality the pro-otic element of the ossified auditory capsule; the epiotic being fused with or represented by a process of the supra-occipital, and the opisthotic being fused with the ex-occipital. The ali-sphenoid must probably in that case be found in the posterior part of the orbito-sphenoid.

Digestive system—

Teeth implanted in sockets, not ankylosed. Number from eighteen to twenty on each side of each jaw; attached to pre-maxillary, maxillary, and dentary bones. They consist of dentine, cement, and enamel; are hollow at the base, but not persistent in growth, new teeth being produced in regular series from pulp at the base of the socket, and extruding the old. The number of teeth constant throughout life.

Tongue. Nowhere free, being attached by its margin within the lower jaw; its base, however, and the hyoid bone, very moveable in a vertical direction, and capable of being raised against the palate, so as to cut off the mouth from the naso-pharyngeal respiratory tract. The bony palate is enormously developed, so that while the nostrils open externally, quite at the tip of the snout, they open internally close under the basi-occipital. This arrangement supposed to allow the crocodile to drown its prey, held in the mouth, while its own respiration proceeds as usual.

Œsophagus of moderate size.

Stomach; two divisions; first, a gizzard; second, pyloric portion.

Small and large intestine.

Cloaca, receives rectum above and posteriorly; dilated

into allantoic cavity in front; genital orifices posterior and lower; ureters still further; a lowest part partly separated by valvular folds to form "vestibule," receiving contents of uro-genital portion. In the vestibule lies a penis or clitoris. Anal aperture longitudinal.

Salivary glands represented by follicles, simpler on the tongue, more complex in the fauces.

Liver large; two-lobed; gall-bladder; hepatic and cystic ducts after communicating, open by separate orifices into the duodenum.

Pancreas, not large.

Spleen, well-developed.

Circulation. Heart consists of four cavities, two auricles and two ventricles, the right cavities for venous, the left for arterial blood; but the large arteries have such free communication outside the heart as readily allows the venous blood in the pulmonary artery to flow into the aortic system. There are two aortæ, right and left, which, after a supply has been sent from the right to the head and anterior extremities, unite behind to form a single aortic trunk for the body and hind limbs. Veins, reno-portal system.

Respiration. Lungs richly cellulated; bronchus passes some distance into the lung before losing cartilage, giving off lateral branches connected with dilated, elongated passages; from the passages air flows by numerous round orifices into the cellular structure. Trachea and larynx, with vocal chords. Inspiration effected by movements of walls of trunk.

Lymphatics, very distinct; valves; no glands; plexuses.

Nervous system. Note disproportionately small size of encephalon.

Cerebellum small, only partially covering fourth ventricle.

Cerebral lobes large; corpora striata in lateral ventricles.

Eye. Provided with muscle-moved upper and lower lids;

within them a third lid, or membrana nictitans, capable of being drawn outwards over the front of the eyeball by special muscle. Lacrymal and Harderian glands.

Globe, nothing noteworthy except the firmness of the sclerotic.

Ear. Tympanic cavity with membrana tympani lying at bottom of a fissure or cavity provided with a pair of closing flaps externally.

Columella, joins membrana-tympani to membrana fenestra ovalis. Remarkable arrangements of Eustachian tubes already noticed. In internal ear, besides sacculus utriculus and three semicircular canals, a commencement of cochlea, in the form of a conical diverticulum of vestibule, subdivided by a vertical, but apically incomplete septum. The cochlea not twisted. The "scalæ" of human anatomy, with their apical communication, thus represented.

Nose. External nostril single, with internal valvular flap; posterior aperture also single; the two cavities, however, distinct.

Kidneys, compact, ureters terminate on projecting papillæ in the "uro-genital" compartment of the cloaca, behind the genital orifices.

Genital organs. Male. Testes, long, in front of kidneys. Single penis of two corpora cavernosa with groove between on upper surface to receive semen as distilled from vasa deferentia. The organ contained in special compartment of cloaca.

Female. Ovaria compact; oviduct in three parts—first, with longitudinal foldings, then glandular, with transverse folds, then shell-forming and dilated, with fine longitudinal ridges. A clitoris in cloaca.

Development. Well-formed amnion and allantois.

Differences—

Skin covered with scales in Ophidia, and most Lacertilia;

with horny plates, joined often to dermal bones, in the Chelonia.

Skeleton. Two main out-goings, leading to high degree of mobility in Ophidia, to high degree of rigidity in Chelonia.

Ophidia. Vertebræ very numerous (more than 400 in Python); procœlian; about six-sevenths support ribs, articulating only with diapophyses by a ball-and-socket joint; these ribs do not find a sternum for attachment, but are fixed to lateral abdominal scales directly or by intervention of cartilage. In the caudal region the ribs are fused with the diapophyses. Sternum nowhere developed. No extremities; nevertheless, corresponding internal arches exist in some as rudiments.

Skull. Arranged so as to allow of excessive dilatation of mouth in swallowing prey. The pre-maxillaries, palatines, and maxillaries united across by yielding ligaments; the dentary bones similarly united below, so that mouth can be extended transversely. To facilitate vertical movement, the joint of the lower jaw is carried far away from the skull upon elongated quadrate and squamosal (mastoid, Owen) bones; quadrato-squamosal articulation, moveable. Malar and quadratojugal bones absent.

Chelonia. The strong trunk-box into which the head and tail can both be safely retracted, is composed of an upper and lower hollow shield placed face to face.

The dorsal shield, more rounded, is called carapace, the ventral, flatter, plastron.

The shields, according to Owen, formed by a very intimate coalescence of vertebral and dermal bones.

In carapace, a central row of discoid bones, composed of neural spines, fused with dermal ossifications; on each side a row of transversely-elongated bones, ribs with dermal ossification; a third marginal series is, according to Professor Owen, entirely of dermal origin.

Plastron, of nine pieces, one median, eight parial; corresponding, according to Owen, to sternum, and sternal ribs, with united dermal ossifications.

But Parker, making good use of Rathke's earlier notes, contends that the whole of the plastron is of dermal origin, and gives to the nine pieces the following names: 1, interclavicle (median); 2, 3, clavicles; 4, 5, post-thoracics; 6, 7, præ-abdominal; 8, 9, post-abdominal.

The centra of vertebræ on the under surface of the carapace are reduced to fixed, narrow, elongated bones.

Extremities. Scapular arch contained within trunk. Scapula, clavicle, and coracoid bones of each side united into one three-rayed bone suspended from the side of a vertebra by the scapula. Scapula rib-like; clavicle (præ-coracoid) a process of scapula; coracoid broad, not meeting its fellow. Only scapula and coracoid enter into glenoid cavity.

Sacrum, of two vertebræ, each supporting a pair of stout lateral processes (pleurapophyses ?). These on each side give attachment to ilium; arch completed by ischia and pubic bones. All three bones enter into acetabulum.

Teeth. Varying modes of attachment. 1. Tooth simply ankylosed at base to surface of jaw, or to pediment sent up to meet it.

2. Tooth ankylosed to inner side of a ridge running along the outer margin of the tooth-supporting surface. (Chameleon.)

3. By addition of an inner ridge a groove is formed, in which the teeth are lodged without ankylosis. (Icthyosaur.)

4. Tooth implanted in a shallow socket, to which it is ankylosed. (Most Ophidia.)

5. Tooth implanted in socket without ankylosis. (Crocodile.)

Teeth mostly attached to proper jaw-bones, but in some

also to pterygoids (Iguana), and to pterygoid and palatines (Serpents.)

Chelonia have a continuous horny beak investing jaw-bones in place of teeth. This, however, developed from a series of papillæ like those from which teeth are formed.

Special note of poison-fangs of serpents.—Long, curved fangs, implanted firmly in the anterior part of maxillary bone; maxillary bone fully moveable upon a transverse horizontal axis, so that the teeth can be laid flat along the roof of the mouth, or fixed at right angles to the palate. Behind the tooth in use at the moment are others ready in turn to take its place. The fangs are either traversed by a fine canal or impressed with a groove for the transmission of the poison from its gland into wounds. The duct not a perforation, but a further development of a groove, the sides of which grow up and meet. Its openings above and below fall short of the ends of the tooth, and are on the anterior aspect.

Tongue often elongated, bifid and extensible in Lizards and Snakes.

Œsophagus very dilatable in Serpents; covered internally with reverted spines in Chelonia.

Stomach, in Ophidia, exhibits a first dilatable portion, with thin walls for reception of prey; a second with glandular inextensible walls for digestion.

Circulation. Heart always with two auricles, systemic and pulmonary. The ventricle single, but usually more or less divided internally by septa, the most constant of which projects between the pulmonary and aortic orifices, and, as we have seen, extends so far in the Crocodile as to form a complete wall of separation between a right and left compartment.

There are always two aortæ, left and right, which wind round the œsophagus, and unite to form a common systemic aorta; the right aorta gives off before the junction the vessels for the head and anterior extremities, and where there are septa these appear to be so arranged as to determine the flow of blood chiefly from the pulmonic auricle into this right aorta. The head and fore-limbs therefore receive a more highly oxygenized blood than the rest of the system.

Veins; always a reno-portal system.

Cavæ; no valves in Ophidia; few in others.

Respiration. Ophidia, only one lung developed, the left.

Larynx simple, without vocal chords; termination of bronchi abrupt; the lung a long sac much resembling that of frog; much more vascular at upper than at lower part. Chelonia have well-formed lungs like those of Crocodile.

Lymphatic hearts in Lacertilia and Ophidia, none in Chelonia; usually placed near posterior part of body.

Nervous system—

Spinal cord uniform in Serpents; with two enlargements in Chelonia.

Cerebellum small, without lateral lobes or pons. Corpora quadrigemina and thalami distinct; hemispheres larger proportionally than in fishes; corpora striata in ventricle; external fissure (Sylvian).

Eye. Ophidia. Sclerotic fibro-cartilaginous; a delicate falciform process attached to capsule of lens; integument continued in a transparent form over the front of the eye, enclosing a conjunctival sac; lids glued together, and made transparent.

In Lacertilia and Ophidia, sclerotic strengthened, and its shape maintained by a circle of inbricating bony plates.

Chelonia have nictitating membrane.

Ear. Tympanic apparatus very imperfect in Ophidia. No Eustachian tube. The tympanic structure more perfect in Lacertilia. In Chelonia a rudimentary cochlea. Tympanic cavity large and complicated.

Urinary organs. Kidneys in Ophidia unsymmetrically placed, and broken up into small moveable lobes. No urinary bladder.

Generative organs—

Male. In Ophidia two lateral penes, consisting of hollow, evertible sacs, bifid or spinulose when protruded.

Lacertilia, penis double, cloacal outlet transverse.

Chelonia, single penis, cloacal aperture longitudinal.

Female. Ovaries in Ophidia unsymmetrical; right usually in advance. In Chelonia a clitoris.

Cl. Aves.

Characters.
1. Oviparous.
2. But warm-blooded.
3. Heart with four cavities; two auricles, two ventricles.
4. Never have branchiæ.
5. Skin covered with feathers.
6. Respiration double—by lungs, and by air-containing cavities prolonged from the lungs into the cavities of the body, interior of bones, &c.
7. Anterior extremities adapted for aerial, posterior for terrestrial or aquatic progression.
8. Amnion and allantois.

As separating them from Mammalia, a number of negative characters, viz., absence of external ears, lips, teeth, epiglottis, diaphragm, fornix, corpus callosum, scrotum.

Classification—

Birds altogether form a group of great compactness; and, agreeing largely in their life-conditions, vary among themselves in few essential points, their differences being nearly always differences of degree. The value of the whole class is perhaps in reality little more than ordinal. Birds simply exhibit the Reptilian type very perfectly modified for aerial life, and the whole class may be compared to one of the four principal orders of Reptilia. It is usual, however, to divide the class into orders (really little more tribes), and the following tolerably natural arrangement may be used with advantage

Cl. Aves.

Sub-Cl. Autophagi.

Natatores.	Swimmers.	Duck.
Grallatores.	Waders.	Heron.
Cursores.	Runners.	Ostrich.
Rasores.	Scratchers.	Common Fowl.

Sub.-Cl. Insessores.

Columbæ.	——	Pigeons.
Scansores.	Climbers.	Parrot.
Passeres.	Perchers.	Sparrow.
Raptores.	Raveners.	Hawks.

But it is necessary to point out that Professor Huxley has put forward a classification in part natural, but, as regards nomenclature, depending chiefly upon modifications of certain cranial bones. The class is divided by him into three orders :—

1. Saururæ. 2. Ratitæ. 3. Carinatæ.

1. Saururæ include only Archæopteryx, a fossil form, in which the caudal vertebræ are developed, so as to form a tail as long as or longer than the body.

2. Ratitæ (having keel-less sternum), include the Ostrich tribe.

3. Carinatæ (with keeled sternum), include all other existing birds, and are divided into four sub-orders :—

i. Dromœognathæ (with palatal structure. Tinamou like that of Ratitæ.)

ii. Schizognathæ (fissured jaws). Bustards, Cranes, Gulls, Penguins, Gallinæ, Columbæ.

iii. Desmognathæ (jaws united). Ducks, Flamingoes, Herons, Pelicans, Accipitres, Parrots, Toucans, Kingfishers.

iv. Aegithognathæ (jaws united with vomer to form a buckler). Goatsuckers, Rooks, Passeres, and probably the Woodpeckers.

External Form. Long flexible neck, firm body, short rudder-like tail.

Feathers. Parts. Quill, shaft, vane, barbs, barbules, sac, and bulb.

Wings.—Feathers attached to bones of hand are the longest (*primaries*) ; those attached to forearm *secondaries* ; to humerus, *tertiaries.* Alula, or *bastard wing,* attached to thumb. *Wing coverts* at base.

Skeleton. Bony tissue exceedingly firm and compact ; sutures obliterated early.

Spinal column—

Cervical vertebræ ; numbers vary according to length of neck, which is determined by such causes as length of legs, aquatic habits, &c. In Raptores, Passeres, and Scansores, 9 to 14 ; in Rasores and Cursores, 13 to 19 ; in Grallatores and Natatores, 12 to 23 (Swan).

Centra joined to one another by true joints ; anterior surfaces convex vertically, concave transversely. In the lower cervical vertebræ, all the processes forming the four canals surrounding the centrum are found. But atlas only a ring, with a single concave facet for the occipital condyle.

Dorsal.—Eagles, 8 ; Sparrow and Parrot, 9 ; Rasores, 7 ; Cursores, 10 ; Swan, 11. Total range, 6–11. Centra compressed laterally. Ankylosis frequent, chiefly in posterior and middle thirds, allowing of lateral movement of posterior upon anterior part of thorax in rapid turning. Adjoining neural spines also often ankylosed, and the transverse processes of adjoining vertebræ often knit together by little osseous splints. Thoracic ribs fixed to vertebræ by angle and head (to di- and parapophyses), and bound also together by diverging processes sprouting from posterior edge of each, and extending backwards over outer side of next posterior, to which they are joined by ligament. The constituents of spinal half of the thorax thus bound together into a compact, comparatively rigid shield. The vertebral ribs and sternum form similarly a ventral shield, moveable upon the dorsal at the junction of vertebral and sternal ribs. The sternal ribs are fitted by wedge-shaped ends into corresponding depressions in the side of the sternum. The sternum is a large buckler-shaped bone, with a longitudinal projection, or keel. The keel and the surface of the sternum are extended or restricted in the ratio of the flying powers of each bird. Note that some of the posterior ribs do not reach the sternum, joining their fellows in front; and that in some cases (Rasorial) the posterior sternal and vertebral ribs do not come into communication with each other, as in Crocodile. The constitution of the sternum not always the same. In the Cursorial birds it is composed of pairs of bones (pleurostea); in the rest of the class it has also a central piece (lophosteon).

Parker divides the sternum into præ-sternal, meso-sternal, and xiphi-sternal regions. Longitudinally, according to the same author, it has five parallel regions. Other ossifications, less constant than the pleurostea and lophosteon, are the metostea, behind the pleurostea; the coracostea, on each side of lophosteon; urosteon, rarely found, at the very end of the xiphi-sternum. In Rhea (Cursorial), there are bone centres in front of first rib, pro-ostea. Parker considers the lophosteon, urosteon, and coracosteon, to be absolutely ornithic.

Note that Penguin has posterior surface of third dorsal centrum concave, anterior surface of fourth convex, and so on to last dorsal. Lumbar region, though definitely existent, obscured by forward projection of ilia.

Sacrum. Vertebræ number from nine to nineteen; all ankylosed, forming a continuous central girder, to which the ilia are firmly joined. The spinal canal here much expanded. The first four or five sacral vertebræ, and the last few have both di- and parapophyses, the middle vertebræ (four or five) have only diapophyses, so that, as seen from below, a long recess is formed in the middle sacral region on each side of the centra; the spinous processes expanded laterally at their summits to join the ilia, which form with them on each side an arch over the transverse processes.

Coccyx. Vertebræ usually moveable; number, six to nine; the last vertebra curiously modified to form a large compressed ploughshare-shaped bone, by which the guiding tail-feathers are mainly supported.

Extremities. Anterior. Scapula and coracoid firmly united; scapula narrow, extending down side of thorax, nearly parallel with spinal column, to a greater or less distance, according to flying powers of each bird. According to Parker, a præ-coracoid and meso-scapula (acromion) are always distinct in development, but small. Coracoid, stouter, runs to sternum at anterior aspect. The coracoid and scapula form the glenoid cavity between them; but in some birds a third small bone wedged in between them goes to complete the articular surface. Clavicles form together the "merry-thought" or furculum (with or without inter-clavicle, Parker); united to rest of arch and to scapula sometimes by ligament, sometimes by bone. In Ostrich, the clavicles are separate from each other, and ankylosed to scapula, as in Chelonia.

Limb. Head of *humerus* much expanded, so as to allow of extensive gliding movement in flight. Air-opening underneath head. Ulna articulation, internal, spherical; radial elongated, curved.

Ulna and *radius;* long, distinct; scarcely any rotation; ulna much the stouter.

Carpals, two, so fixed as to allow only movements of adduction and abduction to the hand.

Metacarpals, three; two large, elongated, ankylosed at their end, free in the middle; the outer supporting the largest digit; third small, rudimentary thumb.

Digits, two. Radial, two or three phalanges; ulna one phalanx.

Posterior. Pelvis includes ilium, ischium, and pubis.

Ilium early united to sacrum in its whole length, and often to the spinous processes of one or two posterior dorsal, and of lumbar vertebræ. Ilium joined both to transverse and spinous processes of sacral vertebræ.

Pubis does not extend to meet its fellow, but is directed backwards as a flexible styliform process; unites, however, with ischuim, to form obturator hole.

Ischium also does not meet its fellow, but curves round and joins posteriorly the ilium of the same side, turning the ischiatic notch thereby into a foramen.

All these curious variations from the idea of the pelvic arch have relation to peculiar needs in the bird. In standing, when the pushing-back of the legs requires great muscular exertion to sustain the anterior weight of the body; in flying, where a greatly extended surface of attachment is required for the wing-muscles, a strong and massive bony centre of support is needed at the pelvic region. On the other hand, it seems necessary that the pelvic arch should be open below, and not rigid, in order that the eggs may pass safely. So to meet these needs the ilia have all the breadth of surface and length of attachments above described. In the Cursorial birds these conditions attain a further development. The ilia meet one another in a solid arch above the spines of the vertebræ, and even the ischia, in certain cases, meet beneath the centra. In Ostrich, the ossa pubis unite with each other, and complete the pelvic arch.

Limb. *Femur* short, cylindrical ; no neck.

Tibia large. Fibula small, articulating with femur, falling short of tarsus, ankylosed with tibia.

Tarsus, early lost by fusion with metatarsus.

Metatarsus represented by one long bone, with longitudinal grooves, indicating primary complexity of structure. (In Penguin there are three metatarsals, ankylosed at both ends.) Lower end presents three articular eminences for three anterior *digits* ; usually a fourth or inner and posterior aspect for hallux, low down in Insessores, higher and higher in Waders, lost in Cursores—according to grasping power of feet.

Digits ; number varies ; in Gallinaceæ, if we count the spur as a toe, five ; in Ostrich, two. The hallux has two joints, the next three, the next four, and the last, outermost, five. The Raptores have these four ; most Insessores, three, four, and five ; Ostrich, four and five.

Skull. Note first its lightness ; due first to the slenderness and compactness of the bones ; secondly, to the small development of face and lower jaw, as compared with the cranium ; the cranial cavity being as large in proportion to the bones as in the lower Mammals. Similarly, the orbits are very large proportionately, and are incompletely separated from each other ; the nares also frequently communicate with each other in the dry skull.

The constitution of the skull, as far as regards the homologies of the bones, much resembles that of Reptiles.

The occiput has a single condyle for the atlas, formed, as in Reptiles, by basi-occipital and ex-occipitals. There is no para-sphenoid.

Supra-occipital sometimes double; parietal double, much expanded in relation to greater proportionate development of brain.

In the face the pre-maxillary, maxillary, and palatine bones are firmly united into one piece, anteriorly; these are joined to the frontal region of the skull by the nasals, or by processes of the pre-maxillaries; to the infero-median region by the vomer, which supports the palatine bones; this attachment being often strengthened by backward prolongations of the palatines, bringing them into connection with the pre-sphenoid, and with each other; to the os quadratum by two lines of bone—1, the pterygoid, usually strong, running from the posterior end of the palatine and side of the pre-sphenoid to the inferior internal process of the quadrate; 2, the jugal and quadrato-jugal, forming together a slender tie between the posterior external angle of the maxillary and the external aspect of the quadrate. The quadrate is moveably articulated with the side of the skull, and the nasal bones in front are usually elastic, so that the bones of the upper jaw have some degree of mobility on the skull. This is best seen in the Parrot. The lower jaw is still compound; its articular piece forms the joint with the quadrate.

Hyoid arch. Basi- and cerato-hyals small; glosso-hyal, and uro-hyals large; the long lateral processes, at first sight resembling cornua, are in reality "thyro-hyals," extra ossifications. (Owen.)

The interior of the bird's skull is divided by a transverse ridge into two depressions; an anterior for cerebral hemispheres, a posterior for the rest of the brain. Sella turcica a deep, round cell.

Digestion.—A *beak*, or horny investment, taking the place of *teeth*, invests the pre-maxillaries, maxillaries, and mandibular bones. Probably, tooth-homologue in origin.

Form of beak or bill varies according to use.

In birds of prey, compressed and strong, with sharp edges, working like scissors; upper mandible ending in sharp, hooked extremity, projecting beyond lower mandible. In "noble" Raptores, the upper mandible toothed on the sides. In voracious but less powerful birds, such as Crows, Magpies, and Gulls, the bill is narrow and straight. In Waders, long, strong, trenchant, depressed or compressed, usually without tearing hook; straight or curved. In most of duck tribe, the bill depressed, with blunt edges, so as to form a sort of shovel.

Tongue, supported by median bony or cartilaginous process of hyoid arch (glosso-hyal); covered by a dense sheath of very thick epidermic structure, and therefore of little use as regards taste.

Note a few variations of tongue.—In Humming-bird, split like a brush; in Toucan, a rasp (for reduction of soft fruits, Bates); in Woodpecker, barbed, and possessed of great range of antero-posterior movement; in Flamingo, broad, grooved longitudinally, with lateral, recurved spines, forming a sort of sieve with the edge of the bill; in some Raptores bifid; in Parrot, a moveable finger; in Rasores and allies, much covered with recurved spines. (Chiefly Owen.)

Salivary glands, of varying development; in Crow, simple separate follicles; in Rasores, Grallatores, and Natatores, large conglomerate glands, with numerous orifices; in Woodpeckers and some Raptores, large, compact glands with one duct.

No epiglottis, or soft palate; faucial pouches in Pelican, Swift, &c.

Œsophagus, crop, proventriculus, gizzard, small and large intestine.

Œsophagus, usually very muscular, wide, dilatable; in many rapacious birds, regurgitation easy.

Crop, a dilatation of œsophagus near thorax, not always present; *e.g.*, Toucans, Hornbills, frugivorous and insectivorous birds; in most granivorous birds a large, globular receptacle attached to the œsophagus; in Pigeon, double, with special secreting apparatus.

Proventriculus, or first part of stomach; a dilatation of various degree, with much-thickened, glandular, little-extensible walls; secretes from tubular (or branched, Ostrich) glands the gastric juice; corresponds to cardiac portion of stomach in Man.

Gizzard, a muscular sac, with orifices of ingress and egress placed close together at upper aspect. The muscular fibres take their origin from two polar (anterior and posterior) tendinous areæ, and radiate from them round the walls; the internal coat hard and horny, with two callous buttons opposite the musculi laterales. The gizzard thick and powerful in granivorous birds, thin and weak in flesh-feeders. Hard foreign bodies are regularly introduced to assist in trituration of food.

Intestines, about twice length of body. Large intestine, short and straight; generally two cæca appended to ileo-colic junction.

Large intestine ends by valvular orifice in upper part of cloaca.

Liver large, usually in two lobes, which receive the apex of the heart between them above, and conceal the duodenum, pancreas, part of small intestine, proventriculus, and gizzard. Note central position of both liver and heart, doubtless in relation to the necessity of preserving the balance of the body in flight.

Two bile-ducts opening by separate orifices into intestine, one of them having gall-bladder appended.

Pancreas; three pieces united into one gland; ducts, two or three. Spleen, small, to the right of proventriculus and liver.

Lymphatics; have valves; in anterior part of body, glands; in posterior, contractile sacs (lymph-hearts).

Circulation.—Heart; shape conical; position nearly median; in a pericardium; not in a thoracic chamber, the diaphragm not being complete; has four cavities; the two right cavities—auricle and ventricle—transmit only venous blood; the two left only arterial.

The left ventricle, with very thick walls, is found, in a section made across the middle of the heart, encompassed on three sides by the right; the right falls considerably short of the apex. The right auriculo-ventricular valve (= tricuspid of Man) formed by a muscular fold, without chordæ tendineæ or musculi papillares.

Arteries. 1. From left ventricle starts aorta, immediately breaking up into three branches—two brachio-cephalic, and one systemic. 2. Systemic aorta arches over right bronchus. 3. No common iliacs, femoral and sciatic arteries arising from abdominal aorta by distinct origins.

Respiration—

1. Lungs. Two; long, flattened, extending longitudinally from second dorsal vertebra to kidneys, transversely from spinal column to junction of vertebral with sternal ribs; fixed dorsally to thorax; covered ventrally by pleuræ. Bronchi divide each into five or six branches, running close along the dorsal surface of the lungs; communicate internally with air-cells, externally, by orifices on the surface of the lung, with large air-receptacles of the thorax and abdomen. The lung is divided into a number of minute hexagonal lobules, each traversed by a central channel, connected with a bronchus, but not limited by special walls, the air freely entering into the spongy substance of the lung, where blood

in the capillaries is exposed with complete freedom to its action. The cavity of the body divided by partitions into a number of large cavities containing air admitted through the bronchial orifices. These sacs are, in fact, continuations of bronchial structure, invested by serous membrane, and are regularly arranged, so that each has its name. Beyond these body-sacs, the system of air reservoirs is continued, in some instances, beneath the skin and into the interior of bones. The number of bones thus entered by air varies. Between Penguin, which has none, and Hornbill, which has all bones penetrated, there are endless degrees; the general rule being, that the amount of lightening bears a close relation to the power of flight. But, in fact, almost each case must be studied by itself. Note, *e.g.*, all birds of flight, except Woodpecker, have air admitted to humerus. Pigeons and Owls, no air in femur; diurnal Raptores have air in femur. In Ostriches, the trunk-bones, cranial-bones, and femur admit air; wing-bones and distal-bones of leg, not. Pelican and Gannet have air in all bones except phalanges of toes.

Uses of this arrangement:—

1. Increase of respiratory surface.
2. Lightness of body.
3. Aid, within body, to mechanism of respiration.
4. Mechanical assistance to muscles of wings.

2. Air-passage, consists of—i. Upper larynx, resting on uro-hyal. ii. A long trachea, with complete bony or cartilaginous rings. iii. Lower larynx, situate just above the bifurcation. The upper larynx consists of four to ten pieces, and has a rima-glottidis internally; the trachea is often curiously convoluted, even within the substance of the sternum, as in the Swan (loud voice?); the lower larynx is provided with from one to five pairs of proper muscles, and appears to be the true organ of voice.

Nervous System. Note first, great proportionate size of encephalon.

Spinal cord has two definite enlargements, the posterior larger.

Cerebellum single, without lateral lobes; marked posteriorly by a series of transverse sulci, separating transverse plications.

Optic lobes, rounded; situate below and behind the hemispheres, in the lateral interspace between them and the cerebellum.

Thalami small; no grey commissure.

Hemispheres large, cordiform, with apex forward; no convolutions; no corpus callosum; round anterior commissure; a mere rudiment of fornix.

Organs of sense—

Smell. Nasal cavities distinct; no cartilages; but little convolution of lining membrane.

Sight. Eye never rudimentary; of great relative size; anterior segment very prominent.

Sclerotic; maintained in form by an anteriorly-placed circlet of osseous plates, thirteen to twenty in number, surrounding cornea.

Cornea much as in Man.

Choroid continuous anteriorly with iris.

Iris and ciliary muscles have striped fibres.

Lens flattened, except in water-birds.

Vitreous humour. Through the middle runs the pecten, a plicated, densely vascular, pigment-coated band, extending from the point of entrance of the optic nerve to the lens. It is not muscular, and is probably supplementary to the choroid in adaptation.

Birds have a third eyelid—membrana nictitans—and Harderian gland. They have also a lacrymal gland, and a nasal (or pituitary) gland.

Hearing—

No external ear, though feathers sometimes arranged so as to collect sounds.

Rarely an external meatus.

Membrana tympani in part attached to os quadratum.

Tympanic cavity has the two internal foramina, and the Eustachian tube. Columella still the one ossiculum. Cochlea like that of Reptiles.

Urinary Organs—

Kidneys, two; elongated, and irregular; moulded into the irregular hollows of the sacral bones from the lungs to the end of the rectum. Relatively larger than in Mammalia. Structure, tubular; no division into cortical and medullary. No dilated cavity or pelvis in the interior of the kidney; ureter placed at inner and anterior aspect; terminating in middle or "urethro-sexual" division of cloaca.

Reproduction. Male Organs—

Testes high in abdomen, never descending into a scrotum; above upper extremity of kidney; greatly enlarged at breeding season. Structure, tubular, with strong investing fibrous tunic (albuginea). Vasa deferentia terminate in papillary elevation in cloaca, placed within and before the urethral orifices. In Gallinaceæ, the papillæ erectile, and cloaca evertible; in Natatores, a long, single, dorsally-grooved penis, placed in lower part of cloaca. In Ostrich, a simple penis, not unlike that of Chelonia.

Female Organs—

Only left oviduct present, and generally only the left ovary.

Ovary; capsule; fibrous stroma, with ovules in various stages of development.

Oviduct. Infundibular orifice large; walls here thin, but increase downwards in thickness. Duct straight when quiescent, convoluted during sexual excitement. Inner surface smooth above, then rugous, lastly densely villous. The tube opens into the urethro-sexual portion of the cloaca, in front of left ureter ; orifice has a sphincter.

Class Mammalia.

Characters :—

1. Not oviparous, but, with certain exceptions, nourishing the embryo by medium of placenta.
2. Always have mammæ, supplying milk for nutrition of offspring.
3. Warm-blooded.
4. Heart with four cavities—two auricles, two ventricles.
5. Never have branchiæ.
6. Skin covered more or less with hair.
7. Amnion and allantois.

The class below (Birds) has been found to be characterized by important negatives ; to have neither external ears, lips, teeth, epiglottis, diaphragm, fornix, corpus callosum, nor scrotum. All these, or most of them, are found in nearly all Mammalia, and by these additions a great advance is established in the class under consideration.

Classification. The class comprehends about fourteen orders, viz. :—Primates, Carnivora, Insectivora, Cheiroptera, Rodentia, Proboscidia, Sirenia, Artiodactyla, Perissodactyla, Cetacea, Bruta, Marsupialia, Monotremata. These have been arranged in groups by different authors upon more or less artificial grounds. In one system the structure of the brain, in another the structure of the apparatus of reproduction has been taken as a determining test ; but the remark is possible, that in both cases lesser things are made to include greater, and inflexibility is attained where comprehensiveness is required.

Cerebral Classification.

(Owen, after Waterhouse.)

Cl. Mammalia.		Order.	Type.
1. Sub-class. Archencephala		Bimana	Man.
2. Gyrencephala	Unguiculata	Quadrumana	Apes.
		Carnivora	Lion, Bear.
	Ungulata	Artiodactyla	Hog. Ruminants.
		Perissodactyla	Horse. Rhinoceros.
		Proboscidia	Elephant.
	Mutilata	Sirenia	Dugong.
		Cetacea	Whale.
3. Lissencephala		Bruta	Sloth. Armadillo.
		Cheiroptera	Bats.
		Insectivora	Moles, Shrew.
		Rodentia	Rat, Hare.
4. Lyencephala		Marsupialia	Kangaroo.
		Monotremata	Ornithorhyncus.

It must be noted that the anatomical determination from which the fourth group receives its name (loose-brained), viz., the absence of corpus callosum, is disputed by highly competent observers. Similarly, the anatomical difference which is held to separate the Archencephala from the Gyrencephala, viz., the possession by the one of a third lobe of cerebral hemisphere, and the absence of the same in the other, is satisfactorily shown by good authorities, at home and abroad, to be of no value, as concerns comparison between Man and the Apes. These animals have the third cornu of the lateral ventricle, and, in accordance with generally received teaching, must have also posterior cerebral lobes.

Reproductive Organs Classification.

(Huxley, after Blainville, Carus.)

Sub-Cl.		Orders.	Form of Placenta.
1. Monodelphia	Deciduata	Primates	Discoid.
		Carnivora	Zonular.
		Insectivora	Discoid.
		Cheiroptera	Discoid.
		Rodentia	Discoid.
		Proboscidia ?	Zonular?
	Doubtful	Sirenia	
	Non-Deciduata	Artiodactyla	Diffuse: Hog. Cotyledinary in Ruminants.
		Perissodactyla	Diffuse.
		Cetacea	Diffuse.
		Bruta.	
2. Didelphia		Marsupialia.	
3. Ornithodelphia		Monotremata.	

In so far as it brings together the first five orders, the grouping is satisfactory, but the great internal and structural differences existing among the members of the nondeciduate group seem disproportionate to the value of the tie by which it is sought to unite them.

General Anatomy of Mammalia.

External form—

Anterior limbs always present.

Integument covered with hair, as opposed to scales and feathers. Hair present in fœtal Cetacea, though absent in adult. Hairs may be altered to vibrissæ, or to spines, or even to horns (as in Rhinoceros), and may be associated with dermal scutes, as in Armadillo.

Mammæ have nipples, except in Monotremes.

Skeleton—

The five regions of the *vertebral column* are usually well marked.

1. Cervical region. Always comprehends seven vertebræ, except in some of the Cetacea, which have only six, and in the three-toed Sloth, which has nine. The vertebræ are united together by concentric ligaments enclosing a glairy matter (remains of chorda dorsalis). They consist of centrum, complete neural arch, upper and lower transverse processes united by a rudiment of rib to form the vertebral foramen. The hæmal arch is not completed, as in birds.

2. Dorsal. From eleven to twenty vertebræ (twenty-three in two-toed Sloth). Ribs, with double vertebral attachment (head and tubercle), are tipped at the lower end with a rod of cartilage, joining them on to a sternum or hæmal spine, which is composed of a series of pieces corresponding to vertebral segments. The costal cartilages evidently correspond with the sternal ribs of birds and reptiles,

and belong to the category of hæmapophyses. Behind the middle of the dorsal region the cartilages fall short of the sternum, and unite with cartilages of ribs in front. At the hindmost end the cartilages are free, and the ribs are called "floating ribs." The vertebral attachments of ribs alter in the posterior part of the dorsal region. Generally, the tubercular attachment is gradually lost, and the head remains articulated with the parapophysial disc. But in the Cetacea the diapophysial and more rigid union persists, the head being carried away from the lower by the great length of the upper transverse process.

Sternum. Varies in extent; from Cetacea, where it may support only one or two pairs of ribs, to Edentata (Bruta), where it is prolonged with numerous attachments of ribs nearly to the ossa pubis. In Man, the linea alba is evidently the homologue of an abdominal sternum, and the inscriptiones tendineæ of the costal cartilages of some of the lumbar vertebræ.

The sternum is divided into pre-sternum (manubrium), meso-sternum (body), and xiphi-sternum (xiphoid process). The pre-sternum supports entirely one (the first) pair of costal cartilages, and joins with the meso-sternum to form the articulation for the second pair. The meso-sternum supports the rest of the costal attachments. It consists of a varying number of segments developed from single or parial points of ossification. The xiphi-sternum supports no ribs. (Parker.)

Lumbar. Vertebræ, two to nine in number; ribless.

Sacral. Number of vertebræ, two in implacental Mammalia, four in most placental; Man, five; Mole, six. None in Cetacea.

Caudal. Vertebræ four to forty in number.

Anterior extremity. Vertebral homologues of Owen.
1. Scapular arch ("shoulder-girdle," Parker).

Scapula; expanded, in three planes from the axial line, to form præ-scapula, meso-scapula (spine), and post-scapula; respectively developed from cartilage.

Coracoid; enters varyingly into glenoid cavity; excepting in Monotremata it does not reach the sternum, but is reduced to a process of the scapula.

Clavicle; extends from inferior extremity of spine of scapula (acromion) to anterior edge of sternum (præ-sternum). Ossification of shaft in membrane; of the two ends in cartilage. Divided by Mr. Parker into meso-scapular segment, shaft, præ-coracoid, and omo-sternum. The bone, therefore, is of complex origin, including, besides its proper membrane-bone or shaft ("splint-bone," Parker), cartilage-developed elements belonging partly to the scapula, partly to the sternal line of bones. The clavicle is often absent.

The modifications of the limb will be noted under the several orders.

Pelvic arch or girdle. Fixed on each side to sacrum; consists of ilium, ischium, and pubis. Ilium alone attached to transverse processes of sacrum; ischium and pubes form lower part of arch, the pubes meeting across at the symphysis, and the ischia bending forward to join them on each side without meeting across the median line, like cartilages of "false" ribs, and so including the obturator foramen. According to Owen, ilium = scapula, ischium = coracoid, pubes = clavicle. All three enter into acetabulum.

Skull. Important differential points.

Articulation with atlas by two lateral condyles, corresponding in position with the articular processes (zygapophyses) of vertebræ, and formed by the ex-occipitals. Pre-sphenoid and basi-sphenoid distinct in origin, *i.e.*, no para-sphenoid. Os quadratum, at first sight, absent, being represented either by incus or by tympanic bone.

Each half of the lower jaw consists of but one piece,

ossified from one (or perhaps two) centres. Condyle always convex or flat, not concave.

Articulation for the lower jaw formed by squamosal instead of quadrate.

No post-frontals, ossa transversa, or, according to Huxley, quadrato-jugals.

In general description, the basi-cranial and basi-facial axes noted; the three segments corresponding to basi-occipital, pari-sphenoid, and pre-sphenoid respectively; relations of facial bones, and of sense-capsules.

Digestive System—

Teeth. Few Mammals have no teeth; such, however, are the Anteaters. In the Ornithorhynchus the teeth are horny; and in the northern Whales calcified teeth belong chiefly to embryonic life, the so-called whalebone afterwards replacing them.

Number. General range from two to fifty, but in Armadillo they approach 100, and in the Dolphins 200.

Form. Where very numerous, they assume one common form, the simple cone. In general, with reduced numbers, a greater differentiation. Stated generally, they assume the following forms:—Certain front teeth, useful in cutting and simple in fang, are called "incisors:" one large conical projecting tooth with single fang, placed in each jaw next the incisors, is adapted for holding and rending, and is called a "canine" or "laniary" tooth. Others, placed further back, useful in the comminution of food, have complicated free surfaces, and are implanted by more than one fang. They are called molars.

Implantation. Always in sockets; with interposition of periosteum; never with ankylosis. Multiple fangs thus implanted belong only to Mammalia.

Bones of attachment. Pre-maxillary and maxillary in upper jaw, mandibular (dentary) in lower; no others.

Succession—

Most Mammals develop two sets of teeth, a first set called the milk teeth, a second called the permanent teeth. (Diphyodonts, Owen.) In the Sperm Whales, Porpoises, and Dolphins, such succession does not occur. (Monophyodonts, Owen.) In the Sloth, also, there is no succession; but the pulps of the teeth persist and maintain an uninterrupted formation of new tooth-structure. Orycteropus.

In the majority of Mammals the teeth of the first set are replaced by corresponding teeth in the second; but in the second set there are always some added toward the back part of the jaw which have no representatives in the first set.

Definitions of several kinds of teeth. Depend upon their position in the mouth. The names "incisor," "canine," "molar," applied originally to certain teeth of man and of familiar quadrupeds in respect of their shape and uses, are extended to their homologues in other animals without regard to analogy.

Incisor; a tooth implanted in the pre-maxillary, and its opposed tooth in the mandible.

Canine; the single tooth implanted on each side of the upper jaw, at or close to the suture, between maxillary and pre-maxillary; the single tooth in the lower jaw corresponding to and underhanging such tooth.

Premolars; teeth which replace deciduous molars.

Molars; teeth placed still further back, having no succession.

The first molar and the last premolar are the most constant of the teeth.

Tongue; usually bulky and soft, and covered with gustative papillæ.

Salivary glands; mostly arranged as in Man. In amphibious Mammalia, in Cetacea, and Anteaters, imperfect or wanting.

Note existence of velum pendulum palati, and of epiglottis.

Stomach ; simple or complex, according to nature of food.

Intestines; distinction between small and large usually well marked ; cæcum coli, and appendix not constant. Liver ; more lobed than in birds ; only one duct enters the intestine, joined previously by cystic duct where gall-bladder exists.

Diaphragm complete.

Heart ; right auriculo-ventricular valve (tricuspid) membranous, with chordæ tendineæ and musculi papillares, as in Man. Aorta arches over left bronchus.

Blood. Red corpuscles circular (except in Camel), bi-concave, non-nucleated.

Lungs ; highly vascular ; minutely cellular ; freely suspended in pleural cavity. Bronchi divide to great minuteness, and have no systemic prolongations.

Lymphatics ; valves in vessels ; glands, and plexuses. (Teichmann.)

Nervous system. Note increase in size of central ganglia. Cerebellum has lateral as well as central lobes, and has a pons Varolii.

Hemispheres united by corpus callosum, transversely, and their anterior and posterior parts united by fornix.

Eye ; no bony plates in sclerotic ; no pecten.

Kidneys ; compact ; smooth on surface ; cortical and medullary parts distinct.

Reproduction. Embryo nourished by intervention of placenta before birth ; young by mammary secretion after.

Detail of anatomy of orders—

Order Monotremata. Includes two forms, Ornithorhynchus and Echidna, both Australian. These have many affinities with the oviparous Vertebrata.

Externally, they are found to have no nipples, external ear, or scrotum; they have claws, and are five-toed. The Ornithorhynchus has a mouth formed like a duck's bill, and the toes are webbed. Hind leg spurred in male of both.

Skeleton. Skull very bird-like in shape, more noticeably in Echidna, an edentulous form with slender jaws. In Echidna, also, the nostrils being curved far forward, are formed by the pre-maxillaries alone, to the exclusion of the nasals; stapes columelliform; rapid obliteration of sutures.

Scapular arch; coracoids stout and flat, extend to join an epi-sternum (or "inter-clavicle"); epi-coracoids are developed in front of them; clavicles developed, extending along expanded front of epi-sternum.

Pelvic arch. Ischia meet in symphysis as well as pubes; to anterior border of each pubis attached a bone projecting into the anterior abdominal wall—the marsupial bone—a structure common and peculiar to this order, and the order Marsupialia. Not regarded as a vertebral bone, but as an ossification of tendon of abdominal muscle (external oblique). Owen regards the marsupial bones as the homologues of the last pair of lumbar hæmapophyses.

As above noted, Echidna is edentulous; Ornithorhynchus has horny teeth.

In both, the genital and urinary ducts and the rectum open into a common cloaca (whence the name Monotremata). The male has a perforated penis applied, during erection, by its base to the cloacal orifices of the vasa deferentia. The embryo is expelled from the uterus at a very early stage of development, and does not appear to be nourished by a placental structure.

Order Marsupialia—

Extensive; limited, with one exception, to the Australian group of islands. The exception is the American Opossum.

External form. Females have pouch (marsupium, giving name to order), placed at the lower part of the belly, containing nipples, and destined for reception of young immediately after birth. In males a corresponding area of integument is everted to form the scrotum, which is, therefore, in front of the penis.

Skeleton. In skull we find always a curious bending inwards of the angle of the lower jaw.

Coracoids never reach sternum.

Marsupial bones always present.

Always calcified teeth.

Genito-urinary passage distinct from rectum, but included in a common sphincter.

Besides two ovaries and two oviducts, there are two uteri and two vaginæ, the latter opening into a single urino-genital sinus; clitoris.

The embryo is not nourished by a placenta (the allantois, according to Owen, never attaining sufficient development), and is expelled in an immature condition from the uterus. Received into the marsupium, it becomes attached by an oral sphincter to the nipple, and having no power of suction, is fed by injection of milk into the pharynx, the mammæ being compressed by a special muscle. (Cremaster, Owen.)

The order, thus sharply defined from all others, includes within its limits a great variety of forms in adaptation to the varieties of local circumstance in the wide region of distribution. The Carnivora among placental Mammalia are here represented by the Dasyures. They have a large number of cutting and tearing teeth, viz.:—

$$\text{Incisors } \frac{4\,.\,4}{3\,.\,3} \quad \text{Canines } \frac{1\,.\,1}{1\,.\,1} \quad \text{Premolars } \frac{2\,.\,2}{2\,.\,2} \quad \text{Molars } \frac{4\,.\,4}{4\,.\,4}$$

making a total of 42. The molars have large projecting sharpened cusps like those of the great cats, and the canines are of great proportionate size. The feet are armed with strong and curved claws.

The Opossum family (Didelphidæ) and the Bandicoots may be taken to represent the Insectivora.

In the Phalangers we find arboreal animals, with dental arrangements indicating that vegetables enter largely into their diet. The incisors diminish in number and increase in size, the canines are dwarfed, and the molars broadened for grinding.

The Kangaroos advance further in this direction, their tooth formula being as follows :—

$$I. \frac{3 . 3}{1 . 1} \quad C. \frac{0 . 0}{0 . 0} \quad P. \frac{1 . 1}{1 . 1} \quad M. \frac{4 . 4}{4 . 4} = 28.$$

The lower incisors are large and declined, so that their long axis nearly corresponds with the axis of the horizontal ramus of the jaw. The upper incisors remind one of those of the Horse. The canines are present in infancy. There is a wide toothless interspace, as in the Horse and the Ruminants, between the incisors and the molars, doubtless correlated with grass-eating habits.

Finally, in the Wombat, a dentition equivalent to the Rodent type of dentition among Placentals is found, viz. :—

$$I. \frac{1-1}{1-1} \quad C. \frac{0 . 0}{0 . 0} \quad P. \frac{1-1}{1-1} \quad M. \frac{4 . 4}{4 . 4} = 24.$$

The resemblance consists not only in the numbers and arrangement, but in the fact that the teeth have persistent pulps. The incisors, however, are less graceful in their form and curve than in the Rodentia.

The teeth are taken for convenience as affording ready indications of variations of habit. It must be noted that, according to M. Flower's observations, the teeth in this order or sub-class do not vertically displace and succeed each other, with the exception of one tooth on each side of each jaw—the last premolar.

Placental Mammalia—

Order Bruta or Edentata. A very aberrant order, including a variety of forms brought together more by their differences from ordinary Mammalia than by any close resemblances among themselves.

Three marked subordinal groups may be noted:—

1. The Sloths, or Tardigrada.
2. The Armadillos, or Dasypoda.
3. The Anteaters, or Myrmecophaga.

These agree in the imperfection of their teeth. The incisor teeth are almost always absent, in relation with a singular truncation of the snout-bones; the canines are frequently absent, and the molars are also wanting in some cases. The Anteaters, indeed, with the exception of Orycteropus, are edentulous. Such teeth as exist in other members of the group have no true enamel, differ but little between themselves, and have no succession. All the suborders have long, strong claws. In the Armadillos and scaly Anteaters, curious dermal scutes protect the body.

In the skeleton, the ribs are very broad and flattened, very numerous (to a Reptilian degree) in the Sloth, imbricate in the Armadillos. The ischium unites with the sacrum. The orbit is not divided from the temporal fossæ.

Brain, very small, and feebly developed.

Testes abdominal; a cloaca.

The Sloths deserve a few special remarks. They are distinguished for great length of body and of claws, in relation with an arboreal life; their movements are very slow, and their tenacity of life very great. In their skeleton we find an interesting exception, before noted, to the prevailing numbers of cervical vertebræ. In the three-toed Sloth these are nine in number; the upper seven corresponding with the cervical vertebræ of other Mammals, the lower two differing in supporting small moveable ribs, which do not meet towards the median line with any sternal structure; rather like the floating ribs at the other end of the dorsal region.

The sternum extends far along the abdomen.

Skull. Face abruptly shortened by imperfect development of pre-maxillaries; zygomatic arch incomplete; malar bone sends down a long, stout, very characteristic process outside the lower jaw.

Altogether, they exhibit many oviparous affinities, to be summed up as follows:—

1. Tenacity of life, slowness of movement (Reptiles).
2. Convolutions of wind-pipe (Birds.)
3. Number of cervical vertebræ.
4. Form and number of ribs.
5. Testes abdominal, without special necessity.
6. Cloaca.

Order Cetacea. Includes Dolphins, Porpoises, Grampuses, Right Whales, Sperm Whales, Narwhals, &c. Fish-like Mammals with no neck, with anterior limbs in form of fins; with no posterior limbs; the body tapering to the tail, which supports a transverse fin, strengthened within by cartilage attached to the sides of the terminal much-depressed caudal vertebræ.

Skin naked, except where a few bristles grow near the mouth; compensatory blubber beneath.

Skeleton. Cervical vertebræ much compressed in antero-posterior direction, and partly fused together; reduced to six. Sternum supports only a few ribs, and in some cases is almost rudimentary. Lumbar vertebræ have upper transverse processes much developed; caudal vertebræ marked by chevron or V-shaped bones, suspended beneath and forming their hæmal arches. No sacrum. Line of centra altogether fish-like in look.

Anterior extremity. Scapula flattened, with small distinc

tion of parts. Acromion and coracoid mostly imperfectly marked. No clavicle.

Digits often have more than three phalanges; are enclosed in common skin or web, and have no nails.

Pelvis represented by a pair of bones not attached to spinal column. They support penis or clitoris, and, as is suggested, correspond to ischia.

Skull. Altogether remarkable in form. Tympanic and periotic bones united into one firm mass, and connected to the rest of the skull only by ligament.

Teeth; a single set, of conical shape, in Dolphins, &c.; confined to the lower jaw in Cachalot; in northern Whales developed in fœtus, but replaced afterwards by the elastic plates of whalebone, or baleen. These are attached by their bases to the margin of the upper jaw and palate, and sweep with a gentle curve down to the lower jaw; they are on their outer aspect firm, strong, and smooth; in their inner, thin and fimbriated, so as to form with the tongue an excellent straining apparatus. They are probably homologous in their origin with dentine of ordinary teeth; secured at their attachments by a representative of cement.

Stomach often complex; notably in Porpoises.

In the circulation are found peculiarities related to the necessity of storing blood during submersion. In the anterior part of the body are remarkable arterial plexuses in the walls of the thorax, and around the spinal cord and toward the base of the skull, evidently storing arterial blood for the use of the great ganglia; in the posterior part of the body are venous plexuses of great capacity, reserving blood for the lungs. The veins have hardly any valves.

Brain with fairly marked convolutions.

Nostrils open on top of head by a single or double orifice.

No external ears.

No scrotum or vesiculæ seminales.

Mammæ enclosed in cavities opening by slits on each side of vulva.

Young well developed at birth.

Order Sirenia. Includes Manatee and Dugong, browsing animals, agreeing with the Cetacea in having no hind limbs, and having a transverse tail-fin, but approaching in organization to the Ungulate Mammals.

The form is less fish-like than that of the Cetacea; the head being divided from the body by a neck; the mouth is surrounded with bristles; the mammæ are pectoral, and the nostrils open at the end of the snout. The digits have not more than three phalanges. The teeth are formed in two sets, and are of two forms—incisor and molar. The incisors are massive, but remain within the gum in the female, and project only in the upper jaw of the male. The molars are large, four or five on each side of each jaw, with a much complicated surface of dentine, enamel, and cement, and come into work only one or two at a time. Compare Elephant.

The *Ungulate* orders are the Proboscidia, Artiodactyla and Perissodactyla, corresponding to the Ruminantia, Pachydermata, and Solipeda of earlier authors.

Order Proboscidia. Includes the Elephants, Mastodons, Mammoths, and Dinotherium.

Massive vegetable feeders, having the nose projected into a long, flexible, sensitive, prehensile trunk. Skin enormously thick, nearly naked in existing, hairy in some extinct forms; extremities hoofed, but pentadactyle. Testes abdominal; mammæ, two, pectoral.

Dentition—Diphyodont.

Incisors or tusks, long, massive, open at the base, of persistent growth. Developed in lower jaw of Dinotherium, in upper jaw of Elephant, in both of Mastodon.

In Elephant, a milk pair, and a permanent pair; composed of a modification of dentine. Molars in Elephant, very bulky; have the surface of the crown folded into a number of long parallel laminar ridges running at right angles to the axis of the jaw; each ridge consists of a core of dentine invested by enamel, and the intervals between ridges are filled with cement. As the surface is worn it becomes regularly broken into ridges of different hardness, and therefore of different degrees of projection. The molars descend in succession from behind forwards, and in a sort of arc, the anterior part of the grinding surface of each projecting first. Only one or parts of two in use in each side of each jaw at one time.

Order Perissodactyla. Includes Horse and allies (Solipeds), Tapir, Rhinoceros, and Hyrax. As compared with order Artiodactyla, has the following characters (Owen):—Dorso-lumbar vertebræ never less than twenty-two; femur has a third trochanter, and the medullary artery does not penetrate the anterior part of its shaft; the fore-part of the astragalus is divided into two very unequal facets; os magnum and corresponding digit large, the digit symmetrical; the same of outer cuneiform in foot; horns, where present, median; a well developed post-tympanic process; posterior nares, mostly formed by palatines, placed opposite last or penultimate molar; pterygoid process perforated by ecto-carotid; crown of one to three last pre-molars as perfect as of molars; simple stomach; capacious cæcum; diffused placenta in all except Hyrax.

Oppose to this character of *Artiodactyla,* including the Ruminants, Hog, Peccary, Hippopotamus.

Dorso-lumbar vertebræ always nineteen; femur has no third trochanter, medullary canal at fore and upper part of shaft; facets at fore part of astragalus equal; os magnum not larger than unciform; their digits equal and parial; horns in pairs; post-tympanic process small, par-occipital always larger than post tympanic or mastoid; opening of posterior nares behind last molar; base of pterygoid process not perforated by carotid; crowns of pre-molars comparatively imperfect; stomach often complex; cæcum small; spirally-folded colon; placenta cotyledonary or diffused.

General remarks on Ungulata, or hoofed Quadrupeds.

The Ungulata have, in common, peculiarities associated with their food and the mode of obtaining it which place them in strong contrast with the Carnivora and their Unguiculate allies. The hoofed feet, defensive horns, great length and calibre of alimentary canal, and correlated great barrel of body, the dentition and correlated form of skull, are all points of this kind.

Thé Ruminant skull may be taken as a good type of the purely vegetable (mainly, grass-) eating modification.

As compared with the Carnivorous skull, the face is found greatly developed in proportion to the skull, this being dependent upon the massiveness of the grinding teeth. The teeth, in fact, form a good key to the whole type. Their arrangement is as follows:—

$$\text{I.}\ \frac{0\ .\ 0}{3\ .\ 3}\qquad \text{C.}\ \frac{0\ .\ 0}{1\ .\ 1}\qquad \text{P.}\ \frac{3-3}{3-3}\qquad \text{M.}\ \frac{3-3}{3-3}$$

The place of incisors in the upper jaw is occupied in the adult by a callous pad; the three incisors and the canine of the lower jaw form with their fellows a continuous crescent, opposed to the pad, and meeting it by their posterior surface rather than by their edge, all these teeth being bent downwards, so that their axes nearly correspond with the axis of the horizontal ramus of the jaw, instead of being perpendicular, as in Carnivora. The canine is of no greater development than the incisors. Behind this cropping part of the dentition is a long toothless interval, succeeded by closely packed, bulky molars, with much folded surface, arranged so as to comminute the food by horizontal triturating movement of the lower jaw upon the upper.

Skull has strong occipital crest, but no parietal crest; small temporal fossæ; perfectly walled orbits; that is to say, all that should give wide attachment and free movement to temporal muscle is dwarfed, and the whole attachment of the muscle is thrown backwards by the great development of the face. The sigmoid notch of the lower jaw is small and shallow, and the coronoid process is feeble, and bent much backwards. The zygoma is also comparatively weak, though the masseter remains much more powerful than the temporalis. The pterygoid processes and the angles of the lower jaw are, on the other hand, greatly developed, to meet the great growth of the pterygoid muscles, upon which the lateral movements of the lower jaw depend. The orbits project so as to allow of the all-surveying prominence of the eye characteristic of the prey, and opposed to the forward direction of the eye of the preyer.

Short notes of a few important details in the organization of constituents of Ungulate orders :—

1. Perissodactyles—

Solipeds. Six species, viz. :—Horse, Dzigguetai, Ass, Zebra, Quagga, Onagga (*cf.* Darwin).

Skull.—Length of face nearly double that of cranium; vertical depth of lower jaw greater than that of cranium; great enlargment between orbits.

Vertebræ. Dorsal, eighteen; eight ribs attached to sternum; Lumbar, six; Caudal, seventeen to twenty-one.

Sternum compressed, almost carinated anteriorly, broad and flat posteriorly.

Anterior extremity—

No clavicle; in scapula, coracoid feeble, no acromion. Carpus; of seven bones in two rows, forming the so-called knee.

Metacarpus; of one large central bone, with two small splint-bones. The large bone, "cannon bone," is chiefly supported by the os magnum, and belongs to the third, or middle digit; digit of three broad phalanges (pastern, coronary, and coffin-bone), with two parial, one median sesamoids (navicular.)

Posterior extremity—

Femur short and massive; third trochanter, and distinct articulation for patella.

In foot, the third digit largest, symmetrical in itself, the second and fourth being represented only by slender metacarpals.

Teeth—

$$I. \frac{3-3}{3-3} \quad C. \frac{1-1}{1-1} \quad P. \frac{3-3}{3-3} \quad M. \frac{3-3}{3-3} = 40$$

End of incisors has enamel folded in so as to make surface when worn complex; the extent to which wearing takes place determines the marking of the surface, and age of Solipeds can thence be deduced.

Canines small; in middle of large space between incisors and molars.

Molars and premolars equally developed; folds of enamel as seen on grinding surface form five subequal crescents, with convexities outward, concavities looking towards centre of surface.

Stomach simple; colon of great size.

Mammæ inguinal; in male their rudiment found on prepuce.

Rhinoceros—

Horns median, placed one behind the other, when more than one.

In both extremities the second, third, and fourth digits are completely developed; the third largest.

Teeth.—Incisors developed in inverse ratio of horns (Owen). Some two-horned kinds have no incisors in adult dentition; one-horned forms have incisors in both jaws; Acerotherium much larger incisors. No developed canines. Four premolars, three molars.

The Hyrax has been usually associated with the Perissodactyla, Professor Owen speaking of it as bearing the same relation to the great Rhinoceros as the existing Sloth does to the extinct Megatherium. M. Flower, following Professor Huxley, forms a distinct order, Hyracoidea, for the genus. Lamnunguia of Wagner.

In form they are rabbit-like, with hair and bristles. Their anterior extremity presents four toes, with flat, hoof-like nails; these are the second, third, fourth, and fifth; the third being still largest, symmetrical in itself; the first toe (pollex) is feebly developed, having either one minute phalanx, or only a metacarpal.

The posterior extremity has three toes.

No tail.

Teeth—

$$\text{I.}\ \frac{1-1}{2-2}\ \text{or}\ \frac{1\,.\,1}{1\,.\,1}\quad \text{C.}\ \frac{0-0}{0-0}\quad \text{P.}\ \frac{4-4}{4-4}\quad \text{M.}\ \frac{3-3}{3-3} = \begin{matrix}32\\ \text{or}\\ 34\end{matrix}$$

Placenta, zonular, deciduate; this being the chief ground for separation of Hyrax from the rest of the order which have the placenta diffused and non-deciduate. (Huxley.)

Tapirs. Heavy-bodied animals, with a short proboscis, but not very large head.

Skull remarkable for great development of sagittal-ridge, and of nasal bones in relation with proboscis.

Fore-foot has four complete toes, the third central in position, and symmetrical in itself, the fifth short, not reaching the ground.

Hind-foot, three toes (second, third, fourth).

Teeth—

$$I. \frac{3-3}{3-3} \quad C. \frac{1.1}{1-1} \quad P. \frac{4-4}{3-3} \quad M. \frac{3-3}{3-3} = 42$$

Canines small ; lower in same series as incisors.

Order Artiodactyla. Subdivided by Owen into Omnivora (Hog, Hippopotamus) and Ruminantia. Mr. Flower, giving the name Suina to the non-ruminating group, divides the old Ruminant order into three sections, each of equal value with the Suina, viz. :—1. Tylopoda, cushion-footed ; Camels. 2. Tragulina, or Chevrotains. 3. Pecora, or true Ruminants, including Deer, Giraffe, Antelope, Sheep, Ox.

Sub-order Suina. Hog, Peccary, Hippopotamus. General characters familiar.

Fore-foot ; four toes ; second to fifth ; third and fourth equal, symmetrical with each other, not each in itself ; second and fifth smaller ; metacarpals distinct. Hind foot ; four toes, subequal, metacarpals distinct.

Teeth—*Hippopotamus.*

$$I. \frac{2-2}{2-2} \quad C. \frac{1-1}{1-1} \quad Pr. \frac{4.4}{4.4} \quad M. \frac{3-3}{3-3} = 40.$$

Incisors and canines very large, molars heavy, and complexly folded in surface. Incisors and canines have permanent pulp. With the heavy teeth related here is an excessive development of facial bones.

$$\textit{Hog.} \quad I. \frac{3-3}{3-3} \quad C. \frac{1-1}{1-1} \quad Pr. \frac{4-4}{4-4} \quad M. \frac{3-3}{3-3} = 44.$$

The surface of the molars much tuberculated, but the enamel folds shallow.

The Hog, Peccary, and Hippopotamus exhibit three degrees of complication in the stomach, folds being formed, partially subdividing the cavities into three compartments, cardiac, œsophageal (median), and pyloric.

Sub-order Ruminantia ; includes Camelidæ (Camels and Llamas, somewhat aberrant, with equine affinities), Cervidæ (Deer, Giraffe), Ovidæ (Sheep, Goat), Antilopidæ, and Bovidæ.

Skull peculiarities. Great bending of face downwards on skull ; feeble pre-maxillaries ; orbit complete ; tympanic bulla.

Fore-foot—

In Camels, only two metacarpals and two digits, third and fourth metacarpals confluent above, distinct below. The ungual phalanges and hoofs are small, the animal resting in walking on a broad cushion, in which the middle phalanges are imbedded. The Llamas have less cushion and more hoof, for progression in rocky, as opposed to sandy soil.

In the rest, the third and fourth metacarpals fused, with, however, remaining indications of their original distinctness, particularly in the distal articular surfaces. The lateral (second and fifth) digits are imperfect or absent ; Giraffe has neither lateral hoof nor digit ; Musk-deer has, on the other hand, both phalanges and metacarpals of lateral digits.

Hind foot, no important variations from characters of fore-foot.

Horns. Camels and Musk-deer none.

Giraffe has bony projections, united by suture with the frontal and parietal bones ; two or three inches long ; covered with hairy skin.

Deer has two processes of frontals, upon which deciduous antlers, formed by dermal ossification, are annually produced.

Ox, Sheep, and Antelope have similar processes of frontals forming cores upon which non-deciduous sheaths of horny structure are moulded; these being chiefly of epidermic origin, and corresponding to a mass of fused hairs.

Teeth. Camels have two incisors in upper jaw, and have prominent canines in both.

The Musk-deer has long, projecting canines in the upper jaw. The canines of the true Ruminants already noted. Molars six on each side; premolars less perfect than molars. Surface complex, the enamel forming two double concentric or parallel crescents in each tooth, the crescents being reversed in the lower as compared with the upper jaw.

Note here, inverse ratio of anterior teeth and horns.

Stomach, much complicated; in four compartments, rumen, reticulum, psalterium, abomasus. 1. Rumen (paunch); villous internally; largest; first receptacle of food. 2. Reticulum; second cavity; "water-bag;" has inner surface extended by hexagonal cells or compartments 3. Psalterium ("maniplies") or omasus; lining membrane in broad laminæ, packed like leaves of a book. 4. Abomasus (rennet); lining membrane filled with true gastric tubular glands; apparently the representative of the simple stomach of other Mammalia. Process of rumination.

Placenta, non-deciduate; cotyledonary.

Unguiculate Orders.

The Carnivora proper here hold a central position, with the Quadrumana, Insectivora, and Cheiroptera grouped around them, and the Rodentia linking them to the Ungulata through Proboscidian affinities.

Order Rodentia, the most extensive among Mammalia, comprehending upwards of thirty genera, and no less than two-thirds of the whole number of species of existing Mammalia.

Their most decided characteristic is to be found in their dentition; in the two large chisel-shaped incisors of each jaw separated from molars, varying in number, by a long interval destitute of smaller incisors or canines.

The order divided into three subordinate groups :—

1. The Murine, typified by the Rat and Mouse, and including the Squirrels, Dormice, Marmots, and Beavers.

2. The Hystricine, typified by the Porcupine, and including the Cape Mole, Capybara, Guinea-pig, Chinchilla, and Agouti.

3. The Leporine, including Hare, Rabbit, and Calling Hare (Lagomys)

They are, with the exception of the Beaver, Porcupine, Capybara, small animals, all Unguiculate.

Skeleton. In skull note the smallness of the facial angle, which approaches that of birds; great size of incisive foramina; orbits not separated from temporal fossæ; two optic foramina united into one passage, in front of which the sphenoid forms a single vertical plate; tympanic bulla, and usually tubular bony meatus. In jaw, coronoid process small, angular part large and strong.

Anterior Extremity. Clavicle absent in some, present in others. Where present, its omo-sternal extremity (cartilaginous) often much elongated. (Parker.)

Coracoid small; hook-like; in some cases a proximal fragment found attached to pre-sternum.

Fore-foot usually pentadactyle, with variations in development of thumb.

Posterior Extremity. Femur usually has a third trochanter. Digits, usually five, but three in Jerboa; all clawed, except in Capybara, which has hoofs.

Dentition—

Incisors. One on each side of each jaw, excepting in Hare and Rabbit, which have one extra on each side in upper jaw.

Curved; enamel in front, dentine behind; deeply implanted, with permanent pulp and open pulp cavity.

No canines; a wide space intervening between incisors and molars.

Molars; in some cases with persistent pulps and undivided fangs (Beaver), in others with closed pulp-cavity and divided fangs. Surfaces simple or complex.

Numbers vary from $\frac{6.6}{5.5}$ (Hares) to $\frac{2.2}{2.2}$ Australian Rat.

Stomach; usually in two compartments.

Cæcum large.

Gall-bladder often wanting.

A scrotum generally present, but only temporarily occupied by testes; prostate; vesiculæ seminales.

Placenta deciduate; discoid. (Huxley.)

Note further, migration-impulses, nest-building instincts, gregarious habit, hibernation.

Order Cheiroptera; Bats—

Unguiculate Mammals; with modification of carnivorous dentition; adapted for flight.

The wings are formed by a membrane—a thin expansion of integument stretched out first between the much-elongated digits of the anterior extremity (the thumb excepted), and supported also by the bones of the arm and fore-arm, thence along the side of the body to the hinder extremity, the foot of which is left free, the thigh and leg being included, and across from one hind extremity to the other, with or without the interposition of a tail.

Skin covered with hair. Mammæ pectoral.

Skeleton—

All have clavicles, and, according to Parker, a rudiment of the sternal end of the coracoid: the sternum is broad and carinated; the sacrum is united to the tubera ischii, and in some species the ossa pubis do not meet in the median line.

In skull, orbits incomplete, temporal fossæ large, zygoma very slender.

The Bats are divided into two groups, the Insectivorous and the Frugivorous.

The Frugivorous are large, have truncate, grooved molars, and have little or no tail. Skull much longer, owing to greater development of face.

The Insectivorous have molars, with sharp cusps; a tail (in relation with rapid turning in pursuit of prey), and a short face.

Teeth formula :—

$$\text{I.}\frac{0}{0}\text{ or }\frac{1-1}{1-1}\text{ or }\frac{2\,.\,2}{3\,.\,3}\quad \text{C.}\frac{1-1}{1-1}\quad \text{M.}\frac{3-3}{3-3}\text{ to }\frac{6-6}{6-6}$$

The high numbers attained in the Frugivorous Bats.

The Frugivora lead towards the Quadrumana through the Lemurina (Galeopithecus); the Insectivorous forms closely approach the order Insectivora.

Order Insectivora; including Moles, Shrews, Hedgehogs, and Tupaia. Small, unguiculate, plantigrade, and pentadactyle Mammals, with small, smooth brains, and with carnivorous dentition.

Skeleton varies much according to habits.

Clavicles are present, with one exception.

In burrowing forms, skull conical and pointed anteriorly; sternum much developed; in Hedgehogs, skull much of carnivorous shape, with slender zygoma.

Teeth—

Mole. $$\text{In.}\frac{3-3}{3-3}\quad \text{C.}\frac{1-1}{1-1}\quad \text{P.}\frac{4\,.\,4}{4\,.\,4}\quad \text{M.}\frac{3\,.\,3}{3\,.\,3}=44.$$

Canine has two fangs ; molars multicuspid ; the cusps long and sharply-pointed.

Shrews ; great preponderance of anterior incisors of both jaws ; their edges notched in some, and their tips sometimes stained as in Rodents ; canines small.

$$\textit{Hedgehog.}\quad \text{In.}\ \frac{3-3}{3-3}\quad \text{C.}\ \frac{1-1}{0-0}\quad \text{P.}\ \frac{3\,.\,3}{2\,.\,2}\quad \text{M.}\ \frac{3\,.\,3}{3\,.\,3} = 36.$$

In Insectivora generally a great development of enamel as compared with dentine ; cement also much organized, so as to resemble true bone, becoming in the Shrews actually continuous with the bone of the alveolus. (Owen.)

Stomach simple ; no cæcum.

Mammæ ventral.

Order Carnivora ; includes five families—Cats, Dogs, Bears, Weasels, and Seals.

All Unguiculate, but differing in the arrangement of their feet for progression, whence they have been somewhat artificially divided into sub-orders—1. Cats and Dogs are Digitigrada, walking on the toes, with tarsus and carpus raised from the ground ; 2. Bears are Plantigrada, walking on the sole of foot and palm of hand—Weasels are intermediate, Semi-plantigrada ; and 3. Seals are Pinnigrada, Pinnipedia, or web-footed, the hind feet being further joined by an extension of webbed integument to the tail.

Skeleton—

Vertebræ. Great development of transverse processes of atlas, and of spine of axis for attachment of muscles moving head in tearing or carrying prey.

Dorsal vertebræ ; thirteen to sixteen, with long spines, directed backward in the anterior part of dorsal region, forward in posterior ; the meeting point of the two inclinations varying according to the axis of movement.

Lumbar ; four to seven.

Sacral ; usually four ; in White Bear seven.

Caudal ; Bear six ; Lion twenty-three.

Ribs ; note that anterior ribs are small.

Clavicle often absent ; slender, and mostly imperfect when present.

Coracoid, as a process, hardly developed in Seals.

Ulna and radius distinct, but with very little movement of rotation ; ulna placed behind radius.

In the carpus the pisiform bone forms the heel or spur of the fore-foot.

The claws are fixed upon the dorsal aspect of the terminal phalanges, and are held in place by a strong, broad, curved lamina developed from the base of the phalanx, and forming with the phalanx a deep groove into which the root of the claw is received. In the Cats, which retract their claws, the middle phalanx of each digit is hollowed out on its outer side, and the ungual phalanx, during rest, is folded back into the space thus left.

Pelvis short ; tibia and fibula free ; metatarsals five, inner only rudimentary in Dogs and Cats ; toes four in Cats and Dogs, five in Bears ; first rudimentary in Weasels ; in Seals all equal.

Skull. Bones of face short and contracted as compared with cranium.

Posterior surface of skull small, directed backwards ; ridges and processes for attachment of neck-muscles very strongly marked ; upper surface arched, with strong median crest, giving large space on each side for attachment of temporal muscle ; orbits and temporal fossæ confounded ; zygoma perfect, much arched outwards, and very strong ; large posterior glenoid process.

In lower jaw, coronoid process greatly developed ; angle very small in comparison.

Bony tentorium—

Teeth. Always two sets; all with enamel; surface never folded as in Herbivora.

$$\textit{Cats.}\quad \text{In.}\ \frac{3-3}{3-3}\quad \text{C.}\ \frac{1-1}{1-1}\quad \text{Pr.}\ \frac{3-3}{2-2}\quad \text{M.}\ \frac{1-1}{1-1} = 34.$$

Incisors not very long, rather broad and thick in the crown; canines deeply planted, conical, slightly recurved, pointed, upper under-curved by lower; molars trenchant, having usually three cusps with convex sharp edges all in one line; the lower molars work within the upper, and fit in with them so as to act like scissors; movement of jaw vertical only.

Compare this dentition and skull with Ruminant; the powerful sagittal crest, and great attachments of temporalis; with short face, giving great leverage for compression of matters between canines and molars.

Bears have face more elongated, and in connection with a less purely animal diet, have the surfaces of the molars depressed and tuberculated, their outer edges trenchant.

Seals have the canines reduced generally to some equality with the rest of the teeth (Walrus a notable exception). The molars are numerous, and have sharp cusps for holding fish.

Alimentary canal very short; in the Lion and Wild Cat not more than three times the length of the body, as compared with twenty-eight times in the Ram. Stomach simple.

Cæcum small; always a gall-bladder.

In connection with the organ of hearing, the mastoid forms a large hollow process acting as an extra tympanic cavity.

Kidneys have in all Carnivora a tendency to lobulation; they are minutely subdivided in Bears and Seals.

Testes—in a scrotum in Bears, Cats, Martens, Hyænas;
under skin of perineum, in Civet;
„ „ groin, in Otter;
in belly, in Seal.

Most Carnivora have no vesiculæ seminales.

Uterus two-horned. Placenta deciduate, zonular.

Order Quadrumana; name derived from the fact that the thumb is opposable to the other digits in both feet and hands; embraces the Apes and Monkeys of the New and Old World, and the Demurs of Africa and Madagascar.

General characters; two incisors on each side of each jaw; a varying number of premolars, and three molars with tubercles of various shapes; perfect clavicles; pectoral mammæ; vesiculæ seminales and prostate; placenta discoid as in Man. Three sub-orders:—

1. *The Catarrhinæ,* which include the large tailless anthropoid Apes, such as the Gorilla, Chimpanzee, and Orang Outan; the Monkeys proper—most characteristic of the order—and the dog-like Baboons. They have the nostrils oblique, approximating below, and opening behind the muzzle.

$$\text{Premolars } \frac{2-2}{2\text{-}2.}$$

In the higher Apes the skeleton has, of course, resemblances to that of Man, but in the lower Monkeys it approaches that of the Carnivora.

Even in the Gorilla and Chimpanzee it is evident that the erect position is not natural or perfectly easy to the animals.

The spinal column is comparatively clumsy, and without the curves which in Man act as springs, preventing jarring of the well-balanced head; the pelvis is elongated, much weaker than in man, with an axis corresponding more nearly with the axis of the body. Again, in the foot, the os calcis is weak, and the foot rests somewhat uncomfortably on its outer edge; by the downward projection of the navicular and internal cuneiform bones the hallux or thumb is made opposable to the other toes.

The anterior extremity is remarkable chiefly for its great length as compared with that of Man.

In the scapular arch the coracoid process is directed more downwards than in Man, pointing, as it were, to the sternum.

The sternum in the Chimpanzee strongly resembles that of Man, particularly in the lateral expansion of its upper part forming the manubrium, but without the semilunar incision.

The cranium in the Chimpanzee is rounded above, but in the Orang, and still more in the Baboons, a strong central ridge runs along the junctions of the parietal bones, as in the Carnivora.

Generally, the squamous portion of the temporal bone is feebly, the supra-orbital ridges enormously developed, giving an aspect of scowling ferocity.

The suture between the maxillary and pre-maxillary bones, which is early obliterated in Man, remains long in the Apes, and in the Baboons is permanent.

The Platyrrhinæ are the Monkeys of South America—of the New World. The nostrils are wide apart, and do not open at the end of the snout. The premolars are $\frac{3}{3}$, making the grinding teeth twenty-four in all; the thumbs of the fore-hand either not opposable or wanting, and to make up for this the tail is long and prehensile. They are generally small and feeble, and in the characters of their teeth, which are provided with prominent sharpish tubercles, carry us toward the Insectivora, much in the same way as the Catarrhines carry us toward the Carnivora. Their form and general position is still less biped than those of the former order.

In the skull we notice chiefly the projection of the muzzle, the backward direction of the occipital foramen, and the narrowness of the forehead.

3. *The Strepsirrhines* have the muzzle very long and pointed, and the termination of the nostrils curved or twisted. Their incisors are usually about $\frac{3\,.\,3}{3\,.\,3}$, and are in some instances curiously indented at their edges; the premolars are $\frac{\ }{3}$ or $\frac{2}{2}$, and the molars with sharp tubercles.

They have the four thumbs opposable, and the second digit of the hind-foot is armed with a long claw. They inhabit Madagascar, Africa, and the Indian Archipelago.

Relations of Man to the Quadrumana—

Professor Huxley nas well shown that, in his bodily anatomy, Man is altogether nearer to the highest Simian—the Gorilla—than the Gorilla is to the Baboons and lower monkeys. The differences between Man and the Gorilla are partly differences of structure, partly and chiefly differences only of size and form of common parts.

The most important structural differences are, that the Gorilla has thirteen dorsal and four lumbar vertebræ, instead of twelve dorsal and five lumbar, as in Man; that there is a diastema or gap in the hedge of teeth in the Gorilla in front of the upper and behind the lower canine, whereas in Man the hedge is unbroken; that certain muscular slips in the foot have different attachments to tendons and bones. There is also a slight difference in the order of succession of the teeth, the second and third molars preceding the canines in the Gorilla.

Other differences have evident relation to different intellectual capacity, different habit of attitude, and different mode of life. The Gorilla has a much smaller brain than Man; assumes a procumbent or semi-erect attitude, or climbs, as opposed to Man's erect attitude and terrestrial habit, and makes more use of his teeth in fighting and in chewing.

So we see the head of the Gorilla suspended to the spine by powerful muscles, instead of being balanced upon it; the neck short and thick, the thorax long, and the loin hardly marked. The curves of the spinal column are almost lost; the buttocks and calves are not prominent, and the fore-arm is of uniform girth.

In the skull we find the occipital foramen directed backwards instead of downwards; and the occipital crest and tuberosity, with the muscular processes around, greatly developed; the brain cavity comparatively small, the facial bones large, and with strongly marked processes; a strong sagittal crest, and great surface of attachment for temporalis; strong coronoid, deep angle, large pterygoid processes. The face is, however, developed downwards (chiefly by the depth of the angle of the jaw) rather than forwards; there is no chin; and an aspect of ferocity is given by the great supra-orbital ridge which over-arches the eyes with a constant scowl.

In the vertebral column, the spines of the last five cervical vertebræ are very stout, and much prolonged obliquely backwards for the attachment of the muscles moving and supporting the head. The curves of the spinal column, so characteristic of Man, and no doubt related with his erect attitude, are almost lost.

The pelvic ring has its axial line much more nearly corresponding with the axial line of the body than in Man.

The arm is longer, the leg shorter, in comparison with the length of the trunk, than in Man.

In the foot, the hallux is smaller relatively than in Man. It consists of a metatarsal bone and two phalanges ; the toe is comparatively free from the rest, and has considerable movement upon the convex anterior surface of the cuneiform ; the os calcis is thinned away, and lets the sole of the foot rest rather on its outer edge, the arch of the instep being lost. The foot is thus unfitted for the support of the weight of the body at right angles, as in Man ; and is more suited for quadrupedal progression or climbing.

But if Man is thus closely allied by his material form to the higher Apes, he is separated from them by a wide intellectual and moral gulf.

He has the power of perceiving abstract ideas, the sense of right and wrong, and of duty ; the power of social organization ; the faculty of articulate speech ; the power of constructing language ; and a steady tendency to change language.

The theory of Natural Selection as applied to the extenuation of these differences.

LONDON : PARDON AND SON, PRINTERS, PATERNOSTER ROW.

LONDON, NEW BURLINGTON STREET,

NOVEMBER, 1872

A LIST

OF

MESSRS CHURCHILL'S WORKS

ON

CHEMISTRY, MATERIA MEDICA, PHARMACY, BOTANY, THE MICROSCOPE,

AND

OTHER BRANCHES OF SCIENCE

INDEX

**** The Works advertised in this Catalogue may be obtained through any Bookseller in the United Kingdom, or direct of the Publishers on Remittance being made.*

A LIST OF

Messrs CHURCHILL'S WORKS, &c

C. L. Bloxam

CHEMISTRY, INORGANIC and ORGANIC:

With Experiments. By CHARLES L. BLOXAM, Professor of Chemistry in King's College, London; Professor of Chemistry in the Department for Artillery Studies, Woolwich. Second Edition. With 295 Engravings on Wood . . . . . 8vo, 16s.

*** It has been the author's endeavour to produce a Treatise on Chemistry sufficiently comprehensive for those studying the science as a branch of general education, and one which a student may peruse with advantage before commencing his chemical studies at one of the colleges or medical schools, where he will abandon it for the more advanced work placed in his hands by the professor. The special attention devoted to Metallurgy and some other branches of Applied Chemistry renders the work especially useful to those who are being educated for employment in manufacture.

"Professor Bloxam has given us a most excellent and useful practical treatise. His 666 pages are crowded with facts and experiments, nearly all well chosen, and many quite new, even to scientific men. . . It is astonishing how much information he often conveys in a few paragraphs. We might quote fifty instances of this." — *Chemical News.*

By the same Author

LABORATORY TEACHING: Or, Progressive

Exercises in Practical Chemistry, with Analytical Tables. Second Edition. With 89 Engravings. Crown 8vo, 5s. 6d.

*** This work is intended for use in the chemical laboratory by those who are commencing the study of practical chemistry. It does not presuppose any knowledge of chemistry on the part of the pupil, and does not enter into any theoretical speculations. It dispenses with the use of all costly apparatus and chemicals, and is divided into separate exercises or lessons, with examples for practice, to facilitate the instruction of large classes. The method of instruction here followed has been adopted by the author, after twenty-three years' experience as a teacher in the laboratory.

John E. Bowman and C. L. Bloxam

PRACTICAL CHEMISTRY, Including Analysis. By JOHN E. BOWMAN and C. L. BLOXAM. Sixth Edition. With 98 Engravings on Wood.

[Fcap. 8vo, 6s. 6d.

*** The intention of this work is to furnish to the beginner a text-book of the practical *minutiæ* of the laboratory. The various processes employed in analysis, or which have been devised for the illustration of the principles of the science, are explained in language as simple as possible. This edition has been embellished with a large number of additional wood engravings from sketches made in the laboratory.

Also

MEDICAL CHEMISTRY. Fourth Edition, with 82 Engravings on Wood. . . Fcap. 8vo, 6s. 6d.

*** This work gives instructions for the examination and analysis of urine, blood, and a few other of the more important animal products, both healthy and morbid. It comprises also directions for the detection of poisons in organic mixtures and in the tissues.

—o—

Albert J. Bernays

NOTES FOR STUDENTS IN CHEMISTRY: Being a Syllabus of Chemistry and Practical Chemistry. By ALBERT J. BERNAYS, Professor of Chemistry at St. Thomas's Hospital. Fifth Edition, Revised.

[Fcap. 8vo, 3s. 6d.

*** A new feature is an Appendix giving the doses of the chief chemical preparations of the "Materia Medica."

"The new notation and nomenclature are now exclusively used. We notice additional notes in apparently every paragraph in the book, and a close revision of the whole."—*Scientific Opinion.*

—o—

J. Campbell Brown

ANALYTICAL TABLES for STUDENTS of Practical Chemistry. By J. CAMPBELL BROWN, D.Sc. Lond., F.C.S. . . . . . . 8vo, 2s. 6d.

T. Griffiths

CHEMISTRY OF THE FOUR SEASONS: Spring, Summer, Autumn, Winter. By T. GRIFFITHS. Second Edition, with Engravings. Fcap. 8vo, 7s. 6d.

—o—

U. J. Kay-Shuttleworth

FIRST PRINCIPLES OF MODERN CHEMISTRY. By U. J. KAY-SHUTTLEWORTH, M.P. Second Edition . . . . . Crown 8vo, 4s. 6d.

"We can recommend the book."—*Athenæum.*

"Deserving warmest commendation."—*Popular Science Rev.*

—o—

Francis Sutton

HANDBOOK OF VOLUMETRIC ANALYSIS, or, the Quantitative Estimation of Chemical Substances by Measure applied to Liquids, Solids, and Gases. By FRANCIS SUTTON, F.C.S., Norwich. Second Edition. With Engravings. . . . . . . 8vo, 12s.

*** This work is adapted to the requirements of pure Chemical Research, Pathological Chemistry, Pharmacy, Metallurgy, Manufacturing Chemistry, Photography, &c., and for the Valuation of Substances used in Commerce, Agriculture, and the Arts.

"Mr. Sutton has rendered an essential service by the compilation of his work."—*Chemical News.*

—o—

Arnold J. Cooley and R. V. Tuson

A CYCLOPÆDIA OF PRACTICAL RECEIPTS, PROCESSES, AND COLLATERAL INFORMATION IN THE ARTS, MANUFACTURES, PROFESSIONS, AND TRADES: Including Pharmacy and Domestic Economy and Hygiène. Designed as a Comprehensive Supplement to the Pharmacopœias and General Book of Reference for the Manufacturer, Tradesman, Amateur, and Heads of Families. By ARNOLD J. COOLEY. Fifth Edition, with Engravings. . . . . . . 8vo, 28s.

NAMES OF THOSE WHO HAVE CONTRIBUTED TO, OR ASSISTED IN THE REVISION OF, THIS EDITION

JOHN ATTFIELD, Ph.D., F.C.S.
J. WORTLEY AXE
LLOYD BULLOCK, F.C.S.
E. L. BARRET, B.Sc., F.C.S.
E. CANTON, F.R.C.S.
SPENCER COBBOLD, M.D., F.R.S.
STEPHEN DARBY, F.C.S.
Dr. DE VRIJ, of the Hague
WILLIAM HARKNESS, F.R.M.S.
C. W. HEATON, F.C.S.
EDMUND NEISON, F.C.S.
GEORGE PHILLIPS, F.C.S.
WILLIAM PRITCHARD
A. E. SANSOM, M.D. Lond., M.R.C.P.
J. B. SIMONDS
JOHN SPILLER, F.C.S.
JOHN STENHOUSE, LL.D., F.R.S.
RICHARD V. TUSON, F.C.S. (*Editor*).

W. G. Valentin

INTRODUCTION to INORGANIC CHEMISTRY. By WM. G. VALENTIN, F.C.S., Principal Demonstrator of Practical Chemistry in the Royal School of Mines and Science Training Schools, South Kensington. With 82 Engravings. . 8vo, 6s. 6d.

Also

QUALITATIVE CHEMICAL ANALYSIS. With Engravings. 8vo.

—o—

R. Wagner and W. Crookes

HANDBOOK OF CHEMICAL TECHNOLOGY. By RUDOLF WAGNER, Ph.D., Professor of Chemical Technology at the University of Wurtzburg. Translated and Edited from the Eighth German Edition, with Extensive Additions, by WILLIAM CROOKES, F.R.S. . . . . . [8vo, 25s.

*** Under the head of Metallurgical Chemistry, the latest methods of preparing Iron, Cobalt, Nickel, Copper, Copper Salts, Lead and Tin and their Salts, Bismuth, Zinc, Zinc Salts, Cadmium, Antimony, Arsenic, Mercury, Platinum, Silver, Gold, Manganates, Aluminium, and Magnesium are described. The various applications of the Voltaic Current to Electro-Metallurgy follow under this division. The Preparation of Potash and Soda Salts, the Manufacture of Sulphuric Acid, and the Recovery of Sulphur from Soda-waste, of course occupy prominent places in the consideration of Chemical Manufactures. It is difficult to over-estimate the mercantile value of Le Mond's process, as well as the many new and important applications of Bisulphide of Carbon. The Manufacture of Soap will be found to include much detail. The Technology of Glass, Stoneware, Limes, and Mortars, will present much of interest to the builder and engineer. The Technology of Vegetable Fibres has been considered to include the Preparation of Flax, Hemp, Cotton, as well as Paper Making; while the applications of Vegetable Products will be found to include Sugar-boiling, Wine and Beer Brewing, the Distillation of Spirits, the Baking of Bread, the Preparation of Vinegar, the Preservation of Wood, &c. Dr. WAGNER gives much information in reference to the production of Potash from Sugar residues. The use of Baryta Salts is also fully described, as well as the Preparation of Sugar from Beet-roots. Tanning, the Preservation of Meat, Milk, &c., the Preparation of Phosphorus and Animal Charcoal, are considered as belonging to the Technology of Animal Products. The Preparation of the Materials for dyeing has necessarily required much space; while the final sections of the book have been devoted to the Technology of Heating and Illumination.

J. Forbes Royle and F. W. Headland

A MANUAL OF MATERIA MEDICA.

By J. FORBES ROYLE, M.D., F.R.S., and F. W. HEADLAND, M.D., F.L.S. Fifth Edition, with Engravings on Wood . . . . . . Fcap 8vo, 12s. 6d.

*** This edition has been remodelled throughout on the basis of the present edition of the British Pharmacopœia. The medicines of the British Pharmacopœia will be found arranged in natural order, the preparations described at length, and the formulæ explained. Other medicines and preparations, mentioned only in the London Pharmacopœia of 1851, are separately described and included in brackets. All remedies of value, whether officinal or not, are noticed in their place in this Manual.

"This Manual is, to our minds, unrivalled in any language for condensation, accuracy, and completeness of information."—*British Medical Journal.*

—o—

Adolphe Wahltuch

A DICTIONARY OF MATERIA MEDICA

AND THERAPEUTICS. By ADOLPHE WAHLTUCH, M.D. . . . . 8vo, 15s.

*** The purpose of this work is to give a tabular arrangement of all drugs specified in the British Pharmacopœia of 1867. Every table is divided into six parts :—(1) *The Name and Synonyms ;* (2) *Character and Properties or Composition ;* (3) *Physiological Effects and Therapeutics ;* (4) *Form and Doses ;* (5) *Preparations ;* (6) *Prescriptions.* Other matter elucidatory of the Pharmacopœia is added to the work.

"A very handy book."—*Lancet.*

—o—

Peter Squire

COMPANION TO THE BRITISH PHARMACOPŒIA.

With Practical Hints on Prescribing ; including a Tabular Arrangement of Materia Medica for Students, and a Concise Account of the Principal Spas of Europe. By PETER SQUIRE, Chemist in Ordinary to the Queen and the Prince of Wales ; late President of the Pharmaceutical Society. Eighth Edit. 8vo, 10s. 6d.

By the same Author

THE HOSPITAL PHARMACOPŒIAS OF LONDON

arranged in Groups for Easy Reference and Comparison. Second Edition. . Fcap 8vo, 5s.

LIST OF THE HOSPITALS

Charing Cross—Consumption—Diseases of the Chest—Fever—Guy's—King's College—London—London Ophthalmic—Middlesex—St. Bartholomew's—St. George's—St. Mary's—St. Thomas's—Skin—University College—Westminster—Westminster Ophthalmic.

J. B. Smith

PHARMACEUTICAL GUIDE.

By JOHN BARKER SMITH. . Crown 8vo, 6s. 6d.

FIRST AND SECOND EXAMINATIONS

LATIN GRAMMAR — FRACTIONS — METRIC SYSTEM — MATERIA MEDICA — BOTANY — PHARMACY — CHEMISTRY — PRESCRIPTIONS.

——o——

John Steggall

FIRST LINES FOR CHEMISTS AND DRUGGISTS preparing for Examination at the Pharmaceutical Society. By JOHN STEGGALL, M.D. Third Edition. . . . . 18mo, 3s. 6d.

CONTENTS

Notes on the British Pharmacopœia, the Substances arranged alphabetically.
Table of Preparations, containing Opium, Antimony, Mercury, and Arsenic.
Classification of Plants.
Thermometers.
Specific Gravity.
Weights and Measures.
Questions on Pharmaceutical Chemistry and Materia Medica.

——o——

J. Birkbeck Nevins

THE PRESCRIBER'S ANALYSIS OF THE BRITISH PHARMACOPŒIA OF 1867. By J. BIRKBECK NEVINS, M.D. Lond., Lecturer on Materia Medica in the Liverpool Royal Infirmary Medical School. Third Edition, Revised and Enlarged.

[Royal 32mo, 3s. 6d.

——o——

Jonathan Pereira

SELECTA E PRÆSCRIPTIS:

Containing Lists of the Terms, Phrases, Contractions, and Abbreviations used in Prescriptions, with Explanatory Notes; the Grammatical Construction of Prescriptions; Rules for the Pronunciation of Pharmaceutical Terms; a Prosodiacal Vocabulary of the Names of Drugs, &c.; and a Series of Abbreviated Prescriptions illustrating the use of the preceding terms. To which is added a Key, containing the Prescriptions in an Unabbreviated Form, with a Literal Translation for the Use of Medical and Pharmaceutical Students. By JONATHAN PEREIRA, M.D., F.R.S. Fifteenth Edition. [32mo,

Henry Beasley

THE POCKET FORMULARY AND SYNOPSIS OF THE BRITISH AND FOREIGN PHARMACOPŒIAS: Comprising Standard and approved Formulæ for the Preparations and Compounds employed in Medical Practice. By HENRY BEASLEY. Ninth Edition . . . . 18mo, 6s.

By the same Author

THE DRUGGIST'S GENERAL RECEIPT-BOOK: Comprising a Copious Veterinary Formulary and Table of Veterinary Materia Medica; Patent and Proprietary Medicines, Druggists' Nostrums, &c.; Perfumery, Skin Cosmetics, Hair Cosmetics, and Teeth Cosmetics; Beverages, Dietetic Articles and Condiments; Trade Chemicals, Miscellaneous Preparations and Compounds used in the Arts, &c.; with useful Memoranda and Tables. Seventh Edition. 18mo, 6s.

Also

THE BOOK OF PRESCRIPTIONS: Containing 3,000 Prescriptions collected from the Practice of the most eminent Physicians and Surgeons, English and Foreign. Fourth Edition. [18mo, 6s.

"Mr. Beasley's 'Pocket Formulary,' 'Druggist's Receipt-Book,' and 'Book of Prescriptions,' form a compact library of reference admirably suited for the dispensing desk."—*Chemist and Druggist.*

——o——

F. H. Lescher

AN INTRODUCTION to the ELEMENTS of PHARMACY. By F. HARWOOD LESCHER. Fourth Edition . . . . 8vo, 7s. 6d.

Sec. I. MATERIA MEDICA: Characteristics of Drugs; Geographical Sources; Detection of Spurious Specimens.

II. BOTANY: Sketch of Organs, with their Functions; Groupings of the Characteristics; Natural Orders.

III. CHEMISTRY: Outline of Physics; Simple Primary Analysis; Detection of Adulterations; Poisons—Tests and Antidotes; Organic and Inorganic Chemicals.

IV. PHARMACY: Pharmacopœia; Preparations; Active Ingredients.

V. PRESCRIPTIONS: The Latin Language; Examples, with Errors and Unusual Doses; Tables of Doses.

VI. PRACTICAL DISPENSING: Groupings of Strengths of Solutions; Emulsions; Pills, &c.; Changes in Mixtures.

THE YEAR-BOOK OF PHARMACY:

Containing the Proceedings at the Yearly Meeting of the British Pharmaceutical Conference, and a Report on the Progress of Pharmacy, which includes notices of all Pharmaceutical Papers, new Processes, Preparations, and Formulæ published throughout the world. Published annually. . . . . . [8vo, 7s. 6d.

——o——

R. V. Tuson

A PHARMACOPŒIA, INCLUDING THE OUTLINES OF MATERIA MEDICA AND THERAPEUTICS, for the Use of Practitioners and Students of Veterinary Medicine. By RICHARD V. TUSON, F.C.S., Professor of Chemistry and Materia Medica at the Royal Veterinary College. Second Edition . . . . [*In preparation.*

"Not only practitioners and students of veterinary medicine, but chemists and druggists will find that this book supplies a want in veterinary literature."—*Chemist and Druggist.*

——o——

Robert Bentley

A MANUAL OF BOTANY:

Including the Structure, Functions, Classifications, Properties, and uses of Plants. By ROBERT BENTLEY, F.L.S., Professor of Botany, King's College, and to the Pharmaceutical Society. Second Edition, with 1,127 Wood Engravings . . . . Fcap. 8vo, 12s. 6d.

"As the standard manual of botany its position is undisputed." —*Chemist and Druggist.*

——o——

W. B. Carpenter

THE MICROSCOPE AND ITS REVELATIONS. By W. B. CARPENTER, M.D., F.R.S. Fourth Edition, with more than 500 Wood Engravings.

[Fcap. 8vo, 12s. 6d.

*** The author has aimed to combine within a moderate compass that information in regard to the use of his instrument and its appliances, which is most essential to the working microscopist, with such an account of the objects best fitted for his study as may qualify him to comprehend what he observes, and thus prepare him to benefit science, whilst expanding and refreshing his own mind.

J. H. Martin

A MANUAL OF MICROSCOPIC MOUNTING; with Notes on the Collection and Examination of Objects. By JOHN H. MARTIN, author of "Microscopic Objects." With upwards of 100 Engravings. [8vo, 7s. 6d.

⁎ The aim of this work is to supply the student with a concise manual of the principles of microscopic mounting, and to assist his progress in the manual dexterity, as far as illustrations and words render it possible, necessary in their application.

—o—

THE QUARTERLY JOURNAL OF MICROSCOPICAL SCIENCE. (Established in 1852.) Edited by Dr. J. F. PAYNE, Demonstrator of Morbid Anatomy at St. Thomas's Hospital, and Mr. E. RAY LANKESTER, Natural Science Fellow of Exeter College, Oxford. [Annual Subscription, 16s.; Single Numbers, 4s.

⁎ The Memoirs are, when needful, illustrated by Lithographic Plates, many of which are Coloured. The Journal contains, in addition, Notes and Memoranda, Reviews of Books, Quarterly Chronicle, and Proceedings of Societies.

—o—

J. Fayrer

THE THANATOPHIDIA OF INDIA; being a Description of the Venomous Snakes of the Indian Peninsula. With an Account of the Influence of their Poison on Life, and a Series of Experiments. By J. FAYRER, M.D., C.S.I., Honorary Physician to the Queen; late President of the Asiatic Society of Bengal. With 31 Plates (28 Coloured) . . Folio, 7*l*. 7s.

—o—

J. Reay Greene

TABLES OF ZOOLOGY: indicating the Tribes, Sub-Orders, Orders, and Higher Groups of the Animal Kingdom, for Students, Lecturers, and others. By J. REAY GREENE, M.D., Professor of Natural History in the Queen's University in Ireland. Three large sheets, 7s. 6d. the set; or, mounted on canvas, with roller and varnished . . . . 18s.

⁎ These Tables have been carefully prepared in accordance with the present state of science, and with a view to remove the difficulties which arise from the various opinions held by different zoologists.

T. H. Huxley

A MANUAL OF THE ANATOMY OF VERTEBRATED ANIMALS. By Prof. HUXLEY, LL.D., F.R.S. With numerous Engravings.

[Fcap. 8vo, 12s.

By the same Author

INTRODUCTION to the CLASSIFICATION of ANIMALS. With Engravings . . 8vo, 6s.

—o—

W. M. Ord

NOTES ON COMPARATIVE ANATOMY: a Syllabus of a Course of Lectures delivered at St. Thomas's Hospital. By WILLIAM MILLER ORD, M.B. Lond., M.R.C.P., Assistant-Physician to the Hospital, and Lecturer in its Medical School. . Crown 8vo, 5s.

"Compact, lucid, and well arranged. These Notes will, if well used, be valuable to learners, perhaps still more so to teachers."—*Nature.*

"We have gone through it carefully, and we are thoroughly satisfied with the manner in which the author has discharged his task."—*Pop. Science Review.*

—o—

John Shea

A MANUAL OF ANIMAL PHYSIOLOGY. With Appendix of Examination Questions. By JOHN SHEA, M.D., B.A. Lond. With numerous Engravings.

[Fcap. 8vo, 5s. 6d.

—o—

VESTIGES of the NATURAL HISTORY OF CREATION. With 100 Engravings on Wood. Eleventh Edition . . . . Post 8vo, 7s. 6d.

—o—

R. G. Mayne

MEDICAL VOCABULARY: An Explanation of all Names, Synonymes, Terms, and Phrases used in Medicine and the Relative Branches of Medical Science, giving their correct Derivation, Meaning, Application, and Pronunciation. Intended specially as a Book of Reference for the Young Student. Third Edition. [Fcap 8vo, 8s. 6d.

"We have referred to this work hundreds of times, and have always obtained the information we required. . . Chemical, Botanical, and Pharmaceutical Terms are to be found on almost every page." — *Chemist and Druggist.*

Lake Price

A MANUAL OF PHOTOGRAPHIC MANIPULATION.

By LAKE PRICE. Second Edition, Revised and Enlarged, with numerous Engravings.

[Crown 8vo, 6s. 6d.

*** Amongst the Contents are the Practical Treatment of Portraits—Groups in the Studio—Landscapes—Groups in Open Air—Instantaneous Pictures—Animals—Architecture—Marine Subjects—Still Life—Copying of Pictures, Prints, Drawings, Manuscripts, Interiors—Stereoscopy in Microphotography, &c., and Notices of the last Inventions and Improvements in Lenses, Apparatus, &c.

"In these days, when nearly every intelligent person can, after a few weeks, master the manipulatory details of our art-science, attention to the artistic treatment of subjects is a matter for the serious consideration of the Photographer; and to those who desire to enter on this path, Mr. LAKE PRICE, in the volume before us, proves himself to be 'a guide, philosopher, and friend.'"—*The British Journal of Photography.*

—o—

C. Brooke

THE ELEMENTS OF NATURAL PHILOSOPHY.

By CHARLES BROOKE, M.B., M.A., F.R.S. Based on the Work of the late Dr. GOLDING BIRD. Sixth Edition, with 700 Engravings on Wood.

[Fcap 8vo, 12s. 6d.

CONTENTS

1, Elementary Laws and Properties of Matter: Internal or Molecular Forces—2, Properties of Masses of Matter: External Forces—3, Statics—4, The Mechanical Powers, or Simple Machines—5, Principles of Mechanism—6, Dynamics—7, Hydrostatics—8, Hydrodynamics—9, Pneumatics—10, Acoustics—11, Magnetism; Diamagnetism—12, Franklinic Electricity—13, Voltaic Electricity—14, Electro-Dynamics—15, Electro-Telegraphy—16, Thermo-Electricity—17, Organic Electricity—18, Catoptrics and Dioptrics—19, Chromatics—20, Optical Instruments—21, Polarised Light—22, Chemical Action of Light: Photography—23, Thermics—24, Radiant Heat.

—o—

H. M. Noad

THE INDUCTORIUM, OR INDUCTION COIL:

Being a Popular Explanation of the Electrical Principles on which it is constructed. By HENRY M. NOAD, Ph.D., F.R.S., Lecturer on Chemistry at St. George's Hospital Medical School. Third Edition, with Engravings . . . . Fcap 8vo, 3s.

The following CATALOGUES issued by Messrs CHURCHILL will be forwarded post free on application:

1. *Messrs Churchill's General List of* 400 *works on Medicine, Surgery, Midwifery, Materia Medica, Hygiene, Anatomy, Physiology, Chemistry, &c., &c.*

2. *Selection from Messrs Churchill's General List, comprising all recent works published by them on the* **Art** *and Science of Medicine.*

3. *A descriptive List of Messrs Churchill's works on Chemistry, Pharmacy, Botany, Photography, and other branches of Science.*

4. *Messrs Churchill's Red-Letter List, giving the Titles of forthcoming New Works and New Editions.*

[Published every October.]

5. *The Medical Intelligencer, an Annual List of New Works and New Editions published by Messrs J. & A. Churchill, together with Particulars of the Periodicals issued from their House.*

[Sent in January of each year to every Medical Practitioner in the United Kingdom whose name and address can be ascertained. A large number are also sent to the United States of America, Continental Europe, India, and the Colonies.]

MESSRS CHURCHILL have concluded a special arrangement with MESSRS LINDSAY & BLAKISTON, OF PHILADELPHIA, in accordance with which that Firm will act as their Agents for the United States of America, either keeping in Stock most of Messrs CHURCHILL'S Books, or reprinting them on Terms advantageous to Authors. Many of the Works in this Catalogue may therefore be easily obtained in America.

M'Gowan & Danks, Printers, Great Windmill Street, Haymarket.

CPSIA information can be obtained
at www.ICGtesting.com
Printed in the USA
LVHW032250100223
739217LV00006B/510

9 783382 102104